Northwest Vista College
Learning Resource Center
3535 North Ellison Drive
San Antonio, Texas 78251

D1563394

Safe Delivery

SAFE

DELIVERY

JIM SANDERSON

University of New Mexico Press Albuquerque

Portions of this novel appeared in a different form as "A Texas Ranger,"
Frontiers 1, no. 1 (fall 1996: 65–76).

Library of Congress Cataloging-in-Publication Data

Sanderson, Jim, 1953–

Safe delivery/Jim Sanderson.—1st ed.

p. cm.

ISBN 0-8263-2191-7 (alk. paper)

1. Private investigators—Texas—San Antonio—Fiction.

2. Women detectives—Texas—San Antonio—Fiction.

3. Mexican American Border Region—Fiction.

4. Revolutionaries—Mexico—Fiction.

5. Illegal arms transfers—Fiction.

6. San Antonio (Tex.)—Fiction.

I. Title.

PS3569.A5146   S24   2000

813'.54—dc21   99-050631

For Gordon and Leonard

CHAPTER ONE

Vincent Fuentes sat on a bench in front of city hall with the old men, pigeons, and lawyers who filled Military Plaza as the workday ended. Despite his dedication to his own welfare, Fuentes felt the presence of ghosts in this plaza. Up until the 1940s, when the health department and Mayor Maury Maverick closed them down, the Chili Queens had sold their chili and tamales here. Fuentes's imagining of the residual smell of the Chili Queens' chili powder and the taste of their bad chili and tamales heavy with *masa* seeped into him and distracted him from his task. Before the Chili Queens, this had been the plaza where produce or Yankee goods were sold. Santa Anna had placed his artillery here. The Tejanos, Indians, and early Anglo settlers had mixed and negotiated in Military Plaza. Later, the ex–Confederate officers, the old ex-Rangers, the cattlemen, the Anglo merchants, who kept the Mexicans farther west, gathered and made their deals in Alamo Plaza, several blocks east, out in front of the old mission and the Menger Hotel. The ghosts here were the leftover spirits of the soldiers, vendors, salesmen, explorers, whores, traders, and con men who, for two hundred years, had bought, sold, bargained, and cheated in this plaza. It was the proper place for Fuentes to renegotiate a love affair with Jerri Johnson.

It was a clear day, and the afternoon heat had gotten up to full force, but the shadows from the buildings and trees in downtown

San Antonio at least kept the sun off him. Fuentes spread his arms along the back of the park bench and let himself feel the first currents of the nightly Gulf breeze. He stared across the plaza and across Dolorosa Street to Sam's Bail Bonds and the smaller office next door: Sam's Investigating Services. Both were housed in a two-story building, the upper floors no doubt condemned and crumbling to the first floor. The renovation of San Antonio had not yet gotten to Sam's two businesses.

Jerri Johnson worked for Sam's. Fuentes remembered petite, anxious, ambitious Jerri—the way she forced herself to learn what was instinctive for most students, her face that contorted itself when she couldn't learn, her pleasing body. Now that she was a private detective, Jerri peeked into motel windows and took pictures of cheating spouses. Some corruption had surely worked itself into her, Fuentes reasoned; that corruption would be his salvation.

He pushed his mind past the dull throb in his head, the sour taste in his dry mouth, and the slight nausea in his stomach to think about corruption. He would have liked to let his mind move where it wanted, to remember looking over his shoulder and seeing Jerri Johnson's toes dangling above him. He would have liked a drink even better, or maybe some of the white powder in his toilet kit, but he had to concentrate if he was to save himself. He would go ahead with the plans and be what the PRI wanted him to be, and he would find out if Jerri Johnson could save him. She might be willing to run away with him and hide. He might be able to make her feel about him as she once did.

Several of the plaza pigeons approached him, their heads jerking like soundless metronomes. Their stiff-legged gait reminded him of prison; convalescing in the sick ward, he had watched pigeons on his windowsill. A bed by a window: a prize location because he had agreed to help the PRI, and clean sheets and good meals were part of the bargain. And he continued to enjoy clean sheets in better beds and fine meals in quality hotels. Even if Jerri couldn't save him from his life, his life wasn't bad.

Four years before, sitting in the chair he was tied to, he'd watched out of the corner of his swollen eye as the Saltillo telephone book came toward his face. It caught him on the temple and knocked him and the chair over. The two Saltillo policemen pulled him and the chair up and steadied him. Then the third policeman took another swipe at him. The blow made his head swing as though it was on a swivel, and his chin hit his shoulder. This telephone book taught him the nature of pain. Pain was pure. At first he felt as though *his* pain, this pain, linked him with all human suffering, especially the suffering of the poor and the dispossessed. It was some approximation of what they must feel every day. Then the pain got much simpler. It became his pain alone. He shared it with no one. He could feel *his* blood in *his* veins. He learned, through pain, what every animal feels: its own being. With this new feeling of his own blood—no one else's, not even his family's—he began to worship the sacredness of his existence, the dependence of every atom in that being on his actions. He gave up on ideas.

His mind conjured up the old image of the prophet Colonel Henri Trujillo. After the third whack with the Saltillo telephone book, Fuentes saw the hazy outline of a suited man. He smoked a cigarette, backhanded, like a European. He stepped into the light of the naked bulb hanging above Fuentes, and Fuentes tried to see him more clearly but could only see shapes. The suited man bent to put his face in front of Fuentes's, and Fuentes could smell the cigarette. Compared to his cell, it smelled clean, like the early San Antonio mornings before the heat dried the dew in the grass. "You are too rough with him," the suited man told the policemen. The suited man sat in a chair beside Fuentes and looked sympathetically at him. Now Fuentes could see that the suited man was bald and had a goatee. When he talked, his hands folded limply backward on his wrists. "Father Fuentes," the suited man started, then shook his head. "Excuse me. Professor Fuentes. I don't like to see you beaten." Fuentes rolled his head away. "Can you speak?" Fuentes tried to move his jaws to see for himself if he could speak. "Sir, can you speak?" The telephone book caught him on the temple and slung his head back toward the suited man. "Please," the man said to the policeman who had hit him. "No more barbarity." The man turned back to Fuentes. "Please, Professor Fuentes."

"It hurts to talk," Fuentes mumbled to him. Later, in the hospital, he found out that his nose and a cheek were broken and that a tooth was gone, but now he knew only that one eye was swollen shut, so he had to twist his neck to see with his better eye.

"Very well," the suited man said, and patted Fuentes's shoulder. He put his arm around Fuentes and got so close to his face that Fuentes could smell the chorizo on his breath. "I am Colonel Henri Trujillo. I represent the Ministry of Defense, not just in Saltillo but for all of Mexico. The minister himself sends me. First, I wish you to know that this is Mexico. It is not El Salvador or Nicaragua. The PRI has no death squads. We are not extremists. We want only to get by. Can you hear me, Professor Fuentes?" Fuentes could feel Trujillo's arm draped around his shoulders and the pat from Trujillo's other hand on one shoulder. "We no longer care if you name your crazy friends who want to arm everybody who has an argument against the PRI. We can forget. But you have to help us."

Fuentes, having given up on ideas but still believing in loyalty, struggled to say that he would name no one. "No, no," Colonel Henri Trujillo said, and patted his shoulder again. "You need not answer now, just listen. We forgive all. We promise you a good job, a career if you choose. We encourage you to continue with your books. We want you to say what you will. We are not censors. We have freedom of speech. We want you only to help us. Occasionally. For this, you no longer stay in jail. You do not take your chances in a trial. You are free. You have my promise, and behind my promise is the promise of the minister of defense, the army, and the PRI."

Fuentes rolled his head toward Trujillo and started to move his lips, not really knowing what he would say. But Trujillo took the cigarette out of his mouth with one hand and put the forefinger from his other hand against his lips. "Shhh." The colonel patted Fuentes's shoulder again and got up. He moved like a woman. He stepped out of the light of the naked bulb, and Fuentes could no longer see him. He heard a door slam; then he felt the hands of one of the policemen untying his hands. When the ropes were off him, the other two policemen helped him to his feet and pain sped up his legs. He gasped when he stood. Because of the telephone book

4

slapping his face, he had forgotten the cigarette burns on the bottoms of his feet. Pain is pure. The specific, intense, and immediate pain blocks all other pain. It becomes *your* pain, like no one else's. *His* pain made his isolation complete. The loneliness of being a priest, a scholar, and a writer was just preparation for the complete surrender of soul to self that *his* pain gave him. One policeman grabbed him under his arms, another grabbed his feet, and the third opened the door.

They carried him to his cell and gently set him down on his feet. *"Excuso,"* one guard said while the other helped him down the steps into his cell. He groaned when his feet hit the six-inch-deep water on the floor of his cell. The rain had seeped in, and then a toilet on the floor above his had overflowed. The policemen closed the door behind him. "Hey, Professor," he heard his cell mate say from the bunk on the far side of the cell. "They teach you about this at the university?" Fuentes lowered himself to his knees and, when he felt the wetness on them, he curled forward toward the toilet. "Hey, I pissed in this slop," his cell mate said. "You're walking in my piss. How you like it?"

Fuentes looked into the toilet, and he saw the reflection of the bare lightbulb that made shadows but not much light in the cell. He felt his guts heave and watched tiny droplets of blood fleck the water floating in the toilet bowl. "Hey, I hear you're a priest besides a professor," he heard his cell mate say. "You going to pray? Is God going to rescue you? Give you wings and let you fly away? Is God going to save you?" The cell mate laughed. "You're on your knees. Are you praying now?"

Fuentes looked into the toilet bowl and saw in the ripples drops of blood shading from dark red to pink. He couldn't tell if he was looking down or lying on his back looking up, if he was looking down into a toilet at drops of blood or up into the sky at dim red stars. Maybe now he was talking to God.

Then what he saw began to spin into a funnel, as though he were looking into a hurricane. Whether ripples in a toilet or a whirlwind in heaven, the specks he saw swirled around his head. He had floated, knew no up or down or right or left. Rationality and thought

5

were gone. He wasn't talking to God; he felt God. He felt the blood in his veins. His blood spurted through his body to the rhythm of his heartbeat. It was his family's peculiar blood, his gangster father's blood, the blood of his great-great-grandfather, that old rustler, the Red Robber Baron Juan Cortina. His causes and gods wouldn't save him. His old selfish blood might. He knew what to do.

Seeing either up or down but not knowing which, he saw the face of a small blond woman, floating as he was. Fuentes's blood, his new appreciation of his own existence, might have washed away loyalty and ideas, but it let him remember. When he first saw that face, the blond woman was sitting in his class at the state university that catered to older students and poor young ones. He knew that she wasn't a young coed but never guessed she was pushing forty. She still wore the bangs and the ponytail of a younger woman. He remembered her breath, how sweet it always seemed to be, even in the mornings when he woke up with her. He remembered sex, her legs rising over him. She was smart, resourceful, resilient. He had loved her. Maybe he could no longer believe, but he could remember and think.

Fuentes turned off the memory to watch the tame San Antonio pigeons cross in front of him. A drop of sweat rolled down his cheek, and he felt his shirt stick to his back and chest. Fuentes liked the moist, hot weather that made green things grow and gave a person a sticky feel on his skin that encouraged him to indulge himself.

Now, after becoming the property of the PRI, after becoming a "safe" and bogus scholar, after the hotels and good meals, he no longer needed causes, or God, or art. Now, finally back in San Antonio, all he needed for salvation was his blood and Jerri Johnson.

☯ Across the street, Joe Parr watched Vincent Fuentes through the passing crowd and cussed the goddamn sweat his hat's sweatband didn't catch that rolled in a few beads down his forehead and dropped onto the lenses of his sunglasses. Joe Parr grabbed the brim of his straw cowboy hat and pulled his arm across his forehead, leaving a smear of sweat across the sleeve of his crisply starched white shirt. He felt sweat soaking into his cotton shirt up under his arms and across his shoulder blades. All his life he had lived in south Texas, but he still hated the sweat. The bunched-up people made him sweat more. So he cussed.

He ran his hand up his forehead and over his head, pushing his thinning white hair over his scalp, and put his cowboy hat back on. Parr looked at the pointed toes of his boots, then lifted his eyes back to Fuentes. Staring but twisting his head to loosen the tight muscles in his upper back, neck, and shoulders, Parr cussed himself again, this time for getting old and not being able to stand as long as he could ten years ago, or ages ago, when he tailed Bud Harrelson. "Whew," he said to himself, blew at the drop of sweat on the end of his nose, took off his prescription sunglasses to see without sweat stains in front of his eyes, and squinted at Fuentes. The pudgy son of a bitch didn't sweat, Joe Parr said to himself.

Parr was the only one to put two and two together and actually come out to watch Fuentes. Four years ago, when the crazy Mexican was teaching at the university and talking all kinds of radical shit, Parr was the only one to suspect that Fuentes might be doing more than talking. With some FBI records and some Bexar County sheriff deputies' help, Joe Parr had just about caught him before he took off with his girlfriend. He had become a cold case, one the SAPD wasn't interested in.

None of the cops in town, neither the FBI nor the San Antonio police, must even read the papers. Less than a week apart, the San Antonio *Express and News* carried a story about Fuentes coming back to teach a few weeks at Trinity University and then a story about some M-16s missing from a federal armory in Louisiana. The *Express and News* printed a schedule of Fuentes's West Coast lecture tour. And only Parr thought to call a professor in Los Angeles to get a report about Fuentes's activities. He preached crazy politics and went to parties thrown by professors and rich people. No self-respecting policeman ought to trust that a gun negotiator like Fuentes was just teaching or visiting an old girlfriend, especially in a city close to the Mexican border and with M-16s missing. Since they had the time or could take their time, Rangers like himself could keep up with cold cases.

Parr started coughing on the stale, fume-filled Commerce Street air. Since he had quit smoking twenty years ago, smoke and strange smells irritated him. Stepping back from the crowd of people waiting for a bus, he leaned against the wall and watched Fuentes watching pigeons and fat Sam's private cop shop on the other side of Military Plaza. Jerri Johnson, Fuentes's old girlfriend whom he had dumped in Mexico, worked at fat Sam's. Parr knew her, had worked with her, had heard she still carried a torch for the mixed-up son of a bitch.

To Parr, Fuentes, dressed in white linen pants and a turquoise Polo shirt, didn't look like some Mexican-style terrorist. He didn't have wild, fanatic eyes, and he wasn't very hard to follow. But Parr knew that if a cop went on looks and habits, he'd end up with his thumb up his ass most of the time.

Parr looked at the other people. Male bankers, lawyers, and clerks wore short-sleeve shirts with ties and carried their sport or suit coats over their shoulders. The managerial-level women and secretaries wore pantsuits or loose-fitting blouses and thin skirts. The tourists, out to look at the river and see the Alamo, wore shorts and sandals or tennis shoes. They pushed baby strollers with crying babies who looked to be on the verge of heat exhaustion. The locals, the street people, wore open collars, shorts, or jeans. The local Mexicans wore khakis and T-shirts or undershirts. They were the only ones other than Parr sensible enough to wear wide-brimmed hats. Even though Parr was born in south Texas, he had never really learned Spanish, but he was used to Mexicans.

❷ Jerri put a pencil on the far end of her desk, then pulled her hand away from it. The pencil rolled halfway down the desk, toward Jerri's face, then, from its momentum, started to roll uphill. It got as far up as it could, then rolled backward and settled in the dip in her desk. Jerri tried to pull open her top-left drawer, but it held firm. If she had finished her degree, she might have been teaching English now in some public school and maybe would have

8

had something other than a warped, scarred wooden desk with a drawer that didn't work.

Sam Ford, her boss, walked around the flimsy partition that divided their two offices. Sam was a bail bondsman. She was Sam's Investigating Services. Sam's Investigating Services tracked down people who jumped bail, served subpoenas for the local judges, and found illegal aliens (and hid others). Before he hired Jerri, Sam had a small window-front office, but after he hired her, he partitioned the small office into two smaller ones and gave her her own front door. Sam desperately needed to hire a new "man." But besides Jerri, the cheap old fart's only employee was the secretary who did their filing, typing, and computing. Irma had papers, a birth certificate, and a social security number but wasn't legal.

Jerri watched him waddle to her desk. Sam was a fat man. Rolls of fat started at his hips and stacked up like tires to his neck. He was one of those fat men who didn't have pectorals but titties. His short, stubby cigar, almost burning his knuckles, was crammed in between two Tootsie Roll fingers. He wasn't bald, but his hair was very fine. He slicked it down and combed it straight back. Even on the sides of his head, you could see scalp between his strands of greasy hair. He had never been married, and some people thought he was gay; others thought he was behind the ring that sold the sexual favors of teenage boys. He rapped her desk with his knuckles. "Hector Domínguez jumped bail again," he said in a higher voice than a person would expect. "Go get him first thing tomorrow morning."

"I'm going to end up shooting him one of these times," Jerri said. "He's getting wilder and takes more risks."

Sam shrugged. "They pay us to get him back."

"No, they pay me to get him back."

"And who gives you the leads? It's a partnership."

"Don't you think *we* could make more money if *I* had some help?"

Sam smiled and crossed his arms. For the last year and a half, Jerri had been more his partner than his employee, but she still trusted his ability to hire a good *man* more than she trusted her

9

own. "You know how hard it is to find good help? Maybe we could put up a display at one of those college recruitment days. Or maybe an ad: 'Needed, smart self-starter who likes crawling in windows, spying on people, and retrieving scumbags.'"

Sam smiled and stuck his cigar in his mouth between his bad teeth. He was a good bondsman and had been a good detective before he got fat and lazy and had to hire Jerri. The San Antonio police, the city council, and the criminals liked him or at least tolerated him because he could balance things. He had no enemies who were important people on either side of the law. Someday Jerri would inherit his business. Worse things could happen. The public schools, especially in San Antonio, were going to hell. Gangs had more control than teachers. Who'd want to be a teacher? And by the time she got a graduate degree, she'd be fifty, broke, and competing with smarter people for fewer and fewer jobs. Jerri thought less and less about what could have been since Fuentes left until she gave up *could have been* and became a private investigator. The only thing she probably would have enjoyed if she had become a poor scholar or a disgusted teacher was more intellectual conversation with less criminal people. Jerri looked at her watch, then said to Sam's back, "I'm going home." In reality, Jerri wasn't going home but to dinner with Palo Fuentes, her other boss, Vincent Fuentes's father. Sam grumbled something about it not yet being five o'clock.

Jerri grabbed her purse, which hung down nearly to her ankles when she held it by its straps, and hefted it to pull the straps over one shoulder. She peeked across her partition and saw Sam bent over several county forms. "Bye, Sam," she said.

He raised his head and actually smiled at Jerri. "Bye, sweetheart," he said. Jerri forced a smile, too. Someday soon she would become Sam's Bail Bonds as well as Sam's Investigating Services. If Sam still couldn't find anyone qualified, she would hire one or two people to help her (maybe two women, "chick private dicks"; she could advertise in the yellow pages). Sam was sleazy but not poor. Jerri would make a good living. She exited from her door and looked across Dolorosa Street to city hall. With its straps over her shoulder, the purse bounced against Jerri's right hip, and she raised one shoulder against the weight of the purse as she walked across the street.

Jerri and Sam's business was in a good spot: across the street from city hall, a couple of blocks west of the Bexar County Courthouse, and a couple of blocks east of the police. The Spanish Governor's Palace had been restored long ago, and more recently the old U.S. military building next to it had been cleaned up and replumbed to house some city offices. The street in front of them had been converted into a parking lot. Historical markers sprouted up all over the plaza. Only the building that she worked in retained its squalor and dilapidation from a time before San Antonio's downtown became profitable and then colorful. Sometimes Jerri wished that they had an office in the suburbs or maybe that she spied on cheating spouses for a divorce lawyer so that she could get a break from the people she had to work with.

She walked across Military Plaza, where bums, lawyers, and old Mexicans sat on park benches. The old Spaniards had governed their northern frontier from here; the restored Spanish Governor's Palace was across the street. City offices surrounded it. Now San Antonio conducted its public and private business in these downtown blocks. You could get building permits, city contracts, or heroin in this area. Jerri figured that she did have a better job than the one in which she would try to convince pubescent kids who smelled like grape bubble gum that literature was important. In a way, the subject matter of art and literature was all around her life as Sam's Investigating Services. In a way, the skills of an investigator weren't far from the skills of a scholar.

❂ Fuentes saw a woman emerge from Sam's Investigating Services, sat up straight and squinted to look at her, pulled his glasses out of his shirt pocket, and put them on to see her more clearly. She wore faded jeans and a white shirt open at the neck, giving her a simple elegance. Her hair was short and wavy now, not the youthful ponytail he had hoped to see. She looked leaner than he remembered; she no longer had the hips that most women get as they

11

move past forty. She walked with her head tilted to one side, just as he remembered. But now she curled her shoulders forward, creating a stooped posture. As she got closer, a chain around her neck and her hair caught the sun and threw reflections toward him. Always in the light and always golden, Jerri either attracted light or was attracted to it. Yes, Fuentes said to himself, she was golden and elegant, even though she wore tennis shoes.

He rose from the bench, and she cocked her head to the opposite side, making herself look, for a moment, like one of the pigeons. She made a tentative step toward him, and Fuentes could see that her wrinkles had etched themselves more deeply into her face. She wasn't beautiful, he thought, but then he remembered that she had never really been beautiful. She worked well with what she had, and she had looked and felt so alive, so sure.

When she started walking toward him with quick deliberate steps, her head still cocked, looking like she would do some harm to him, he smiled and tried to say her name, but before he could, she was in front of him. He felt the corners of his mouth droop, and he said very slowly, "Jerri?"

The wrinkles in the corners of her eyes grew deeper and reached farther on her face. She bent her head forward but put a foot behind her as though to brace herself or spring away. "Jerri Johnson?" Fuentes asked.

It wasn't exactly a smile that filled her face but a look that showed warmth and recognition. Fuentes stepped toward her and extended his hand.

She moved quickly toward him, and he almost stepped back. But she was faster, for Fuentes felt her arms reaching up behind him and then tug at him. She was pulling herself up toward his face. She kissed him long and hard on the lips. In prison, he had amused himself and tortured himself with the memory of sex with her. She had short but shapely legs that she couldn't wrap quite around his torso. But she hiked her short legs straight up over him, raising them slowly across his outer thighs and, with her toes high over him, she sometimes grabbed her feet. He had been so stupid before. He had given up Jerri Johnson for what he assumed was Mexico's welfare.

❷ For five years Jerri had nursed a slowly fading sting that came with knowing that no matter how she looked at it or whose advice she asked, she had been used and betrayed. From the moment she had stuck her fingers through the pickets of the fence that separated Lukeville, Arizona, from Sonoita, Sonora, and watched Fuentes walk away, she had made herself harder, made herself distrust her emotions and initial judgments, all to combat the sting that developed inside her. She had made herself a better realist, a better detective.

She had listened as he told her that he wasn't coming across the border with her and his father, and she'd tried to poke her whole fist through the picket to touch him. When he turned to go, he said, "AMF," and tried to laugh at their private joke. The good-bye ended with her crying and his trotting away. That was when her tissues and organs, everything under her skin, turned molten, became like acid, and created a sting that burned out hope, ideals, and her old life. Detachment, distrust, and work were the only things that had cooled the acid.

For five years she longed for someone who could give her just some hint that she could feel the sting she felt for Fuentes. So the litmus-test kiss was the only proper reaction to seeing him again. When she drew away, her stomach gurgled but didn't burn. He pulled off his round glasses and put them in his shirt pocket. He rubbed the top of his head and flicked at the dangling hair from his cowlick. He smiled at her. She stepped back from him. "I thought you were dead. Palo said you might be," Jerri said. After a second's thought she added, "Did Palo know?"

He smiled and stepped toward her, and Jerri, almost anticipating his moves, stepped back from him. "I was a prisoner. Now I'm an original Latin American voice," he said. He dropped his head. "Though I haven't written in years."

"You didn't write me, either. You're a writer, and you couldn't

13

write me a letter, a note—hell, a postcard?" Jerri said, and slammed her closed fist into her thigh. She turned her head away from him.

"Did you read anything of mine? Have you read anything about me?"

"My interests have changed." Jerri turned back to look at Fuentes.

"Surely you still read Márquez, Welty, Updike?"

"No, Danielle Steel," Jerri said.

Jerri looked up at his face, then slowly pulled her eyes down to his belly. He had gotten fatter. His jowls had started to droop into a middle-aged sag. He wasn't as old as he looked. And the smell of his breath was a little like liquor.

"How did you know where I worked?"

"Palo," Fuentes said, and Jerri felt an ache somewhere above her stomach because Palo, her confidant and benefactor, had never told her he had talked to her former lover. "I asked him not to tell you." Fuentes stepped toward her, and this time she didn't move away. "Did you miss me?" he asked.

"God, did I miss you," Jerri said, as though exhaling, but then breathed in to add, "and that makes what you've done to me even worse."

"In two weeks I'll be back for a short seminar at Trinity University. The Yanquis still hire me." He reached toward her, but she didn't touch his hand. "Will you see me?"

Jerri was surprised how easy it all seemed. She had dreamed of seeing him again and confronting him, cussing him, making him apologize. But now she wanted him back because, with him back, maybe her world would again have the possibilities she had dreamed about when she loved him.

✪ Joe Parr stood on his toes to look over the heads of the other people at Jerri Johnson kissing Fuentes. He took off his sunglasses with the sweat stains on the lenses to try to see better. The kiss was no little peck, not just a hello kiss from a friend. To Parr, Fuentes looked excited enough about seeing the woman, but he didn't look like a lover. He even looked like the kiss scared him a little. Fool-ass

14

Fuentes ought to act like he enjoyed it, Parr thought. If he was just conning her and anybody else who'd be watching, he ought to play out the con. Parr knew about conning women suspects. Besides, Jerri was an attractive woman. She dressed a little too much like a teenager to suit Parr, and he couldn't remember ever seeing her in a dress, but Joe Parr liked the way she carried herself—simultaneously leaning to one side and forward, like a girl and yet like a jock.

Parr knew that kissing the son of a bitch didn't make Jerri a criminal. To most people in town, she seemed honest. But all she really had verifying her honesty was a private detective's license and a pistol permit. And Sam Ford and Palo Fuentes helped her get those. And love or lust accounted for a lot of ordinarily sane people doing a lot of crimes.

The two lovebirds chatted a while longer, hugged, then turned in opposite directions. Fuentes walked toward him, so Parr pressed his back into the hot bricks of the building behind him and crossed his arms. He let Fuentes pass him, then followed him down the street and down the stairs to the river.

Bars and restaurants lined the river, really a canal, flowing under the curving, tangled downtown streets between the buildings that made up the San Antonio skyline. People crowded the narrow sidewalks between the flower beds or decorated brick walls and the river. Parr heard a mixture of music: jazz, rock and roll, and Mexican mariachis—the musicians setting up and warming up for the night's performances. The air was cooler down on the river, and the evening Gulf breeze picked up and ruffled the tops of the cypress trees.

The Spaniards founded San Antonio where they did because of the river. Now it was the primary reason for San Antonio's tourist industry. In 1897 his widow and old friends buried the old Ranger Rip Ford in a Masonic cemetery full of ex–Confederate officers. The cemetery had been somewhere along this river and had long since been moved to make way for the tourists. Now ol' Rip probably stared up at some tourists' asses as they drank strawberry margaritas or some other ladies' drink in some chichi bar. But Parr felt good on the river. Parr and his wife Melba used to like to meet after

15

he got off work and eat good cheap Mexican food at the Casa Rio or the Mexican Manhattan. Sometimes they tried the Italian, Indian, or Chinese food. If they had extra money in their pockets or wanted to celebrate, they'd go to the Old Rhine Steak House.

Fuentes edged through the crowds and went into the first bar that he came to. Parr ducked into the bar, spotted Fuentes at a table, ordered a glass of water, and felt the slight chill of his sweat drying in the air-conditioning. In between the time Parr had closed, then opened, his tired eyes, Fuentes had stepped up to the bar to whisper to a very young Hispanic girl. The girl left, then after downing two drinks Fuentes left, and Parr followed him to the next bar, then the next, then the next. As the sun sank below the trees, shadows spread across the river, and the Chinese lanterns blinked on; Parr took off his sunglasses, put them in his pocket, and felt in his other shirt pocket for his reading glasses, but he had forgotten to bring the damn things. He didn't feel like spending the night watching another Mexican get drunk. So he said to hell with Fuentes, left for the world above the San Antonio River, and walked all the way back to his office in the Bexar County Courthouse. Parr's office was less than a block from Jerri Johnson's. It too faced Dolorosa, just where it turned into Market Street. Across from it was Main Plaza, and to the side of Main Plaza was San Fernando Cathedral and the City Municipal Office Building. Between Jerri and Joe Parr a whole lot of the city's and county's business got done or dealt with.

A few people were leaving as he walked up the steps to the old courthouse, built with large block-sized stones quarried up in the hill country. Parr remembered when most buildings were built with native limestone instead of steel and glass. The Bexar County Courthouse had a World War I memorial statue out front, and old men and pigeons gathered under the shade from the old cotton-woods surrounding the courthouse. The assistant county sheriff, dressed like an accountant, complete with a lizard skin briefcase, nodded at Parr and said, "You're working late," then giggled. Parr only shrugged.

A black custodian opened the locked glass door for him and let him in. She looked down at his boots and frowned. "They're not muddy," Parr said. But the custodian mopped over the part of the floor where he had walked.

Parr took the stairs to his third-floor office. With the lights off and just one yellow ray of the setting sun coming down the hall, Parr had to feel his way along the wall to guide himself to his office. He fumbled with his key and opened the door. With the last sunlight coming in through the open blinds and reflecting off the old waxed wood floor, his office was orange except for the corners. Parr squinted and saw his half-frame glasses lying on his desk next to a spine-down book. When Parr walked around behind the desk, the wooden floor squeaked.

He sat in the golden color of his isolated office, grabbed his half-frame glasses across the lens with his thumb and middle finger, and stuck them on his face. Captain Jack Dean of Company D of the Texas Rangers had his office at what was mostly the DPS station out on the South Side, across from the state hospital for mental patients. Crazy people sometime leaned against the high cyclone fence around the state hospital and stared at the Texas Department of Public Safety's San Antonio station. Captain Jack had two secretaries and shared the office with Sergeant Joey Montavo, but Parr had been in this office before the Rangers' San Antonio Sector Company moved out to the South Side. So the state of Texas and Bexar County let him keep his office. Parr's occasional drinking buddy and colleague, FBI agent Ollie Nordmarken, had a large modern office over in the federal office building, with its glass and steel walls. But Parr much preferred his hidden office. He was closer to the county and city cops. He could walk to the police station or the jail. He could find out more about criminals in downtown San Antonio than in the quiet Highway Patrol station out on the South Side. When Parr retired, the county would probably put some tax assessor's assistant or whatnot in his office and Parr's replacement would work in the South Side office.

Parr looked down at the book but couldn't remember what he had been reading. Damn, you old son of a bitch, he said to himself. When he looked at the title, *Grant Takes Command: 1863–1865,* by Bruce Catton, his memory came back.

He didn't want to go home to his big empty house over in Alamo Heights. Except on weekends, when he mostly liked to sit out in the backyard, he never much saw his house in daylight. After work he'd stop at one of several bars or icehouses where old men still gathered and told stories about being old. He wasn't as old as most of the old men, but he liked their stories.

He forced himself to read on about Grant's background in what was then the West, but his mind kept leaving the pages. Since he had helped track down Bud Harrelson, the triggerman who gunned down Judge Woods, and helped arrest Fred Carrasco at a South Side motel, he had become a stud duck in the courthouse. Anymore, he mostly spent his time in his office or in somebody else's office. He tried to find information about people for the FBI, the IRS, *la migra,* and the ATF. And he knew which people the SAPD didn't want to hassle, so he tried to steer any federal people off the locals who did only a little harm to the law.

In one corner of his office, on a rickety table, was a Ranger-issued notebook computer with its screen clicked open. He had banished it from his desk. He stared at it. It looked to him like one of those giant Amazon snakes that could unhinge its jaws and swallow a whole pig. He wasn't scared of being swallowed. He had learned how to work the goddamn thing; he had surfed the web and knew he could plug into all sorts of private government files. But Parr figured he was weighted down enough already with what he knew how to do. And besides, even though it took more time, he liked to call the sweet secretaries at county, state, or city offices and ask for their help.

Joe Parr heard his backbone creak as he got up and twisted his neck to get the stiffness out of his shoulders. He might as well go home and read. As much as he worked anymore, he might as well be retired. Several people around the state were trained and ready to take his place. All the judges, prosecutors, and cops figured that Joe Parr had earned the easy years before his retirement, and they tolerated his bitching and his theorizing. So not a one of the sons of bitches would believe that Fuentes was doing any more than vacationing.

18

CHAPTER TWO

Jerri drove her Suburban west down Commerce Street and tried to push Vincent Fuentes out of her mind. But it wasn't the Vincent Fuentes she had just seen who was in her mind; it was the Vincent Fuentes she heard and saw as she sat in his class years before. His light coloring gave him the Tex-Mex claim to some kind of aristocratic, Creole background, like the rich enclave of old San Antonians descended from Canary Islanders, who claimed to be Spanish and denied any link to Mexico. Fuentes combed his black hair straight back. But a cowlick, a tuft of unruly hair, dangled in front of him as he read from his manuscript. If he'd had blue eyes, he'd have been the perfect lady-killer. Instead his eyes were a green that changed tints behind his round scholarly glasses. As he himself said, from childhood he had been called a "pretty boy."

His voice had a trace of an accent. Though sexy, that trace was irritating to him, for he had worked for years to speak English like a native. His accent twisted the midwestern-American English into some strange, not quite lyrical poetry. When he read, lectured, or talked, he would pause at convenient spots and lift his slender, almost feminine fingers into a gesture, as though they were exclamation marks. He moved—lips, head, arms, gait—with a deliberate and graceful style that Jerri had come to think of as attractive in refined, educated men. She always thought of him as gloriously young, just over thirty, even though he was older even then.

On their first date, he asked her to a concert, the San Antonio symphony. A week later, in bed, he told her that he was an excommunicated priest and that his present passion was smuggling guns to small radical groups in Mexico. That night, nearly six years ago, he kissed her good night and said, "AMF."

She laughed and asked him what he thought he meant. " 'Adios, my friend,' like the students say," he told her.

"When the students say that, they mean, 'Adios, mother fucker,' " she told him.

"I am a poor ignorant foreigner. A *pelado,* as the Chicanos here say." She laughed then and now at what became their term of endearment.

Now, after just a few quick moments of reinspection, Jerri thought that he looked as though he had caught up to her age. He had the start of a gut and wrinkles. His eyes had the dull look of those middle-aged men she saw who were resigned to their own peculiar pain. Jerri wondered what she must look like to him.

A veteran of boring, neurotic postdivorce dating—snapshots of kids, separate checks, talk of settlements, quality time, and separate but equal homes for the kids—she had saved some money working at the Visitors and Conventions Bureau, borrowed from her parents and ex-husband, and entered school, for the second time, and met Fuentes. She thought, Fuentes could make her her imagined best self. What must his history have done to his looks?

For Jerri a photo, a painting, a poem, a story could show the weight of being human and so made her own weight lighter. Jerri wished that she could somehow create a soul out of nothing. Being married to an artist, appreciating art was not enough. But for all her desire, in Vincent Fuentes's writing class, as in her classes in sculpting, pottery, and printmaking (even with the help of her ex-husband), Jerri had bumped into her limitations. She would never be a writer, an artist, or even a potter.

What Jerri learned in her second attempt at college was that although she couldn't create, she could juggle what she saw. She could have become an intellectual. Jerri loved the chill of excitement when she left herself, carried by the words of a lecture or a book, when she truly, really left behind the world to understand. Returning to herself and the world from the ideas and finding the world and self so much fuller and richer was aphrodisiac. Fuentes gave her this and love, too. He gave her her imagined best self. A man like Fuentes could, through words, grace, manner, and thought, turn human weakness into art, or at least make it stand still so that she could understand it. Art, intellect, and Fuentes made her feel less lonely.

With the discipline and self-knowledge that she had acquired since Fuentes left her, Jerri shifted her mind to what she needed to do. Driving West on Commerce Street, under the I-35 bridge, she entered the heart of the West Side: the place in all the United States where Palo Fuentes decided to settle, the place, as luck or fate would have it, that best suited him. When she had crawled under the paloverde at the pickup point in Arizona and helped him into the Suburban that had just become hers, he had asked her, "Where would be a good place to live?" Then he asked her where she lived. And when she told him, "San Antonio," he said, "I've heard it is a good place to live."

Palo's face, showing the burden that he had carried, could have been the subject of a photo or a poem; for a moment it eased the sting of Fuentes's betrayal. The acid burn started. She felt more alone than anytime in her life. She at first wondered what good it all was. But taking Palo to San Antonio tested her, then made her sharper. She saw inevitability.

After crossing under the freeway, she started up the Commerce Street Bridge, which crossed the old Southern Pacific tracks. From the middle of the Commerce Street Bridge, looking east, she knew you could see the skyline of downtown San Antonio: the Tower of the Americas, the Bell Telephone Building, the Life Tower. Downtown posters, signs, and billboards read NCNB National Bank (the old Alamo Bank), Dillard's (the old Joske's, which used to advertise itself as the greatest store in the greatest state), Southwestern Bell, The San Antonio Folk Life Festival, and Visit the Lone Star Brewery. Signs mostly for tourists and Anglos.

Driving west, Jerri saw billboards that said *La Cerveza Nacional de* Texas: Lone Star, *La Es Mejor:* Budweiser, and *"Centeno* 24-Hr. Supermarket." Small signs, some hand painted, said Davila's Golden Arcade, Asar and Solomon: Pecan Shellers, and Rudy Mendoza's Bail Bonds. Farther down Commerce were the old icehouses (not the newer convenience stores), where Palo sometimes liked to sit and drink beer with his buddies. Jerri drove four blocks down Commerce and turned south on a side street. A few more blocks and she came to Palo's large white house, the finest in the neighborhood. Almost ninety years old, it looked new with a manicured lawn, fresh white paint, and well-trimmed hedges. The tall pecan trees spreading shade over the front and back yards made the house look stately and, even more important in San Antonio, cool.

Palo could have bought a house almost anywhere he wanted to in San Antonio. But Jerri knew why he chose this one. Living on the West Side made Palo both a Mexican and an American. Living in this Mexican neighborhood among these people who had little money, he could immediately buy himself friends and a position. As a Mexican, an illegal one, too, he wouldn't stand out as he would among Anglos. He could start his own kind of business. And he could hide from or buy those with official power. Palo's old house was on one of the few rises on the West Side, so you could see the skyline of downtown San Antonio. Jerri liked to think that both she and Palo lived in the shadow of the moving and shaking of official Bexar County and San Antonio business.

Jerri walked up the long gravel and caliche driveway toward the garage. The pickup truck with the camper over its bed was half out of the garage. A stocky pair of legs stuck out from under the front of the truck; Medina slid out on his back. "Palo's in the back," he said. Medina stood, stared at Jerri, and wiped his hands on a once red rag faded to pink. Bouncing on his toes and dipping his shoulders even when he stood still, Medina was a real *cholo,* a mixture of Mexican machismo and American cockiness. Jerri could only take him in small doses, not only because of his *cholo* act but because Jerri knew that Medina couldn't understand why Palo trusted a *gringa.*

Jerri heard a buzz and looked over the hedges at the front yard. A newly arrived Mexican, still feeling servile and so smiling broadly and looking stereotypical, pushed a lawn mower across the lawn. He waved at Jerri. Jerri smiled and waved back. "Who's he?" she asked Medina.

"New *mojado*."

"He got a family?"

"In Mexico," Medina said, lay back down, and slid across the gravel and underneath the truck. Palo was old enough to know that even if he ran a business that was technically illegal, he could get by if he treated everybody well. He tried to help the wetbacks he brought across until they got jobs. They in turn wrote to their friends, who paid Palo's coyotes in Nuevo Laredo to get them across the river and to a dry place to camp. Then they paid Medina or Ramírez to drive them to San Antonio, where Palo hid them for a while and told them what bus to take and where cheap apartments were and who might give them a job. And when Medina and Ramírez gave Palo the money they had gotten, he gave them a generous cut. And when the police wanted to know about somebody or some crime, if it was somebody who Palo didn't know or owe, he told them.

Jerri stepped off the gravel and opened the gate that led into the big backyard and immediately felt the temperature drop as she walked under the pecan trees. She ran her fingers through her hair, making her head feel cooler. Even with the lawn mower buzzing, Jerri heard the whir of the cicadas. She dabbed at the sweat on her face with the back of her hand. Then she took her compact out of her purse and checked her makeup. The ponytail she had worn in Fuentes's class was gone. Shorter hair made her work much easier, but with her hair cut to stay out of her way, she was afraid that men might think her butch. Dresses or skirts were too cumbersome for her work. Slacks looked nice, but jeans or L.L. Bean khakis were best. Tennis shoes also worked well. A bracelet (silver or turquoise, Santa Fe style), a hair ribbon, or a pearl necklace resurrected some past feminine beauty. Her mother, who lived in an overly expensive retirement community way out north of town, couldn't hide her concern about Jerri. Every Christmas and birthday Jerri's mother gave her makeup, toiletries, jewelry, Victoria's Secret lingerie that

Jerri herself would have been embarrassed to buy, or blouses with lace or sequins.

Palo sat in one of his padded lawn chairs in the shade of a pecan tree with a bucket of last fall's pecans sitting beside him, a handkerchief full of bits of pecan shells in his lap, and a box filling with neatly shelled pecans. Jerri heard a pecan crack in Palo's silver nutcracker and watched as Palo gouged the meat out of the shell with a silver nut pry. As usual, Palo had his feet soaking in a plastic tub of cold water. For some reason, the San Antonio humidity made his feet and his distorted knee hurt.

Jerri first saw Palo the summer Vincent Fuentes had asked her to his father's house in Puerto Peñasco. Palo was trying to retire from being a gangster and so was hiding from his government and rival gangsters in a highly guarded group of condos owned by rich Mexicans and retired Americans. Palo liked to think, as Vincent claimed, that the American money would protect him. She first saw him on the picture-postcard semiprivate beach just south of Puerto Peñasco: a small, wiry man, poking holes in the sand with his cane as he limped down the beach toward her. He had gotten in nearly violent arguments with his son. And with his father poking a rolled tortilla over the breakfast table and into his son's face, Vincent had said, "You live with the rest of the bourgeoisie. You don't have to look at Mexico. All you see is a beach. No trash. No poverty. No crime. No corrupt state. The rich don't like to see the poor because they don't want to help the poor. Same as the powerful. Same as the PRI. One day they will have to shoot. And when they do, Mexico is Nicaragua." Vincent had told Jerri that he wanted desperately to give something back to Mexico for what his corrupt old father had taken. But Jerri could see that if nothing else, Vincent had inherited his graceful manner and style from his father.

Now she approached Palo, and he smiled at her just as he had smiled at her when his son introduced him to her on the beach in Puerto Peñasco. As Jerri got closer, Palo sloshed his feet in the water and cracked another pecan. As always, he wore a new Panama, a crisply starched white short-sleeve shirt, and white linen pants. "Hello," she said. Palo didn't hear her. "Palo," she said

24

louder. He looked up, then smiled. "No, no. Don't get up," she said, and motioned for him to stay seated.

"A chair," Palo said.

"No, this is fine." Jerri sat in the grass and leaned against the trunk of the pecan tree and, for the first time that day, really felt cool. Palo periodically offered to let her live with him.

When she first brought Palo to San Antonio, she put school out of her mind. She got back her old job with the San Antonio Visitors and Conventions Bureau and showed fat cats around town, wined and dined them. Soon Palo got enough power to hobnob with Anglo criminals and met Sam Ford and got Jerri her job after she got tired of the sanitized tourists. Jerri pressed the back of her head against the pecan tree to look up through the branches at the sky and listen to the cicadas. Since she had been working for Sam, she no longer saw much wrong with what Palo did. In fact, she believed that she and Palo had done what most people do: what they absolutely have to. She saw some inevitability in her working with Palo. But she still couldn't live with him. She had, for example, just found out that Palo, by keeping silent, had lied to her.

"You see J. R. in the last *Dallas* show?" Palo asked her. Palo didn't watch much TV at night, but he was addicted to afternoon reruns.

"No."

"Mean son of a bitch."

"You ought to try going to the movies. Or get yourself a video recorder."

Palo said his version of "phooey," shook his head, put a big pecan in his nutcracker, and slowly squeezed until he heard a sharp crack; then he began to pry the shell from the meat.

"I'm a little worried about Medina. I think that coyote, that Najereda boy, and Medina got some things going on the side. I think maybe they got wetbacks wading across with dope taped to their bellies."

"Medina?" Jerri said, thinking that Medina wouldn't have the guts to cross Palo.

"Mario got raided by immigration last week. They find several wetbacks in his kitchen, but everybody knows there's wetbacks in Mario's kitchen, no news. Anyway, these wetbacks are being deported, and Ernie Davila says this guy he knows says they're glad they are. 'Cause you see, they can come back across with some dope. Somebody has to be paying for the dope, and since most of Mario's help comes across with us . . . " Palo smiled for having figured everything out. Then his smile dropped. His tone shifted. He talked to a friend now. "Do you think you could find out who or where?"

"I'll ask around at the police station."

Palo reached toward Jerri but couldn't stretch far enough to touch her. She leaned toward him, and he rested his hand on her shoulder. "I learned something in Mexico. I got too greedy. You get too greedy, you get too much, people want what you got. Dope is too much money. You can't hide. You got dope, people start looking for you. I don't want no dope anymore. Tell the police if I know who does the dope, I turn them in myself."

Palo smiled again and picked his pecan cracker up out of his lap. He wiggled his feet in the water, then rubbed one foot with the sole of the other. "This dope has got young people thinking about nothing but money." He shook his head. "You want to help me shell some pecans?" Jerri knew that she could yet force herself to hurt this man by telling him what she had just found out.

"Hector Domínguez jumped bail again."

Palo shook his head and looked in his lap. "He's got to learn." He looked up at Jerri. "He's in the Aztec Hotel with Oscar Benavides."

Jerri stood and dusted off her butt. "Thanks," she said. She bent to hug Palo.

While she hugged him, Palo said, "Lili makes chicken enchiladas, the kind you like. Dinner is almost ready. A Mexican has to eat before six o'clock. No late dinners." Jerri lost her urge to choke him for not telling her about Vincent and helped him shell a few pecans while they waited for dinner.

After dinner Jerri and Palo sat in Palo's expensive Sears' best padded lawn furniture on his screened-in back porch. They listened to the distant sound of cars on Commerce Street and felt the Gulf breeze as it blew through his trees and through the wire screening surrounding the porch. It was dark, but the lights from Commerce Street and from downtown made shades of gray in Palo's backyard. The different types of bugs, drawn by the faint light shining from the kitchen door behind Jerri and Palo, smashed into the screen and shredded their body parts through the tiny squares of the wire mesh. Jerri, even if she really couldn't, liked to think she could hear the squish the insects' bodies made as they hit the screen because she appreciated the nearly tragic inevitability of the insects' desire for light.

As usual Palo and Jerri each had a bowl of ice cream. Palo, like most old men Jerri had known, had gotten his sweet tooth back from childhood and insisted on some dessert after dinner. In summertime he wanted ice cream, in wintertime flan or *buñuelos* from the bakery down the street. "You should go back to work with me. It's less dangerous."

"What I do is legal. I like that assurance." Palo looked at her like he couldn't believe what she had said, and Jerri felt sorry.

Palo shrugged and scooped up a bit of his ice cream with his spoon. "I said my work was safe, not legal."

Jerri took the last bite of her ice cream and set the bowl on the porch. She rubbed the back of her neck with her hand and then dabbed at the sweat on her forehead. "The breeze is nice tonight, but it's still hot." Palo reached into his pants pocket, pulled out a handkerchief, and handed it to Jerri. Jerri wiped the sweat from her face. It was nice to be friends with an old-fashioned man who still carried handkerchiefs. A man with a handkerchief, grace, and an older sense of style offered comfort, loyalty, accountability.

"Except for how it hurts my knee, I like the hot," Palo said, and scraped the last bit of ice cream from his bowl, then he also set his bowl down on the porch. "*Cabrónes* blew off the kneecap and one of my *huevos*." Jerri and anyone else who got within earshot heard him say this at least once in any conversation.

Jerri pushed herself up from the lawn chair she was sitting in and said, "Why didn't you tell me about Vincent?" She knelt to see his face. "His letters to me stopped years ago. I thought he was dead. Why didn't you tell me?"

"He showed himself to you?"

"Bigger than Dallas. You should have told me."

"He went to jail."

"You should have told me where he was."

"The police got him. Who knows, they might have killed him. I thought sure they would."

"You told me that."

Jerri stood up and sat back in her chair. "He sent me all kinds of letters, mostly about politics. Then he sent me a translation of his book, then of his novel. Then nothing, Palo. Nothing. Why didn't he write when he got out, like before? What happened to him?"

"Maybe he couldn't write."

"Oh, to hell with him." Jerri shifted her weight in her chair and looked across the porch and into Palo's backyard and thought she heard the splattering of insects.

"Where is he?" Palo asked.

"He hasn't seen you?"

"No," Palo said. In Puerto Peñasco, Palo and Vincent had violent arguments about politics, and Palo had begged Vincent to give up his causes and schemes. "First he tries to be a priest. I listened to all that stuff they call liberations theology. Shit. Then he starts to write. Then he wants to be some kind of communist. All that stuff about guns for some revolution that only him and some wild hombres think about. He's at the Palacio del Rio. He wants you to come by."

Jerri jerked, swiveling her butt in her chair, to face Palo. "What's he doing here?" Palo shrugged. "If you know, you tell me, goddamn it," Jerri said with her finger pointed at Palo.

"He wants you to help him. He wants you to help him get some guns." Palo looked at Jerri, breathed deeply, then went on. "He is watched, he says. He wants you to call this man named Domenic Carmona. He says in your business, you can find him." Palo looked away from her, then turned to face her. "There, I said it. I told you. I did his request. Now, you tell him go to hell. Mexicans are going to become guerrilla fighters? A Mexican, he don't care. Mexicans are used to the way it is."

Jerri could see that the old man—who used to control most of the vices in Monterey until a bomb, supposedly planted by the PRI, went off in his car, killing a brother and wife—was more upset about his son than she was.

Jerri put both her hands on Palo's forearm. "Palo, what do I do?"

"Tell him you want none of this gun-smuggling shit." Palo pulled his arm out from under her grip. "All this talk about revolution and liberation and his country. He has no country. His country is with me." Palo paused. His arms rested in his lap, and he looked at Jerri. "And with you." He looked away from Jerri and out to his backyard. "And my only country is here." He waved his hand toward the backyard. "Him and me is all. We both gave up country. When you see him, you tell him to come here and live with me and you."

Jerri grabbed Palo's forearm and squeezed it. "I'm going to go see him."

Palo thought for a moment, then said, "You see him, but you tell him you don't do none of his political shit. You tell him to quit. You tell him." And Palo's delicate, almost feminine finger wavered slightly as he pointed it at her in order to punctuate, like a visual exclamation mark, his speech. Like father, like son.

☻ Fuentes pulled his right arm out from under Jerri's head, laced his fingers, and leaned back against the headboard of Jerri's bed with the back of his head in his hands. The room was dark, but he could see some shadows. And once in a while, light from the downtown lights got in through her window and made sparkles on the wall. He had just made love to Jerri, and her legs and his mind had worked as well as ever. Looking at her face while feeling her thighs against the outside of his hips, knowing her toes were dangling above him, matched the sweet-and-sour pork he had eaten at the Chinese restaurant and the martinis they had drunk afterward in Jerri's living room. Life should be composed solely of good food, better liquor, and Jerri's thighs.

Fuentes stretched out, and Jerri curled up into a ball and laid her head on top of his chest. Both of them were sweaty; he didn't want to touch her yet. He wanted only to lie in the cool stream of air made by her rattling air conditioner and feel the sweet exhaustion that comes after sex and the warm glow in his chest that came from gin.

After a few moments he felt her gently patting his right cheek. Then he felt her trace the scar on his left cheek with her forefinger. "This is new. It wasn't on you last time in Peñasco."

"You remember so much."

"So much is so vivid." She kissed him on the right cheek, and he thought it wise to show her affection now. He slowly slid his arm around her neck and felt the beads of sweat on her back, and Fuentes again felt hot, but he could feel the beating of her heart on his chest and the peculiar pleasant warmth that comes from lying with another person. Though he had been in bed with several women, mostly girls he could find in bars, during this past tour, he hadn't felt as comfortable in bed as he did with Jerri.

"I got it in jail," he said.

Jerri kissed the scar.

Fuentes's thoughts picked up speed and obscured the gin and the comfort. "In prison, I realized that I loved you. I come back now because I love you." He hadn't actually lied. In prison, in his deal, he exercised the guile that his new dedication to his continued existence demanded. In prison, during a crisis, when you are aware of being and blood and aloneness, you must forget other people. You love only your blood. He had started his tour and his guise concerned only with keeping himself intact. Everything was a threat against self. But with some booze, with the coeds, the waitresses, he began to feel comfort. With Jerri's toes above him, he not only felt comfort but he remembered, and part of what he remembered was that somewhere before prison, she was as important to him as his ideas. He felt Jerri kiss him gently on the cheek again.

"Tomorrow I can take off work. I can spend the day with you."

"My flight back is tomorrow, and I must meet with the department chair at Trinity." Fuentes thought for a moment. "But maybe . . . "

"Please, give me another day."

"I will be back for my seminar in two weeks."

"That's too long. Please. I need." Jerri hesitated. He rolled to see her. Her face was contorted and showed the wrinkles that had spread around the corners of her eyes. On her upper lip were very faint wrinkles. "I'm trying to say what I need. But I don't know what it is. I just need."

"I need, too." Fuentes turned and kissed her. "I'll stay," he pledged both to her and himself.

A former priest, who took a vow to reject carnal, erotic love, Fuentes, after priesthood, gave his love to his disciplines, to his study, to his work, to violence against the oppressors. As he looked at her, at the smile that appeared, then disappeared as her eyebrows grew together, he could see that she too was glad to be with him but also being pulled someplace else in her mind. He rolled away from her and stared at her ceiling to give them both a short respite.

He had been a "pretty boy," the light-skinned descendant of a pure Creole line. He had patrician features. For a while, his hair was even blond. And besides his looks, he excelled at thought. Palo, his gangster father, a man caught in the long history of Mexican politics, where politicians, the ruling elite, and gangsters all eat at the same table and sometimes switch positions, saw the promise in his son. So Palo hired the private tutors and sent Vincent to the best schools and then the best colleges. And Palo gave a lavish party with politicians, gangsters, and clergy attending when Vincent decided to become a Jesuit. Thus the pretty Hispanic boy had the weight of his family on his shoulders. He would lift the family to respectability and a higher place in Mexican society and government. Because he was a pretty boy, Fuentes had on his shoulders the weight of ethnicity, history, promise, hope, and disappointment that comes with being Mexican. With privilege, money, looks, education, he owed his Mexican blood. He used to believe that if he could reproduce the suffering and hope of Mexico and then analyze the causes of it, he would alleviate it. Later he decided that words and example were not enough, that he would overthrow the power structure.

So he endured the self-restrictions and loneliness of a priest, a writer, a scholar, and a revolutionary. He forgot about appetite and desire. When he had loved Jerri, he had feared that love might dilute the debt to his Mexican blood. But in prison, a phone book hit him on the head and showed him that it was *his* blood, not some family's, country's, or people's. His concern and his cause became microcosmic—the vitality of his being. At times he regretted his inability to absorb human suffering. His consolation for rejecting other people's suffering was avoidance of his own suffering—through comfort and indulging his appetites, and then through oblivion.

He looked around the apartment. Jerri, Jerri, Jerri, he repeated her name in his mind. He couldn't yet tell her what she promised him. He asked, "Where is your son?"

"J. J. goes to Trinity now. It must be the most expensive school in the state. He lives in the dorm."

"Coincidence."

"Yeah, but he won't be around to see you. He's too busy studying science and math."

Fuentes laughed and remembered the boy's dour face. In a way, he had liked J. J. for his commitment to his half-formed values and to science. J. J. had been another problem when Fuentes had loved Jerri. He had just given up being a Jesuit and was being seduced by the promise of carnal love. Sudden responsibility for a son, even another man's, was too much. "And you moved," he said.

"I sold the three bedroom, moved here. I like living downtown. I used that money to help J. J. I still have some left in case I do ever decide to go back to school."

"You should. You have such intellectual possibilities." Jerri again kissed him, and Fuentes smiled at his choice of a compliment though it distressed him that the new, wiser, more selfish Jerri still regarded causes, beliefs, intellect, or study so highly. He rolled away from her and looked at his watch. He was tired. His mind was numb. Without a jump start from his white powder, he would soon be asleep. "Did Palo say why I need you?"

32

"Let's not talk about it yet," Jerri said, and rubbed Fuentes's shoulder.

"I have to know."

"I can't do something that's illegal."

Fuentes rolled toward her and, nose to nose and looking into her eyes, he began whispering. What he whispered, he had said so many times, about so many incidents, about so many people. At first the rehearsed tone, gestures, and look came back. But then thoughts about what Jerri might do for him changed his voice and his look. Thinking about what he wanted to say almost made what he did say true. "In Saltillo is a housing development. The people are there because a man claiming to represent the government sold them a vacant lot. They formed a community, then a movement, a housing coalition. They got him to reduce his rent. They have talked the city government into providing water. They police their area. They have built laundries and toilets. They have civic meetings. They are what democracy is supposed to be. Now the city and the PRI want to close them down. All negotiations have stopped. The bulldozers are about to roll over them. They have decided to oppose the government. So they came to my group. And we have decided to get them guns. Their leader is Angel Martínez. He will pick up the guns. If they can do this, if they can just show up with guns, even if they get killed, they become a symbol for Mexico. The revolution starts again."

"And they're dead."

Fuentes squinted to see the torment on Jerri's face. He touched her face and recalled their lovemaking and their past love. He wished that he had chosen her instead of his "pretty boy" destiny. "Deaths never justify a cause. But one has to make choices. Their choice is honorable death if need be." Jerri's skin, his new hope incarnate. "We have a chance here to help history progress." Fuentes had learned about human weakness. If he had absorbed anything from Mexico, it was human weakness. He was the PRI's monument to human weakness.

"I can't take that kind of a chance. My license."

Fuentes looked into Jerri's eyes and stroked her cheek with the back of his finger. He felt a tear against his skin.

"You say it's illegal. It is. But it is also right and moral."

"Oh, Vincent, you can't just come in here and ask me to do this." Jerri rolled away from him, leaving his finger in the air where her face just was and breaking the spell of memory and want.

"Dearest Jerri," Fuentes said to her, then placed his cheek over hers. He was still hot, but she had cooled. He could feel the coolness in her cheek, and her coolness made him feel the warmth in his own cheek. "You don't have to do much. Just three things, and they are mostly safe. In fact, just as when I was here in San Antonio, you must be the safe delivery."

She rolled back toward him. "Okay, tell me," she said.

Fuentes smiled at her and stroked her cheek again. "I would like you to call this Domenic Carmona, set up a meeting between him and me in Mexico. If all goes well, we will make a sale. And I will pay him when I get back to this country."

"You said three things."

"You will have to keep the guns for us. Then, with Palo's help, if not his knowledge, you will pick up Angel and bring him here. He will drive the guns back."

"Why can't you do all of this?"

"I could do all of this, but I will be or could be watched too closely in this country." As soon as he shut his mouth, Fuentes thought that what he had said was too close to the truth.

"So what you want me to do is dangerous?"

"I'm not going to hurt you."

"Dumping me in Sonoita isn't hurting me? You shouldn't have done that to me." She pulled away from him, got out of bed, stood at the foot of the bed, and looked down at him. Fuentes could see the bits of light catch patches of her naked skin. She was beautiful in her own way, but leaner. Her body and her mind were harder, more streamlined than five years before.

She crossed her arms and sat at the foot of the bed. He wanted another drink of gin and her legs rising above him again. "If you wouldn't have left me, I could do what you want. I wasn't this scared then."

Fuentes scooted to the edge of the bed, taking the sheet and the bedspread with him. He leaned over to kiss her on the back of her neck. Enough with business and hope. He would try some new position with her, then go into the kitchen for another martini.

CHAPTER THREE

Jerri parked her Suburban in front of the Aztec Hotel and tried not to think about Fuentes. When he left that morning to go back to his hotel, he hugged her out on the walkway in front of her second-floor apartment. He whispered, "AMF" in her ear, then giggled. She had expected something more, almost a trumpet blast or crashing symbols. She wanted to know if she was through with him, if she could muster up the old feeling, if she could be, should be angry with him. The whole night seemed a flashback. The past was there but as though viewed from the present. It didn't give her any answers. But now she couldn't think about him. She could get hurt if her mind wasn't on her job. She was waiting for Hector Domínguez.

The Aztec Hotel was a flophouse. A black woman, Jessie Walker, used to run Mexican whores out of the Aztec, but the vice squad had closed her down two years before. Now an old eccentric with French lineage who lived in the King Williams area rented rooms out to drug addicts, winos, and people wanting to hide. Jerri watched through the passenger side window.

The sex felt good just in and of itself. Furthermore, that pleasure confirmed that she could still enjoy sex and enjoy it with him. It was sex specifically with him and not just welcomed arousal, yet there was something a bit different, a bit strange in his movement, manners, and desires. He seemed to abandon all except his own gratification, then just as quickly, his attention or gratification switched to something besides sex. He left her wanting to know more.

Jerri shook her head to clear it of Fuentes and decided to give up this waiting shit and to go get Hector. She got out, grabbed her purse, and walked toward the house, but halfway to it, she thought about Hector, on his third bail jump, and walked back to the Suburban to get her gun. She got into the passenger side seat, opened the glove compartment, and pulled out her gun and a roll of athletic tape. She pulled up the right leg of her jeans and taped her gun to her calf. No man would dare shave his legs just to hide a gun, so Jerri was glad that she had that advantage. With her gun taped to her calf, she began thinking of herself as a woman, so she twisted the rearview mirror and checked her makeup.

She wore little makeup on the job because the sun usually melted it. But she had enough stored up, gifts from her mother, to last for years. She wondered if Fuentes still thought her sexy and pretty or if he was as surprised at what the years had done to her as she had been at his appearance. On the way to the hotel porch, she stopped and looked at the weeds and rusty cans littering the front yard, found a good size rock, hefted it, then put it in her purse. A purse as a mallet was her idea. Sam had told her the proper way to use a Swiss Army knife for protection. You could lay the knife in your palm, stick the corkscrew out through two fingers of your fist, and slice somebody up. Jerri once laid open a coyote's cheek. If she'd aimed for his nose and pushed in rather than just taking a swipe at him, she could have killed him. As it was, he ran off into an alley in Nuevo Laredo, holding his hands under his chin to catch his blood; later, Palo fired him and threatened to kill him.

After she went to work for Sam, Jerri passed the state private investigator exam administered by the Department of Public Safety. Typical of her, Jerri had studied, but the exam was really a piece of cake, all just common sense. When she passed, she dreamed of high-tech equipment—infrared cameras and binoculars, tracking devices, notebook computers. But Sam was too cheap to buy high-tech equipment that she really didn't need. With her license verifying her, she had become little more than Sam and Palo's delivery person for questionable goods. In a sense, she had become a reputable thug. God, maybe she was turning as violent and as tough as any man and would stop being a woman altogether. Maybe she was becoming so tactful, so careful that she would never find love, that she would be able to lose herself just to sheer arousal.

Once on the porch, she lifted the straps of her purse, slipped her head under them, and walked into the decaying lobby of the hotel, which smelled dank from the leaking air conditioners in the windows of the rooms. Spiderwebs festooned the corners of the ceiling. The residents weren't discreet about where they threw their trash or even where they pissed. Stepping over the trash, Jerri walked to a row of mailboxes and looked for Oscar's name. She tried to become totally calculating, totally aware of every move, absorbed by the task at hand, careful. As she walked up the creaking steps to the second floor and down the dark hall to Oscar's door, she made her mind once again dismiss Fuentes.

In front of Oscar's door she raised her right leg, checked her gun, and stuck her thumb under the straps of her purse to ease their bite into her shoulder. Most city cops would yell from outside the door. Some private cops might try heroic stuff like kicking in a door or a window. She liked to knock on the door or ring the doorbell. Most people were agreeable if they knew the inevitable, and most didn't like to hurt a lady.

Oscar opened the door. She stuck her hand in her purse and pulled out a *Watchtower.* "Have you let Christ into your life?" Oscar took the magazine from her and looked at it, then turned away from the door to show it to someone else. When he put his back to her, Jerri slid inside the door and saw Hector sitting on the sofa watching *Days of Our Lives.* Slack jawed, eyes rolling, Hector jumped up and glowered at Oscar for betraying him. Before Jerri could yell at him, his panic got him, and he ran into the bedroom.

When Jerri got into the bedroom, Hector had his left leg and head through the bedroom window and was about to pull his right leg and butt through. The stupid son of a bitch was going to jump out of a second-floor window. Jerri got to the window before Hector could pull himself through and pushed down on it with both hands. She heard something crack. Then she grabbed Hector's right foot and yanked. Bracing her feet against the wall, Jerri pulled back and finally let her butt fall to the floor. Hector groaned. "Please let go." She yanked again, then thought about Oscar.

She turned to see Oscar moving toward her with a metal chair over his head. "You make me let go, I'll shoot you. Or you hit me before I shoot you and you'll go to jail. Either way, you're in worse shit than Hector." Oscar's face bunched up like that of a monkey trying to figure out arithmetic. "Put down the chair and help me."

Oscar raised the chair a bit higher. "I'm warning you," Jerri said.

"And so am I, only I already got a bead on you," she heard a voice say behind her, then saw a tall man in pointed boots, khaki pants, straw cowboy hat, and starched white long-sleeve shirt casually pointing a gun at Oscar. He looked, Jerri thought, like Marshal Dillon, except that he had his head cocked back to see through his half-frame glasses. Oscar looked over his shoulder and between his upraised arms to see the man. "I see nearsighted, but I shoot pretty good," the man said.

Oscar lowered the chair.

"Why don't you help the lady reel that fish in," the man said, and Oscar helped Jerri pull Hector in through the window.

"*Cabrón,*" Jerri whispered to Hector. When they got him in, Hector doubled over and tried to grab his crotch, but Jerri dug into her purse, pulled out a pair of handcuffs, and cuffed one of his hands before he could get it there.

"*Puta,*" Hector said, doubling over and grabbing his crotch with his other hand as Jerri locked the other cuff to the metal bed frame.

"All right, I'd like to see you drag that through the window," Jerri said to him. She looked back at Marshal Dillon and slowly smiled at him.

"Can we trust this other one?" he asked, and jerked his head toward Oscar.

"I think so," Jerri said.

The tall man watched them and put his pistol in the small holster on his belt. He took off his hat, showing his thick silver hair pasted along the side of his head and the thin strands of silver pointing up from the top. With his hat off, he looked like John Connally. He smiled at her and twirled his hat in his hands, hanging his chin to his chest to see over the tops of his half-frame glasses. Then he turned to speak to Oscar. "What about it there, *vato?* Can we trust you?"

"Oh yeah, man, sure," Oscar said.

"Okay, then," Jerri said. "You got no problem unless I decide you do. Just stay where I can see you." Oscar reached in his pocket and brought out a pack of cigarettes. He offered one to Jerri. Jerri shook her head.

"Pendejo." Hector groaned.

"Shut up," Oscar said. "I didn't give you no invitation." He looked back at Jerri. "Want a beer?" he asked.

"No, thank you," Jerri said.

"I might like one," the man said. "But I'm gonna help you get it." He put on his hat and followed Oscar into the kitchen. Jerri took one step after them, then Hector spit out, *"Puta."*

Jerri turned around to look at him, then bent to look him in the face. "Who's gonna question a short little white lady if you end up dead?" She smiled.

"Shit," Hector said.

Dillon and Oscar walked back in. Jerri cocked her head, squinted, and then remembered that Marshal Dillon was the lean Texas Ranger who once hired her to transport a prisoner to an out-of-town trial. He had sent her other business. "I was on my way to work and saw your car. Thought you might need some help," he said.

"You know what I drive?"

"Sure," he said.

"Hell, maybe I ought to change cars if everybody knows what I drive."

"No. The old Rangers always believed you should let them know you're coming. It scares the hell out of them." He took a drink of his beer, then with the opposite hand grabbed the temples of his half-frame glasses, pulled them off his head, somehow got the arms folded back, unsnapped the pocket of his western shirt, and stuffed the glasses in his pocket.

Hector yelled at Oscar, *"Chinga tu madre!"*

"What did I tell you about that cussing shit?" Jerri said.

"I took the liberty of asking for a police car," the man said, and stepped toward Jerri. "If you don't remember my name, it's Joe Parr." He stuck out his hand. Jerri shook it.

"Hey, really. What about me?" Oscar said in Parr's direction.

"I'd just shut up if I were you. Ms. Johnson here probably figures you just got involved with the wrong kind of crowd."

"Watch your buddy," Jerri said, and put her back to the wall and slowly slid down.

But before her butt could hit the dirty floor, Joe Parr held out his hand and said, "Wait." Jerri straightened up, and Parr reached into his back pocket, pulled out a handkerchief, and spread it out where he thought Jerri's butt would hit.

Jerri giggled, then sat on this kindly old gentleman's handkerchief. She thought that she might be a Texas Blanche DuBois in a miscast San Antonio version of *A Streetcar Named Desire*. "Thank you, Mr. Parr, but your handkerchief is hardly necessary. I've already drug my butt across most of this floor trying to catch Hector."

"Nevertheless, we should remember our manners," Parr said. Jerri turned her head to check on Oscar and Hector. They both cocked their heads as they tried to figure out what was going on. And while Joe Parr and Oscar sipped their beers and all of them waited for the police, Jerri let her mind drift back to the sweetness and misery of remembering Fuentes.

❂ When a knock sounded on his door, Joe Parr shook, lunged forward, and got lost in the moment between sleep and consciousness. He tried to make his eyes adjust to the gold tint that the afternoon sunlight and smooth wood made in his office. He shook again as a chill from the air-conditioning ran down his back and found he could say, "Come in." Then as the door opened, Parr noticed his stocking feet propped up on his desk. He looked around for his boots but couldn't see them.

Charlie Hoestadter, the San Antonio chief of police, stepped into his office and walked to the chair in front of Parr's desk. As

Parr pushed his stockinged feet under his desk, Charlie Hoestadter bent over and came up with Parr's boots between his thumb and forefinger. He smiled and put the boots beside the desk. "Excuse me," Parr said. "A little nap."

Hoestadter smiled that shit-eating grin that politicians sooner or later learn how to make and said, "No, no, no. Don't apologize. Ranger Joe Parr deserves all the little catnaps he can get." Then the smiling son of bitch patted the top of Parr's desk and sat in the chair.

Parr leaned forward with his elbows on his desk and looked at Charlie Hoestadter. But Hoestadter looked over Parr's head, and Parr guessed that the patronizing bastard was looking at the newspaper clippings Parr kept on the wall behind him. "Proud moments for the entire town. No sir, every law enforcement officer in the city is proud of you. Normally I'd have asked a law enforcement officer to come down to the station. But for the man who tracked down Bud Harrelson . . ."

Parr butted in, "I just went to get him. The FBI, and specifically Ollie Nordmarken, found him." He was tired of being treated like a voter. Hoestadter's smile never drooped; it was the smile that TV preachers and car salesmen wear, the smile of somebody trying to get into your wallet. "I asked you to come here because I can't get to you at the police station. And your boys don't like me." Hoestadter tugged at the lapels of his expensive double-breasted suit. To wear that kind of suit, thought Parr, the glad-hander either never stepped out of air conditioning or never sweated.

Hoestadter's smile vanished. He got a serious look now. "Tell me who doesn't like you. Who's ever given you trouble? I'll talk to them."

"I've busted your cops for reselling contraband—dope, furniture, guns, you name it—for running whores, and for strong-arming wetbacks, so most of your cops don't like me." Parr planted the tip of his forefinger on his desk, then looked around for his half-frame glasses.

"All that was before my tenure."

"Bullshit," Parr said, then smiled.

42

"Goddamn it, Parr, you still haven't learned about etiquette, have you? When the hell are you going to retire?" Hoestadter said. Hoestadter had never been a real cop, always some managerial sort who got degrees in city management and appointments in city government. Parr spotted his glasses and put them on. He cocked back his head and squinted through the half frames to see that Hoestadter now looked like he had just smelled a turd. It was one of the few times that Parr hadn't seen Hoestadter smiling.

"At least we got through the preliminary bullshit quick," Parr said.

"You come by this gift naturally, or do you work at it?"

"Sorry," Parr said, hung his head, then looked back at Hoestadter. "I guess I'm just getting old and cranky."

Hoestadter smiled again. "Fix your hair," he said, and jerked his chin toward Parr's head. "It's kind of frazzled." Parr rubbed his hands along the sides of his head, then patted the top. Hoestadter tapped his forefinger against the corner of his mouth.

Parr stared at him. "What?"

Hoestadter dropped his eyes. "You've got a little spittle on the side of your mouth." Parr wondered what the hell it mattered if he had slobbered all down his neck and chest and stained the front of his shirt. Charlie Hoestadter was probably just used to cameras being around, and so he always thought about looking good.

"Excuse me," Parr said, reached into his pocket, pulled out his handkerchief, and dabbed at the corner of his mouth.

"Better," Hoestadter said. "Now, no more common courtesy, or bullshit, as you say. Why did you want to see me?"

"A couple of years ago, I almost got Vincent Fuentes for smuggling guns. Now he's back in town."

Hoestadter interrupted and smiled again. "Who is Vincent Fuentes?"

"Don't any of you cops read the papers?" Parr asked. Hoestadter's grin dropped into a turd-smelling frown, and Parr said, "Okay, okay, I'm sorry. Fuentes is a college professor. He taught here for a year or two back when I first started looking at him. The son of bitch had some nutty idea about starting urban revolutions in Mexico, so he smuggled guns to these poor starving bastards in the cities."

"He's a communist?"

Parr huffed. "He's no goddamn communist. Nobody is a communist anymore. We don't care anymore if they are. And you don't got to be a communist to be crazy." Hoestadter leaned back in his chair. "Sorry," Parr said. "Sometimes I get wound up."

"More than sometimes." Hoestadter pulled himself back to the rigid position in his chair. "So he's back, you say."

"Yeah. And from hanging out over at the federal building, I found out from some FBI agents that some M-16s are gone from a U.S. armory." Parr waited and looked at Hoestadter.

"And so?"

"Am I going too fast for you?"

Charlie smiled like he was smiling at an obnoxious kid or an old lady in a nursing home, like the smile kept him from hitting the child or the old lady. "Go on," he said.

"Real soon now, I bet somebody is going to try to sell them. And here's Fuentes in town now and scheduled to come back once school starts. I bet my boots, he's dealing for those guns."

"So what do you want me to do?" Hoestadter leaned all the way back in his chair, trying to get as far away from Parr as possible. "This isn't exactly substantial evidence you have." The gladhander spoke like he had convinced himself that Parr had gone senile. "And technically now, Joe, guns being sold is not a city matter."

"I need some help."

"So why can't the FBI or a federal attorney help you?" Hoestadter's shit-eating grin appeared. He had guessed that Parr couldn't get any help from the federal people, not even with the influence of his aging ol' buddy Ollie Nordmarken.

"Because I'm asking you. Giving you first shot."

"Now who's bullshitting?" Hoestadter straightened up like he intended to go. "The feds don't investigate anything that they can't prosecute. They can't even issue a warrant with what you have."

44

Parr straightened up, too. "Now, wait a minute. I'd like some surveillance."

Hoestadter turned his head away from Parr and giggled slightly. "How am I going to get a court order with what you've got?"

"You got your people," Parr said.

Hoestadter turned back around to face Parr. "I'm not going to go to 'my people' and ask for a court order on your word."

"Your word is worth more than mine." Parr stood and stepped around from his desk in his stocking feet and faced Hoestadter. Hoestadter smiled and looked down at Parr's feet. "Then just a couple of men," Parr said without following Hoestadter's gaze.

The condescending son of a bitch stood up, reached out, and patted Parr's shoulder. "Not without something firm."

Parr let his shoulder go limp so that Hoestadter's hand slid off it. "What do you need?"

"Something that won't embarrass me as well as you."

"Fine," Parr said, and turned away from the smiley bastard so he wouldn't hit him.

He heard the door open, then he heard Hoestadter say, "Bye-bye." Parr turned around to see his door close. To hell with them all, Parr told himself. He had never liked any of this high-tech stuff, anyway. All that bugging shit just made cops lazy. He turned and paced into the sunlight coming from his window. An informer with just enough information was better than all the bugs you could plant in somebody's car, telephone, or toilet. In ancient times, before wires and bugs and telephoto lenses, Joe Parr was by-God good at seducing information out of people, especially women.

❷ Jerri was a hit at the Alamo Heights dowager's party because she showed up with the biggest celebrity: Vincent Fuentes, a real writer. Though she rarely rubbed elbows, or any other body parts, with these people, she knew them from her days when she had been married to her artist husband and from her job at the Visitors and Conventions Bureau. Starting out giving tours to the representatives of groups looking for convention sites, wining and dining these representatives, Jerri made her way into promoting the city and bargaining with hotels, the city, and the reps. So she met people who were interested in the city, people with votes, power, or money. Many of them lived in Alamo Heights, which was really its own city surrounded by San Antonio.

These people at the party were the political and artistic elite. They wore their finest clothes to the symphonies and operas and paid for the high-dollar seats while the students or the under-employed musicians who really appreciated the music wore jeans and tried to sneak in backstage. Mrs. Townsend, the blue-haired hostess, was trying to win a fight between art and chugholes, so she surrounded herself with politicians and artists. The city council, with federal funds for civic improvement, could repair the streets on the West Side or renovate the aging municipal auditorium, where the symphony played. Mrs. Townsend, of course, wanted to see the threadbare symphony get hot water in the dressing rooms and an extended stage. She flowed through her party in her painter's pallet chiffon and spread gossip about her enemies and good news about her friends.

Jerri had met Mrs. Townsend and received her invitation because she was good with these people. If she'd gotten her degree and stayed with the Visitors and Conventions Bureau, she might have advanced her way to the periphery of this circle. Without money, though, she never would have made it to the inside, and this fact disturbed her. She grew tired of begging. So she left for Puerto Peñasco with her writing teacher, stayed the summer, then returned to San Antonio and created her present life. She now worked with a different class of people.

While Fuentes squeezed her hand, she looked around at what she might have given up. The symphony conductor chatted with the housing contractor who represented the predominantly white North Side. Several people from the Guadalupe Arts Center whom Jerri knew from giving tours for the Visitors and Conventions Bureau made polite conversation in order to get private contributions for public programs. Mexican council members from the West Side, Jerri's district, chatted about the deplorable shape of their neighborhoods. These same council members were wary of Jerri because they were just a bit afraid of what she knew. Art, politics, and social reform mixed in this rich lady's soup bowl. No one served or ate from it as well as Jerri Johnson's distinguished guest.

Fuentes, attuned to the political fund-raising potential of showing off a live, influential Mexican writer, graciously signed books and chatted and in turn told everyone about his seminar at Trinity. He took care to specifically invite Mrs. Townsend to come to his reading that was open to the public. Mrs. Townsend told Fuentes and a councilwoman standing within earshot how lucky San Antonio was to have the likes of him visit and how much more San Antonio could have if the city were willing to give up chugholes for art. Fuentes told her how "delightful" her wine was, smiled at Jerri, and then told the dowager that San Antonio owed its cultural preservation to the likes of her.

As the evening progressed, the rich took Fuentes away from Jerri, or he let them take him away, so she ended up sitting on the end of the sofa and listening to the mariachis playing out by the pool. At first she hadn't wanted to come to the party. She wanted to have Fuentes all to herself this last night of his stay. But having him and his celebrity with her at the party, wearing again a shoulderless evening gown (a gift from her mother), jewelry on her fingers and neck, and perfume on her neck and behind her ears, where Fuentes liked to kiss her, gave her a chance to be feminine. And she had done her own politicking this night. She could get clients. In the future she might be hired to follow one of the ladies' husbands to a motel for a hefty price.

Sam Ford, looking almost elegant in slacks that actually fit his bulk and a large Guayabera shirt, waddled to the sofa and sat by her. "Is this guy for real?" he asked Jerri.

"Are you jealous that he's with me or that I showed up with the star of the party?"

"I mean, what do you know about him? Some hotshot Mexican national writer, okay. But what do you know about him?"

Jerri was growing irritated with Sam's mother act. "He's one of the best men I've ever met." She smiled at Sam.

Sam sipped his cocktail and didn't even smile at her joke. "He's Palo's son, right? That's who he is."

"Right, Sam."

"God, be careful, Jerri."

Jerri didn't know why Sam was at the party. He was certainly more peripheral to these people than she was, but he seemed to have some connection to the city's official business, like he had something on everyone. Jerri patted his knee. "I know what I'm doing, Sam, and I wouldn't bring any harm to our business." Sam looked out of the corner of his eye at her and the sofa beneath him groaned.

Later in the night, standing in the backyard by the pool while the mariachis strolled around serenading the rich, the politicians, and the artists, with bugs incinerating themselves in the Chinese lanterns, Jerri spotted Fuentes in the dowager's huge kitchen. He and a young city councilman had cans of beer raised halfway to their mouths. A woman dropped her hand once, twice, then a third time, then Fuentes and the councilman started to chug their beers. Fuentes finished first and crushed his beer in his fist in mock-macho fashion and laughed. The councilman tried to laugh, then started to cough, so Vincent gently slapped his back. Two more men stood across from each other and got ready to duke it out with beer cans. These were the people who would repair the streets or the symphony. Once the two men started their duel, Fuentes staggered back from them, then walked unsteadily out of the kitchen. On his way out, he grabbed a glass of champagne from a silver tray on the kitchen table.

As the party was breaking up about eleven (time for dowagers to go to bed), Jerri took Fuentes's hand and led him out to the old lady's backyard, where they stood by the pool and watched the mariachis packing up their instruments. "I haven't seen you all night," Jerri said to Fuentes, and led him to a table covered with food. Fuentes's eyes were cloudy, and his unsteady ankles seemed to make his body rotate in a tight circle when he stood up.

Fuentes grabbed a tamale and took off the shuck. "I had fun. Some more food would be good," he said, and put the end of the

48

tamale in his mouth. Jerri stood on her tiptoes and took a bite out of the other end of the tamale. Then they both took quick bites on their ends of the tamales and ended with their lips together, trying to chew and kiss. Jerri could feel his breath on her lips and smell the wine he had drunk. Fuentes finally pulled back, laughing.

Jerri held her open hand up to her mouth and laughed, too. When she looked at him, he suddenly grew serious, the corners of his smile dropping, his green eyes no longer smiling. Jerri pushed at the cowlick at the top of his head and said, "You ask for too much."

❂ Old Joe Parr sat in his backyard in a folding chair and sipped a scotch on the rocks. He had on shorts and a T-shirt and ran his bare feet through the cool carpet of grass. He was listening to the maria-chi music that came floating up over the ivy-covered picket fence that separated his house from the rest of the world. Parr imagined himself to be one of Lee H. McNelly's rangers, camped in Browns-ville and listening to sad Mexican music from across the river in Matamoros. Back in 1875, after reconstructed Texas reinstituted the Rangers, the attorney general sent McNelly down to the Nueces country to stop that old bandit Juan N. Cortina, Rip Ford's foe and later friend. Parr wondered what some east Texas farm boy from up in Washington County must have felt as he heard Mexican music and reflected that he was in the area to kill Mexicans. But this music was chichi-style, rich Anglo mariachi music. So Parr's mind returned to his backyard.

Parr knew that one of the blue-haired neighbor ladies was throw-ing a party. When he came home from work, he had found a small card shoved into his front screen door, inviting him to the party. Cheryl Lee Townsend had signed it.

He thought about going to the party since there would be people there to talk to, some good food, and booze. Then again, he would have to be social and make the idle cocktail party chatter. He'd slip and say "goddamn" or "fuck" this, that, or the other and end up embarrassed or pissed off. Melba had always tried to keep him civi-lized like decent people when she took him to the Alamo Heights parties, but he wouldn't have Melba to tug on his elbow when he said something dumb. Then again, without Melba to nag, maybe he ought to go.

Then again, one of the scourges of being a widower was that you became a piece of prize stock for lonely blue-haired ladies. No sooner was Melba in the ground than troops of widowed ladies began bringing him plates of food and offering to do his laundry. He wasn't about to let any of those uptight neighbor women see his dirty underwear. They would leave notes in his mailbox and ask him to have lunch or give a talk at one of their ladies' club meetings. By now most of the old bitches had given up.

No, Joe Parr didn't like the old women, and the younger ones didn't seem to notice him. Once, in the olden days, when he had a way of getting female suspects to talk, he had a reputation of being a ladies' man (of course Melba never knew this). Criminals had easy morals and wanted more than they had. Sometimes female criminals wanted sex, romance, or just a little attention; sometimes they'd tell all for romance, just a hint of sex, or just a little attention. He was told that he looked like John Connally. So when a scared, needy woman had some information the law wanted, Joe Parr was sent in to investigate. He never told Melba about the extent of some of his investigations. Now he was just too old for such nonsense.

The widowed Mrs. Townsend had nice legs for a woman her age. He had seen her in shorts when she came out to water her front lawn. But if he went to her party, he'd have to talk to the men. Most of them would be younger and boring. And all of the men would want to talk about investments or careers or smart buys rather than old times, drinking, fucking, working, or hunting. He said no to himself, said he'd stay home and listen to the mariachis Cheryl Lee Townsend with the good legs had hired.

❷ Jerri spent that night with Fuentes in his room at the Hilton Palacio del Rio. Just before dawn, she woke and lay quietly while Fuentes, gently snoring, continued to sleep beside her. He would be gone in a couple of hours, and she wanted to remember rather than sleep. The drapes to the room were open, and nighttime downtown shone into their room. The reflections of the lights made shadows in the hotel room, not just dark and light but pastel blues, pinks, and greens.

Puerto Peñasco was a fishing town on the Sea of Cortés that only a few Americans had found. The dry air of the Sonoran Desert mixed with the cooler, fishy-smelling air of the ocean. The public beaches were scattered with dead fish, beer bottles, empty cigarette cartons, and other debris from the fishing boats. Vendors sold *ceviche* and fresh shrimp. Grandmas held their bare-bottomed grandchildren by the wrists and dipped them waist deep in the waves. Skinny dogs slept all day long in whatever shade they could find, sometimes in the middle of one of the sandy, unpaved roads. The Mexicans drove around and didn't even honk at the sleeping, starving dogs. With her boss at the Visitors and Conventions Bureau, her ex (Royce) and her son (J. J.) begging her not to go, Jerri flew to Tucson, where Fuentes met her in a brand-new Suburban and drove her to Puerto Peñasco. She had planned to stay for two weeks but stayed the whole summer.

Jerri folded the sheet away from her and looked at Fuentes sleeping beside her. She bent to kiss him gently on the cheek, then got up from the bed, walked naked toward the light, and stopped at the mirror on the dresser. A light flashed, and she caught a quick image of her naked body. She cupped both her hands under her breasts and lifted a bit until, with another flash of neon reflection, she caught another glimpse of herself. She let go of her breasts and stared as they again sagged. Curling her neck to look closely at her belly, she saw the stretch marks left from the birth of J. J. With her forefinger, she slowly traced the path of one of the stretch marks. Then, turning her back to the mirror and looking over her shoulder, she stared at the reflection of her butt and waited for another flash of light. Her butt too sagged. She then took both forefingers and poked them into the indentations, the waffle marks, on the sides of her legs, just where they joined her butt. She could be in worse shape, she decided, but she didn't have too many years left. Then she turned back to look at the gunrunner and political idealist sleeping in the bed. She turned and stood at the window and looked down at the well-lit San Antonio River.

After a month in Puerto Peñasco, she went native. In the mornings, when Fuentes would lock himself in his room and write the political manifesto that he had composed in his head, Jerri would drive into Peñasco for breakfast with Palo. Sometimes Jerri drove the Suburban to Cholla Bay, walked out in the mudflats at low tide, and collected shells and clams with the wives of retired Arizonans. She made soup from the clams. She wore shorts and T-shirts and an expensive Panama hat that Palo had mail-ordered for her. In the afternoons she would drive to the Pitaya Bar with Palo and Fuentes and drink margaritas on the beach with vacationing Americans. She wrote J. J. and begged him to put a little adventure in his life and come down for the summer. But he said that his dad wouldn't let him and that he had to study for the SATs.

On a warm September night, after the conversation she finally had to have with Palo, the one in which she asked him just what he had done in Monterrey ("Sold people what they wanted," he had said), Jerri and Fuentes walked to the beach out behind Palo's condo and tried to dance in the sand to a sad Willie Nelson song. After the dance, Fuentes led her into Palo's dark house and told her that unless Palo got into the United States, some policeman or enemy would find him and kill him. Fuentes asked her to help smuggle Palo into the United States. At Sonoita a coyote met them and guided Palo cross-country to Arizona. Vincent gave her the title and the keys to the Suburban, kissed her, told her "AMF," then left her to return to Mexico and work on its liberation. The next day she picked up Palo and drove him to San Antonio.

When Fuentes walked away from her five years before in Sonoita, Jerri cried and cussed him but thought he looked like he could indeed lead Mexico into whatever dream he had for it. Now he was pudgy. He didn't look trim or young or capable of leading Mexico anywhere. She remembered his belly sagging and rubbing against her as he pushed himself up from her with his arms as they made love. He had gotten drunk, too. Before, when and if he got drunk, he talked politics or philosophy. Now, once drunk, he wanted only more drinking, eating, or fucking. And none of them kept his attention for long.

Jerri, not a creator but a researcher, prided herself on discovering the inevitable. Among the things that she had researched was that knot of feelings that indicated love. She had listened to other women talk about love. If she believed them, not love but some *it* happened to them just once or happened all the time. *It* occurred after the third or fourth meeting, date, lunch, or casual encounter, when the woman realized that because of some charge in the air between them, something so nearly physical and real she had to push against it, she truly could be content with the man in question. *It* was separate from the giddiness, the pain, the agonizing want of love. *It* sneaked up sometime after the initial realization of lust or love. *It* turned into a confidence in herself and her chosen other that loyalty, faith, comfort, a life together would follow. *It* was the knowledge that she could settle *with* or *for* this man.

Jerri decided that the women who said it happened only once secretly (and desperately) guarded against it happening a second time for fear of screwing up that first feeling. She decided that the women or "girlfriends" who said or showed that it happened all the time secretly (and desperately) forced it to happen because it just felt so good. So either the wish for it or the fear of not having it could lead a woman to lie to herself.

For Jerri, it had happened twice. First with her ex-husband. And then, well into the marriage, Royce must have lost it. Jerri was so sure of her feeling that she never realized that Royce had lost the faith, the comfort, the loyalty. So their being together ended and left her with an acidlike sting that started in her stomach and spread throughout her body. She endured through study, through watching J. J. grow up, through preparing to live without it ever happening again. And then it happened again. Vincent gave it to her. And then when he deserted her, she dabbed at the sting, never fully letting the sting go, by helping his Palo and letting Palo help her.

Sex with an ordinary, pleasant-enough date was different. If he didn't excite the air around her and make it thick, then there was a mutual relief, a massage for wanting. Regular sex wasn't quite real; it didn't leave promise; you could recall it but not feel it long after the lover was gone. Sex with the man who created the promise was sacred, real, always with you, confirmation of the *it* that led to sex. Jerri, for the last five years, hadn't even had enough regular sex.

Sober or drunk, fat or slim, trustworthy or not, Fuentes had once created promise for her. Jerri could anticipate the acid sting in her stomach, but after five years she wanted to feel *it* again. She put Fuentes out of her mind and concentrated on his plan.

Basically she had a managerial task, not unlike the scheduling she did for the Visitors and Conventions Bureau. She just needed to find a gunrunner named Domenic who had access to some fresh M-16s from a U.S. armory. Jerri already knew which local people to talk to. It couldn't be a mistake to help Fuentes. And maybe, by helping him, she could get him to stay and could take a chance at loving him again.

She waited an hour, then bent over him to kiss him awake. He came to, groggily looked at her, and smiled, as though he at first doubted her existence but suddenly took comfort that she was real. She said, "I'll do whatever you need me to do." They needed to hurry. His flight left in another two hours.

CHAPTER FOUR

Parr, with the eyeliner in his hand, stared into his bathroom mirror at his upper lip. Through the steam vapor he could see the mustache he had just drawn. He had thought it might improve his looks. It did add some horizontalness to his mostly vertical face, and it made a straight line among the jagged lines caused by smiles, sun, and sagging skin. But this artificial, too dark mustache shocked Parr, mostly because he had somehow passed through the sixties and seventies without any hair on his face. Melba once tried to get him to grow some face hair, but all he had ever done was let his sideburns go long. "Aw, the hell with it," Parr said, and rubbed at the eyeliner with his wet hand. It just smeared a little. He grabbed a bar of soap, rubbed at his lip with it, then scrubbed his lip with a washcloth.

Having just taken a hot shower, he couldn't fully towel off the water on himself in his steamy bathroom. He would be hot and wet when he walked into his bedroom.

So he sat on his toilet, stared at his black hand, and considered if he could be considered handsome. In the years before Melba died, Joe had given up on his reputation as a ladies' man. He gave up some of his activities that created such a reputation. He gave up on his investigations that required a little romance, attention, or just a hint of sex toward a woman. Joe got so used to being with no other woman that he had forgotten about looking good. Melba had always seen to it: ironed and starched his shirts, picked out his suits, shirts, and ties—everything but choose and shine his boots. Now a Mexican maid (probably illegal)—whom he never saw, just left her cash in an envelope, who rode the bus over from the West Side—ironed and starched the shirts and did his laundry. Melba should have goddamn known about dressing people, Parr thought; she did it for a living for a while, charged women and men ten dollars an hour to pick out their clothes for them. She called herself a "fashion consultant." Another con job, Parr thought. Then she opened her own shop down next to the other fancy-ass shops in the ritzy Alamo Heights shopping center. Parr sometimes wished they had lived south or west of downtown with the Mexicans. He had never really gotten used to living among all the rich Alamo Heights people. He had never gotten used to being rich. Hell, he wasn't really rich, just "comfortable" as Melba would say, but certainly better off than most state or city policemen. He wasn't even "comfortable"; it was Melba's people who had the money.

Parr coughed and looked down at his chest and belly: no bulges of fat but several loose flaps of skin, like a goddamn old lady, Parr said to himself. If he was at home, he even preferred to sit to pee. Jerri Johnson wasn't old enough or desperate enough to take an interest in him. She wasn't one of the local widows or longtime divorcees who gathered in the arts, flower, civic, and symphony clubs that Melba had sponsored. Some of the old ladies with nothing to do still called him and brought over covered dishes. But maybe with some flattery and an easy manner, he might be able to get Jerri to relax around him.

Parr got off the toilet and washed the rest of the black eyeliner off his lip and hands. He picked up the eyeliner pencil he had found in the medicine cabinet and threw it in the bathroom wastebasket. Goddamn dead and she's still leaving shit around the house, Parr almost said. He walked naked into his bedroom and slipped into his jockey shorts. The air conditioning gave him a slight chill, so he reached into his top drawer and pulled out one of Rosa's neatly folded T-shirts and put it on.

He walked from his bedroom into his study. When they added

the study, he asked Melba why they really needed it. Melba said that she was tired of him bringing his after-hours paperwork into the living room and messing it up. So now he had a study and a living room. That's what goddamn money will do for you, give you more rooms than you need. He hardly ever went into the living room; he hardly ever went anywhere in his house. He kept most of the rooms dark, blocked the air-conditioning vents, and let Rosa dust those rooms only occasionally. Sometimes he feared that Melba was still roaming around in those rooms. Balcones Fault, the fault line that made the hills that were Alamo Heights, could go ahead and shift and let the earth swallow most of the house if it left him his bedroom and bathroom, the kitchen, the backyard, and the den.

He sat in his easy chair and felt the cool leather against the back of his thighs. Sleep was what he wanted, but he couldn't yet get to sleep. He wasn't tired enough. Sometimes, if he wasn't tired enough and lay in bed, Melba's voice would come from out of the walls. She'd chatter on about the roses in back, about painting the inside of her shop, about selling the shop and waiting for him to retire, about maybe moving to Hawaii. What the goddamn hell would he do in Hawaii? Sometimes she'd scold him for not retiring early, for not matching his belt and boots, for not keeping up the front yard. Of course, Parr knew she wasn't really talking to him. It was just his mind trying to fool him. But sometimes he got scared that his mind would forget that it was just remembering and not really hearing and he would become one of those pathetic old bastards who couldn't talk to real, live people without mixing them up with ghosts. He hated to think of himself retired, living in this house, and talking to a dead woman.

He reached for the book on the arm of his easy chair. Goddamn it, didn't bring his glasses. He squinted and saw the title of the book, Walter P. Webb's *The Texas Rangers*. He had read it twice before he was forty. It was about the olden days before the Rangers became mostly decorations. At times he wished that he were a nineteenth-century Ranger: one of ol' Rip Ford's boys who chased the Comanches and Cherokees north of the Red River, or with Major Jones shooting up the Comanches in North Texas, or with Lee H. McNelly putting a stop to Juan Cortina's cattle thievery down on the Nueces Strip. He threw that book down and looked at the other books with yellow and red marks on their spines shelved around him. Since Melba was gone, he was turning his study into a library, and he had gotten a couple of Magic Markers and put a yellow slash on the books he figured he had to read before he died and a red one on the books he would like to read but wouldn't feel bad if he died without reading them.

He looked around at all the books in his dark room and thought for just a moment about what kind of excuse he could use to see Jerri Johnson; then he felt himself, wondrously, fall asleep.

❷ Jerri was on the phone to the assistant DA and telling him what she knew about a suspected burglar when Marshal Dillon walked into her office, dressed, as he was two days before, in a starched white shirt, khaki pants, pointed-toe boots, and a straw cowboy hat. Joe Parr immediately took off his cowboy hat, and Jerri motioned to the chair in front of her desk. She kept the telephone to her ear but heard nothing that the assistant DA said; instead she smiled at Joe Parr, something she rarely did in her office, as he sat. Most of the men she dealt with, Anglo or Mexican, were bums or cons who had their faces and their psyches scarred. And she mostly didn't like the crude yet sanctimonious cops of the SAPD. She said, "Good-bye," not knowing if the assistant DA was finished or not, and hung up the receiver.

She heard Sam's heavy, fat-man breathing and swiveled back to see Sam leaning up against the wall, staring at Joe. She slightly jerked her head and motioned with her eyes for Sam to leave them alone. Fat Sam stayed, huffing to get his breath and staring at *the* Joe Parr. "You Joe Parr?" Sam asked. Parr nodded. "That's the man that got Bud Harrelson and shot it out with Fred Carrasco," Sam said to Jerri.

Joe Parr smiled at Jerri. "I don't like to rest my name on old-time laurels."

Jerri shooed Sam away with the back of her hand and said, "Well, let him talk to me."

She swiveled back toward *the* Joe Parr. A single drop of sweat rolled down from his forehead toward the bridge of his nose, but before it could roll any farther, Parr wiped at the sweat with the back of his hand, grabbed the corners of his half-frame glasses between his thumb and a middle finger, pulled them off, folded the arms, and stuck them in his shirt pocket. Jerri heard Sam's heavy breathing and shuffling as he walked into his own office. "I never thanked you for rescuing me the other day."

"From what I hear, you can handle most anything." Joe Parr crossed his legs at the knees to dangle one leg over the other and set his hat in his lap. "I hear you do real well for yourself."

Jerri leaned back in her swivel chair and put her fingers together. A lean, mature man in a freshly starched shirt, boots, and a hat had a hard, rough kind of appeal. Except for the thin strands on top of his head of white hair, he looked like John Connally or a poor girl's Clint Eastwood or Gary Cooper. "What can I do for you, Mr. Parr?"

Parr leaned toward her. "I got a hundred dollars for you if you'll just take a little drive with me."

"Sounds like you want more than a ride," Jerri said.

"Come on, I'm not like that. I represent the great state of Texas."

"Well, it sounds like you want information."

"I hear you're a woman of high professional standards." Joe Parr smiled at her. She laughed inside herself at the thought that whatever she had was high professional standards.

"Mr. Parr, you're not going to insult me by asking me about somebody, are you?"

"Some guns turned up gone." Parr hesitated, and Jerri let her swivel chair rock her forward. She waited several long moments, expecting to hear Vincent Fuentes's name.

"Yes, yes," she said.

Parr smiled again. "Excuse me, ma'am. I talk slow."

"I listen fast. What do you want?"

59

"I want you to drive me to that little section of Mexican ghetto that the city doesn't claim and show me where Juan Maynez lives."

"What do you want with him?"

"He used to do a little gun dealing before being sent up."

"Jesus, Joe, he lives with his mother."

"Darling," Joe started, and Jerri pulled away from him. Another one of those old rednecks who called every woman "sweetheart" or "darling."

"I'm nobody's darling or sweetheart." Jerri repeated the lines she used for the old SAPD cops who were still chauvinists. "Just call me Jerri."

"Excuse me, Jerri, I sometimes have a tough time catching up with the times." Jerri excused him in her mind. He was, after all, a dinosaur.

"Jerri," Parr said. "I'm kind of like an old dog that you just have to tolerate. Mostly everybody down at the courthouse just leaves me alone. Federal courthouse, too. Everybody I work with is just waiting for me to retire. So I get a free rein. They humor my schemes. You want to humor me?"

"For a hundred dollars, I'll humor you."

Joe Parr smiled at her as she got up and hefted her purse. "And such pretty company," he said.

Jerri wondered if she was going to have to keep certain parts of her body out of his hands. "I'll get my car and pull up out front." Joe Parr pushed his tall frame out of his chair, put on his hat, tipped it, said, "Ma'am," like he was in an old Western movie, then walked out the front door.

When Parr left, Sam wallowed into Jerri's office. He leaned against the wall and seemingly filled up the whole room. He tried to cross his arms, but his belly and chest stuck out too far and his arms were too short. "He's an important man in this town," he said.

"Yes, indeed he is," Jerri said, and clicked her tongue.

"He's widowed, too. And better looking than that Fuentes guy you got the hots for. And white."

"Sam, you racist," Jerri said as she watched Parr walk past her window.

"So what's he paying you for this sightseeing tour?"

"You listened, didn't you?"

"I couldn't hear how much he offered you."

"More than I've ever made for any of your cases."

"Yeah, uh-huh," said Sam, and he nodded. "So he probably wants more than sightseeing."

"Who knows? He might get it," Jerri said, and slung her purse over her shoulder.

"Well, whatever. Fine with me. Him and that Fuentes certainly improved your disposition. I guess it's true about what they say about you older women. Keep you happy in bed, and you're happy everywhere else."

"Why, Sam, are you jealous?" Jerri asked. He scooted his feet to move himself back to his office. Then she saw Joe Parr's Continental, as long and as lean and as out of style as he was, pull up outside her office. "Let them know you're coming," Jerri remembered Parr telling her.

❷ Parr had been in this urban blight pissant neighborhood before; most lawmen had. Sooner or later someone in this area committed a crime on your beat. Tourists or Yankees, who might have thought they were used to seeing crumbling downtowns, couldn't imagine that this was part of the United States. To them the dirt wasn't American. But if you were dirt-poor, like those Mexicans, dirt was the least of your problems.

Jerri Johnson sat beside Joe Parr, feeling the leather upholstery of his old Lincoln. Maybe this old car, which he had never really got used to driving, could impress her. "Got over a hundred thousand miles on her," he said.

"This is an old car, isn't it? I mean, they don't make them this big anymore."

"No, ma'am," he said. "Nothing but pimps and old Rangers drive these anymore. But like I said, Rangers like to let them know we're coming." Jerri smiled at this, so Joe Parr knew that he could be crude or funny; he wondered, though, how much honesty to give her. "Really, this is my wife's car. I drive it since Melba died.

My car's an old pickup that's slowly dying in my garage. Next to it is the Dodge Intrepid that the Rangers gave me. But I like this one." Parr's radio was in the standard issue car, along with the DNA testing kit, the fingerprinting kit, and his Kevlar vest and helmet. But he had a cell phone for Melba's Lincoln. He also kept a second red flashing light and his Asp baton under the seat of the Lincoln. What he didn't have in Melba's car was a siren.

"This looks like a Ranger's car."

"Most Rangers drive Crown Vics, Chevy Caprices, or those Dodge Intrepids like I got. They load up their trunks with bazookas and all kinds of dangerous weapons. I just got a silly little automatic rifle and a shotgun mounted in my—excuse me—Melba's trunk." Jerri pointed ahead at a chughole in the half-paved, half-dirt-covered road. Joe Parr jerked the wheel and cussed himself for not looking at a road he knew was rough.

"Should have brought my Suburban," she said.

Joe Parr swung his head to look at her. "I didn't want to impose on the first date."

She smiled back at him. "We've already had our first date, Mr. Parr, at the Aztec Hotel."

Jerri was almost making this fun, he thought. Maybe he ought to forget about this investigation, like everybody was telling him to do, and just enjoy her company.

Jerri looked out his window. "Turn here," she said. As Parr turned, Jerri said, "Just look at this. Damned city ought to do something."

Parr knew damn well the city would never do anything. He couldn't blame the city council. Making this place into an acceptable American community with sewage lines and garbage pickup would just be too expensive. The houses had electricity, but most had outhouses in the backyards instead of toilets. With no garbage pickup these Mexicans, most illegal (another argument against incorporation), piled their trash up outside their houses. Wind scattered some of the trash to bare front yards and into the gutters. Some of the Mexicans burned their garbage in charred trash cans.

Mixed-breed dogs chased the Lincoln and snapped at the tires. "This is almost Mexico," Jerri said. She seemed indignant.

"Might as well be," Parr said. "If I had my choice, I'd rather look for criminals amongst the tourists down on the river. But all you find there are pickpockets." Parr smiled at her. "The FBI and the IRS get all the white-skinned, white-collar crimes."

"I like Mexicans." She said *Mexican* the way Mexicans did, not like Parr and other Rangers said the word. She put the *i* in the word and emphasized it.

"I know you're not Mexican," Parr stated, pronouncing it in the Texas way, emphasizing the first syllable, with no *i* and almost no *x*.

Jerri chuckled. "I'm just sympathetic. You ever been to Mexico?" Parr glanced at her as she turned her head to look in the backseat.

"Border towns," Parr said. "The wife liked Hawaii and Europe."

"You go to Mexico and you seeing starving dogs sleeping in all the roads, and nobody bothers the dogs. They let them starve, but they don't wake them up. You go along the back roads, and you see these enormous mounds of beer cans and paper cartons and empty bottles. And you say to a Mexican, 'Look at that trash.' And the Mexican looks real hard and says, 'What trash?' He says, 'That's cans, and paper, and bottles.'"

"Yeah, Mexicans think different from a white man," Parr said, looked at Jerri again, and saw her try to hide a wince. She clearly must like Mexicans, must be something real strong between Vincent Fuentes and that old bandit Palo.

"A friend of mine used to say that Americans refuse to look at a real Mexico. We either look the other way or stay in a resort. Another friend says Mexicans just accept things. Life is your own needs and the needs of those you love. Everything else is secondary."

"Which friend is Palo?" Parr asked, then turned to look at her to see if he had made a mistake bringing Palo into the discussion. Parr thought that with a few of his hints, she might stumble into giving him the information he needed.

She turned the back of her head to him and stared out the window. "Look out, you're getting close to the curb."

Parr turned away from her as he jerked the wheel. Goddamn old fool—losing your touch, Parr thought.

"How do you know Palo?" Jerri asked, still gazing out the window.

"In our circles, Palo's as well known in this town as me." Parr didn't look at Jerri this time. "He doesn't seem to do much harm in this country. But I hear he was a pretty bad hombre, a real *bronco,* back in Mexico."

"He misses Mexico."

"And you?"

"Mexico's got some passion left." Now Parr turned to look at Jerri, and she smiled at him. "Juan Maynez's mother lives here," she said. Parr stepped on the brakes. "This is really a nice car, Joe," Jerri said, and hiked up her leg and rested the heel of her Reebok tennis shoe on the dash. "Excuse me," she said. She slid up her pants leg and fingered the gun taped to the side of her leg, and Parr thought that a gun taped to her shaved leg was about the sexiest, cutest, and smartest thing he had ever seen a woman do. She pulled her leg down and wiped at the dust that her tennis shoe left on Parr's dash. Parr was even more impressed.

Dogs barked, and children playing in the yard across the street pointed. "I brought you along to shoot the dogs if they try to bite us," Parr said. Jerri giggled. "Would you just kind of step off to the side and cover me in case?" he asked.

"Sure," Jerri said.

"I'm getting old and clumsy," Parr replied, and walked to the front door of the house. As he knocked on the door, Parr glanced over his shoulder and saw Jerri as she lifted one foot, then the other. She hopped to a dry spot and lifted one foot, then the other to look at the mud on her soles, muttering "shit" under her breath.

Parr heard the door open and turned around to face it. He saw oafish Juan Maynez staring at him. Before Parr could say anything, Juan's eyelids pulled up into his sockets, and he said, "I got nothing to tell you." Holding his hands out in front of him, Parr tried to shush him, but he went on, "My mother's here, goddamn it. You got no rights busting me in front of my mother."

"Shut up," Parr whispered firmly but under his breath. Juan looked like a wide-mouthed bass gulping down air as he moved his mouth out of anger but kept himself from saying anything because of Joe Parr's warning. "Don't worry, Juan. Just act like you're talking to me, okay? I'm on a job."

"What kind of a job?" Juan's mouth stopped working like a bass's, and he smiled. Parr looked back at Jerri, then reached into his pocket for his wallet. It cost him ten dollars to fake a conversation with Juan.

❂ "Sorry about the mud," Jerri said, and bent over in the seat to rub with her bare hand at the carpet in Joe Parr's car.

Parr looked straight ahead and said, "No problem." But as he drove down the narrow back road that cut from the sewerless ghetto to Mission Park, through the Berg's Mill area south of downtown, Jerri could tell that he did mind. Despite his manner and the way he dressed and drove, with one wrist resting on the steering wheel and his hand dangling over it, he was particular; he liked his world ordered; maybe he even saw his job as bringing his type of order into the world.

They crossed a large, modern bridge over the rechanneled San Antonio River, and Jerri looked at the graffiti, mixed Spanish and English, on the other side of the bridge. This was the deep South Side. San Antonians forgot about the South Side. The suburbs and most of the Anglos, including Jerri's mother, moved to the expanding, bustling North Side. Close to the South Side Bridge, the city just met the mesquite and the country fields and stopped. Jerri grew up on the South Side, a blonde among Chicanas. Royce was the smart, sophisticated, artistic Anglo she felt destined to meet once she left the South Side. Fuentes was the smart, sophisticated, artistic Mexican she hoped to meet when she was going to high school on the South Side.

Joe Parr turned down a small street and pulled up to the old Spanish aqueduct. The city had made a small park around this little bit of canal that still flowed between the houses in this broken-down residential area. It looked like a roadside park for poor Mexicans. "You said you liked Mexico," Parr said. "This seems like Mexico, at least to me, maybe." Parr opened his door and stepped out. Then Jerri stepped from the air-conditioning into the hot noon sunshine.

"You ever been here?" Parr asked.

"Oh, yes," Jerri said as she walked along the long front fender of Parr's Lincoln. "My mother and father used to bring us here for picnics."

"Sometimes for lunch my dead wife and I would come here," Parr said. Jerri looked at Parr to sympathize with him and then at the large Mexican lady sitting in a lawn chair in her front yard. She smiled as though she kept guard over the place.

Parr walked across the carpet of grass and down the gully to the old riverbed. Jerri followed him. A trickle of smelly water flowed around rocks and through mud. Joe lifted one long leg over the water and planted his boot on a rock; then he pulled his other leg next to the first one and crowded himself on his rock. He turned to face Jerri and reached toward her. She grabbed his hand and skipped to the rocks. They turned to look at the delicate, meticulously made but sturdy arch of the Roman-designed aqueduct. The old priests in the Spanish missions had built the aqueduct to irrigate all this land. The dammed and polluted San Antonio River water still seeped through its mossy sides. But nobody used that water anymore.

Parr stepped to the other side of the riverbed and turned to hold out his hand for Jerri again. When she hopped across, he turned from her and walked along the edge. Jerri stayed where she was because Joe Parr's eyes didn't motion for her to follow. He moved silently down the path as though he were communing with some ghost and disappeared behind some cottonwoods.

While she waited for Parr, sweat beaded on Jerri's forehead, and she blew at the gnats that circled her head. He seemed a bit deliberate, and clumsy because of that deliberation, but Jerri remembered that he carried a handkerchief, and along with a handkerchief he had a grace, a civility, a manner that only a man who carried a handkerchief could have. She knew Joe Parr. He was completely a Texan, just like her father. Her father would cuss the Mexicans, the South Side, and San Antonio, but he had become so much of a part of what he cussed, he couldn't live anywhere else. He refused to move to the North Side, and he refused the transfers. He died of a heart attack while at work in the trucking company's South Side office.

When Parr returned, trickles of sweat were running out from under his hat and his shirt, still crisply starched, stuck to his chest. He smiled, noticing her again, and taking her hand so that she felt the rough palm and the thick fingers, he helped her across the riverbed, then pulled her up to the park. "Time for our own picnic," he said.

Parr walked back to his Lincoln and opened the trunk. Sure enough, Jerri saw an automatic rifle and a shotgun mounted on the underside of the trunk. Parr pulled out an ice chest. "There's an old sheet in there. Would you mind getting it?"

"Do we have time?" Jerri said, and looked at her watch.

"Hell, all I got is time," Parr said.

Jerri spread the sheet out in the shade of a pecan tree, and Parr set the ice chest on the sheet. He opened it and pulled out two beers. "Hope you like Pearl," he said. "Or I brought a couple of Cokes."

"The beer," Jerri said. And when he handed her the cold can of Pearl, she held it against her forehead to cool it down. She sat on the white sheet.

"And I got my maid, who I hardly ever see, to make us some pimento cheese and tuna sandwiches." Parr began pulling sandwiches out of the ice chest.

"Mr. Parr, did you intend for me to help you find Juan Maynez or did you just want to have a picnic?"

Joe Parr's thin-lipped smile spread across his face. "You're a pretty woman, Ms. Johnson." Parr sounded like he really saw some beauty in her.

Jerri was about to answer him when she saw movement behind

her in the aqueduct and had to look. She pointed to get Joe Parr to turn and look, too. Two bare-chested Mexican boys ran toward the aqueduct, shucked their jeans, then jumped into the stagnant water. Their mother walked behind them with a baby under one arm. When she got to the aqueduct, she held the baby by the arms and slowly lowered the child's bottom half into the water. She fussed at the two older boys, who splashed each other and their younger brother.

"When I was a boy, these Mexicans used to do their laundry in that water," Parr said. "Those boys are either out of school for lunch or playing hooky." He said some more, but Jerri left him. Her mind got stuck in Puerto Peñasco. Now, for a moment, she was with her ghosts. She wished that she were in Mexico with Vincent.

She focused her eyes and ears back on Parr just in time to see him pass her a sandwich. She took it and began to take off the plastic wrap while he bit into his own sandwich.

"Jerri, how about you and me having dinner tomorrow night?" Joe said.

Jerri took a bite of her sandwich and chewed deliberately to keep Parr waiting. "Why did I expect that question?"

"I'm an old man. I don't have that much time for patience or subtlety."

It was an honest answer, from a tall, handsome man, who seemed to know himself and yet seemed to have some substance and complexity to him. Of course there was no charge in the air between them, but Joe Parr, she could tell, would be a fine man for the right woman to settle with or for. "Joe, I'd be happy to." Jerri bit into her sandwich again and shoved Fuentes out of her mind.

❂ When he had dropped Jerri back at her office with only an hour left in the working day, Parr left his pistol in the glove compartment of the Lincoln and walked across Military Plaza to Commerce Street, then along the steamy downtown main street to the Esquire Bar. Parr pushed opened the door, walked alongside the long polished wooden bar with the brass rail beneath it, planted an elbow on the bar, and soaked up the cool air. The whole Esquire, with

mopped but not shiny floors, looked like the worn mahogany that
the bar was made from. It had no plants or uniformed girls waiting
on customers like the more modern bars that Melba used to like to
go to with him. A jukebox played country-western songs. Some of
the regulars looked up from the bar and from the booths that lined
the opposite wall. Most were Mexicans. Some waved to Parr.

Parr walked down the narrow space between the bar and the
booths. Most of the customers were dirty—people who worked
with their hands. A few secretaries sat in booths. Bums, winos, and
bag ladies sat at the bar or in booths and mumbled to themselves.
He spotted two businessmen in suits exchanging shots of tequila:
an afternoon high. Two Mexican men with guitars went to the
jukebox. One unplugged it. Nobody moved; then they both started
singing Mexican songs.

Parr had been coming to the Esquire since he had first gotten a
job as a Ranger. He and Ollie Nordmarken used to come to the bar.
Melba seemed to know that this bar meant more to him than their
big house in Alamo Heights; she refused to set foot in the Esquire.
Parr turned the corner that the bar made and planted his elbows in
the scooped pockets in the wood, made by the elbows of drinkers
over the last hundred years. A bartender came to him. "Beer, Sheriff?" This kid liked to call him sheriff.

"Let me sip on some scotch today, Reuben," Parr said, and dug
the two dollars out of his pocket. A beer cost you a dollar a draw
and a dollar-fifty for a can or bottle. A highball was just two dollars.
Joe Parr, like his buddy Ollie Nordmarken, knew that an old man
needed a quiet but crowded bar or two where he could bullshit
with people he respected and get cheap drinks. The two of them
had put the Esquire on their list of haunts for the empty days after
retirement. Then they realized that they did a lot of their business
in the Esquire, too.

The old Mexican everybody called Harry came up and stood
with Parr. They talked about how hot it was, and Harry said he
thought it was going to be a cold winter. Then Parr lost the conversation because he was busy thinking about his date with Jerri
Johnson. As far as he knew, he hadn't cussed anything all day,

thanks to Jerri. As he looked at her during their lunch, he noticed how compact she was, a hard, lithe body. But he also noted that though her butt was spreading and though lines were settling into her face, she was an attractive woman for any age.

Parr thought he'd better get his mind back on business, so he moved away from Harry and carried his beer to one of the cardboard tables at the back of the Esquire. If you squinted to see between the stacked cases of long-neck bottles and out one of the screened windows, you could glimpse the trees shading the river. Trying to squint out at the tourist's never-never land a floor beneath her was Angelica.

Parr walked up behind Angelica, but she never turned to face him. He sat across from her, and she turned around to smile at him and say, "Hi, sugar." When she recognized him, her smiled dropped. "I got a razor in my purse, Joe Parr, and I don't mind cuttin' a lawman." She smiled at the ridiculousness of her bluff.

"It's been a hot day. I just want to buy you a beer," Joe said.

"I've got my own." Angelica held up her bottle of Coke and took a delicate sip, like she was a debutante. For all Parr knew, the whore, who was just now beginning to show signs of wear and tear, might have been a debutante in the small Louisiana town she ran away from. She was white, talked black, did a good business. "I've not done a thing you can charge me with, so don't even try. I got a new lawyer."

"You got me confused with the vice squad, darling. I want to buy something a little different from you," Parr said.

Angelica smiled and purred at him like he was her date to the cotillion. "I'm open-minded. What do you have in mind, sugar?"

"Some information."

"Jesus," Angelica said, and pulled away from Parr. "I could get cut talking to you."

Parr smiled. "I don't want anything you could get cut for." He reached across the table and patted her hand. "Trust me, sugar."

"I can listen," Angelica said, and took a masculine slug of her Coke.

"With your varied clientele and the company you keep, I thought you might know if anyone in town is looking for guns?"

"Jesus, Marshal Dillon, I sell sex, not violence."

"But your boyfriend and some of the other people you associate with would know about sex, violence, and a whole lot of other commodities."

"What kind of guns?"

"Heavy duty. Military stuff."

"Why should I tell you?"

"Because the money you'd get from me is a lot safer than the way you normally get it. No risk of AIDS for my hundred dollars."

"Marshall, I figure there's no risk of AIDS with you even for my normal services. You want to give me two hundred dollars?" Parr kept his leg firmly planted while Angelica rubbed it.

He smiled again. "Haven't you heard, Angelica? Us cops get it all the time for free."

Angelica pulled her hand away, but she left her smile on her face. "I've always had a soft place in my heart for you, and in a spot a little lower." She stopped and looked around. Old habits were hard to break, so Parr slipped a hundred-dollar bill to her under the table for something perfectly legal. "A female detective called my old man to ask about getting some stolen army guns to town."

"Your old man involved?" Parr asked, and stared down at the card table.

"Shit, no. No wild, federal shit like that. He just gave her the name of the guy to talk to."

"Who was the guy?"

"I don't know. He said something about New Orleans."

Now Parr cussed, but only inside his head: Goddamn Jerri Johnson for getting mixed up in this. Chances were that he would have to bust this attractive, lithe woman who was so pleasant to be around. Parr pushed back his chair, got up, and managed a smile for Angelica, then turned away from her. "Hey," he heard Angelica say behind him. He turned to face her. "You want to spend another hundred dollars?"

Parr pressed his forefinger against the underside of his brim to push his hat farther back on his head. "I just gave you all I got." He turned away from her but thought that maybe it would be less foolish to give her another hundred dollars than to keep his date with Jerri Johnson. And from somewhere way back in his mind Melba said, sweetly, without any viciousness or jealousy, "Have a good time on your date, Joe," as though she were concerned for him.

CHAPTER FIVE

Jerri sat at the outdoor table next to the San Antonio River in her white shoulderless evening gown and gold necklace, her hair pulled back, and took a bite from her fried fish sandwich; then she stuck a french fry, dipped in ketchup, in her mouth. As she chewed, she watched Parr, dressed in a tan suit his wife had no doubt helped pick out, sip his wine, then look over his shoulder at the river. Jerri liked to play that she was a tourist or a sophisticate on this series of canals with its shops, restaurants, bars, cypress trees, lush flowers, and river barges. It was tony and commercial but not really too far away from her San Antonio. It smelled of dampness like the mossy aqueduct, of the cumin and cilantro used in Mexican cooking, of the car fumes from the streets above, and of the gasoline from the river barges that cruised up and down the river with their cargo of tourists eating and pointing up at the hotels and office buildings above the river.

Jerri knew San Antonio to be a casual place, and she knew that the Kangaroo Court, a mock-English tavern in a Hispanic city that catered to Anglo tourists in Bermuda shorts, was a casual hangout. But Jerri had dressed elegantly because she knew a man as dated as Joe Parr would wear a suit. Since she so seldom wore a dress, she wanted to be on a very formal date. She wanted to impress Parr, too. So she again wore her evening gown, which she had just worn for Fuentes at the Alamo Heights dowager's party. And she had taken special care to hide the creases around her mouth and at the corners of her eyes with makeup. She was surprised at how good a time she was having with Joe Parr. Jerri was the tough PI, the former lover of Vincent Fuentes, the flirtatious date of Joe Parr. She had worn a sleeveless evening gown twice in two weeks, yet she had crawled in a window after a bail jumper and coerced his criminal friend. Jerri sometimes worried which face to wear. But she had needed this one: a woman worth a gentleman's attention.

"You couldn't have wanted to grow up to be a private detective," Joe Parr said.

"Don't I look the part?"

"Private detectives aren't beautiful women. They're shabby old men." The old Ranger knew how to flirt. She liked the flirting, though. It seemed some long-forgotten, archaic custom, something to make your time together pleasant, whether sex or love were anticipated or not.

"There are women private detectives on TV."

"That's on TV. I don't like TV much," Parr said. "But I guess you do. You're young enough."

"Joe, you're the first man in a long time to refer to me as young." Jerri took another bite and started to chew. When she had swallowed, she asked, "Did you always want to be a Ranger?"

"No. My mama, like most mamas, always said I should be a doctor, lawyer, or preacher. I wanted to be a historian. But then I found out they didn't make much of a living."

"So you've been to college?"

"Way back when college was real simple. Before math." He stared down at his plate and chewed in one corner of his mouth, but he lifted one eyebrow to look at her.

"Well, why a Ranger?"

"I was working for Immigration as an inspector. Seemed more exciting and glorious to be a Ranger. I was tired of chasing poor Mexicans. Seemed like maybe I could do some good as a Ranger. We believed in right and wrong in the olden days."

Jerri giggled and put a napkin up to her mouth to keep from

spitting out bread crumbs. "A cop thinking about right and wrong is as funny as a lawyer thinking about it. It's just a game."

"Maybe, but I figure I'm better off than the guy smuggling dope."

"Yes, you are," Jerri said. She cocked her head and looked at Parr to see if she could tell what he was really like. He was smarter than the words he used. She put down her sandwich and turned from Parr to look at the river, wanting at once to laugh at him and to consider what he had said. "Not many people think about a job in terms of right and wrong. You just do what you do." She thought of Palo and then Vincent and the arguments they'd had in Mexico, the debates about the Mexicans as potential revolutionaries or as quiet, resigned, passionate realists. She chose to tell about Palo. "A friend of mine," she said, then thought, What the hell? With a smile she looked at Parr and continued, "Palo says we should value only our impulses and needs."

"Kind of a credo of selfishness."

The word *credo* sounded funny in Parr's mouth. "Do you operate from a sense of selfishness?" she asked.

"Yes. I try to get what I want," Parr said, took a sip of his wine, leaned back in his chair, and smiled as though he were somehow dangerous. She giggled.

"So I'm not a lady-killer," he said. "But you ain't as tough as you pretend, either."

"Playing tough is an occupational necessity," Jerri said. "I used to want to be something else."

"What?"

She thought of Fuentes and Mexico, then back to Royce and the fascination of being in love with an artist. Too bad that Fuentes dumped her and the artist turned out to be neurotic and conservative. "A princess," she said. "I wanted to be a princess, just like every other woman." She laughed. Parr looked at her and wrinkled his brows. "Then an English teacher," she said. "Both ideas were fairy tales."

❂ After their dinner they stopped for more drinks at another bar on the river, then walked along the river, their hands brushing until

Jerri grabbed Parr's and held on to it. So Parr let Jerri pull him along the river. She pulled him into the Marriott hotel, built right over the river, to look at its design and its fountains. And as they started to leave the Marriott, Jerri heard a trumpet playing. She pulled Parr along as she followed the sound to the bar where Jim Cullum and his Happy Jazz Band were playing, so Joe Parr found himself sitting in a bar with shiny floors and polished brass with tourists and the type of people Melba liked. Jerri ordered a martini, Joe a beer, but he tasted Jerri's martini, the first time ever, and found he could stomach the goddamn Yankee drink. While he drank his second overpriced beer, Parr squirmed and tried to figure out what was so great about the music he heard. If he were with Melba, she would have wanted to donate to some jazz fund.

Around midnight the band took a break, so Jerri pulled Parr up out of his seat to walk back to the car. Grabbing for her purse, she spilled a drink on her white dress. "Crap," she said, and wiped at the stain with a paper napkin. Parr reached into his pants pocket and pulled out a handkerchief. When he offered it to Jerri, she slowly turned it in her hands, as though she were fascinated with a simple, silly goddamn handkerchief. Then she dabbed at the stain and turned the handkerchief around once more in her hands. She handed it back to him and said, "Thank you," in a sad way. "Very few men carry handkerchiefs anymore," she added.

The nightly Gulf breeze was cooling the city. Parr pulled Jerri up to a street where a heavy street sweeper slowly rounded a corner. "Where are we going?" Jerri asked.

"A real bar," Parr said. He held on to her hand as they walked the six blocks to the Esquire. When they walked in, the rough after-midnight crowd stared at the two gringo tourists dressed to kill. Parr pushed Jerri into a slot at the crowded bar, then stood behind her.

"This is not the place to be dressed like this," Jerri said to Parr.

"You scared?" Parr asked.

"Order me a beer."

Reuben, the bartender, worked his way to Parr. "Hi, Sheriff," he said. He looked at Jerri. "Beer or a scotch, Ms. Johnson?" Jerri beamed up at Parr. Parr forced himself to keep a smile from his face, but he was smiling inside his head.

After three beers apiece they walked back down Commerce. Parr insisted that he walk Jerri back to her car before he went to his. When they got to her Suburban, Parr said, "Strange car for a lady," and held open the driver's door for her.

"It was a gift," she said, then reached up to pat his cheek, then kissed it.

Parr stood holding open the door and looked at the short blond lady in the shoulderless evening dress who could drink martinis, scotch, and beer in hotel bars and honest-to-God genuine bars. She bunched her skirt up with one hand, grabbed the steering wheel with the other, and pulled herself into the Suburban. From the driver's seat she turned to look at Parr. He saw a bit of reflection from the dome light catch on one of her nearly gold shoulders. She wrinkled her nose and her brow as if to ask him what he was doing.

What the hell, Parr said to himself, and stuck his head into the driver's side of the Suburban to kiss her on the mouth.

As he pulled back from the kiss, she wrapped her arms around his neck and let him pull her out of the seat so that she was standing in front of him. He lowered his head as she rose on tiptoes to kiss him hard and long.

Gradually Jerri pulled away and looked at Parr as she backed into her Suburban.

"Maybe we ought to do this again?" Parr said.

"Maybe," she said, and Parr closed the door rather than jumping in with her as his mind was telling him to do.

"It's late," Parr said.

"Yes, it's late," she said. She started her car and pulled away.

"Holy good goddamn," Parr said to himself. He walked back to his car, risking a mugging, and thinking about Jerri Johnson in her evening dress, eating a sandwich. Joe's mind got crowded. Jerri was rougher than Melba but more beautiful, not just in physical ways but in ways that could become recurring memories and feelings and sights and smells. This strange woman could dress like she was meeting the president and dip a french fry in ketchup.

"A nice girl," he heard Melba say in his head as he walked into the parking lot where he'd left his car. He shook his head a bit to clear his mind of Jerri so he could know where he was. He wandered a bit, then spotted the Lincoln. He drove back to his house, careful to keep his mind on exits and traffic.

Parr went into the dark house and made his way by memory down the long dark hall to his study. He turned down the air-conditioning, stripped to his shorts, and climbed in bed. He couldn't yet go to sleep because of all the walking he had done.

After a while Parr got out of bed, stumbled to the kitchen to grab a beer, slid open the plate glass door, and went out to his backyard. He sat, sipped from his can of beer, and felt the cool Gulf breeze and the cold plastic of the lawn chair on his all but naked legs. The breeze caught the spray from the neighbors' sprinklers that automatically turned themselves on late every other night. And the breeze carried the smell of his neighbors' fresh-cut lawn, honeysuckle, and chlorine from the pool. Between some of the hedges Parr could see the shimmering lights reflected in the neighbors' pool. They must have been swimming tonight and forgotten to completely shut down. His Alamo Heights neighbors liked backyard parties on summer nights.

"Good evening, Joe."

"Hello, Melba," Joe replied.

"It's a nice evening. You can smell the neighbors' flowers." Joe sipped his beer and didn't answer Melba. He could almost see her fidgeting there in his mind. "The yard really looks nice, Joe. You're doing such a good job with it." Parr grumbled into his can of beer. Melba, he knew, would get to some point sooner or later. "Do you ever regret not having kids?" Melba finally asked.

"I don't miss them," Joe said, and sipped his beer. So that was what she thinking about tonight.

"But do you regret not having any kids to miss?"

"I was busy. You were busy. Money was tight before your folks died."

"But what if?"

"I don't think about it."

"Oh, Joe," Melba said, then giggled. Now that she was dead, Melba always let up before he got bothered or they got into an argument, thank God. "You know what I think you ought to think about?"

Joe smiled and played her game. "What?"

"You ought to think about taking that pretty girl somewhere nice," Melba said.

Joe smiled to himself and to the Melba in his head. "I will, Melba," he said to both.

❷ The next day, drowsy until noon, Joe Parr called Jerri Johnson to tell her he had had a nice time. Melba's coaching had taught Joe Parr that politeness and manners always made a man more attractive to a woman. Besides, when he let himself think about it, he just wanted to talk to Jerri again. She thanked him and suggested that they have dinner at her house the next night. She wanted to grill chicken and serve it with a special salad that she made and some kind of pasta. She mentioned wine. Joe accepted. But then he got to wondering. He knew of course that Jerri Johnson couldn't trust him, but he wondered if he could trust Jerri Johnson. An old man, he knew, could be foolish when it came to younger women.

So Joe called his oldest friend, Ollie Nordmarken. Ollie suggested that they meet after work at Jack Neal's Icehouse for a beer and some horse trading. Joe could have hiked over to Ollie's office rather than meeting him at Neal's, but Joe hated Ollie's office. It was with the rest of the FBI agents and federal judges and marshals over in the Federal Building, one of those modern structures made of steel and glass or fiberglass or whatever it was they used for glass. In Ollie's office the top half of the wall facing outside was all glass. And the old bastard kept the blinds open so that his office had no shade or shadows, no gold color like Joe's office in the Bexar County Courthouse; Ollie's office was bright even in the late afternoon.

After work, the sun still blazing, Joe drove to Jack Neal's Ice House. He bought a beer inside, then walked to the picnic bench sitting out under a scraggly scrub oak beside the old building. Joe Parr cussed the 7-Elevens and Stop-N-Gos and other silly-named goddamn convenience stores that closed some of the old-style icehouses, which were left over from a time when the hot, humid city didn't have air-conditioning. Parr was about to cuss air-conditioning for closing down the icehouses, but then he remembered how he sweated from April to October.

Ollie Nordmarken was sitting at the picnic bench with his head slumped forward over a can of Budweiser. Ollie had taken off his FBI man's official-looking coat and tie and left them in his pickup. Joe sat across from him and poked at Ollie's shoulder. Ollie's eyes twitched, then he shook his head to come to. "Damn, it's hot!" Ollie said.

"You've lived here now, how many years, and you still don't know how hot an afternoon gets," Joe said. Ollie had circles of sweat under his arms and drops of sweat running down his forehead. "We could go someplace with air-conditioning," Joe said. The truth was, as Joe well knew, that Ollie was a Yankee, born in Pittsburgh. When he became an FBI agent and got assigned in the South, he found out that he loved the sunshine and the heat. Joe continued to tease him. "The Esquire? The East Side Club? That it? That black bar on the East Side you like?"

"Esquire's too far, and old men like us would get cut up in the East Side Club. It'll cool off. I like the evenings here," Ollie said. Joe knew that Ollie came here (and to other bars) too often. Ollie had given up cigarettes because his doctors told him to stop drinking and smoking, but he still liked to have a couple of beers in the evening. Joe wouldn't have let doctors scare him out of an evening beer, either.

Ollie leaned back, held on to the picnic table with one hand, and took off his glasses and pinched the bridge of his nose with his other hand. They were two drowsy old men, Joe thought, who maybe ought to just be waking up from an afternoon nap. Joe was beginning to realize, as he was sure Ollie was discovering, that old people sleep in the day because they don't sleep enough at night. And each old person is kept awake by his or her own peculiar thoughts or aches. "Joe, you treat me like some back alley informer, some pimp or hooker," Ollie said.

Joe Parr sipped his beer and leaned on one elbow toward Ollie. They had been pals for years, but several times, because of their horse trading, they had cussed each other and nearly ended their friendship. "I just want to know what's happened to those stolen guns."

"Officially, I'm not supposed to know nothing. This is only for FBI ears," Ollie said, and looked up at the tree limbs. The sagging skin on his neck quivered, and Joe had noticed that the softening muscles in Ollie's chest and belly were starting to quiver, too. "The evening Gulf breeze is coming in." Ollie pulled his head down to look at Parr. "Joe, why are we still fucking around like this? We're both too old to give a shit anymore."

"I got a hunch," Joe said.

"Joe, as a lawman, your dick's gone limp. They're going to make you retire soon as you get of age. The Texas Department of Public Safety is not about to have some seventy-year-old Ranger on its payroll when it's got all kinds of young men, women, and minorities waiting to be Rangers. Hell, you don't even have to retire. The Rangers have that special retirement program thing. You can be eighty years old and still legally shoot people." Ollie pulled a handkerchief out of his pocket and rubbed at the lenses of his glasses. "You and me need to start thinking about what we're going to do when we've got nothing to do."

"You talk like we're dead," Parr said.

Ollie smiled and slipped on his glasses. "Just as a favor, I'm going to tell you that those guns have traded hands a few times but haven't gone nowhere. Latest word is that some New Orleans wise guys now own them. They got the power to cut a deal."

"If you were going to suspect somebody of making the deal, who would you suspect?"

"You don't want much, do you? Bet you ain't even gonna kiss me afterward, are you?"

"Any ideas?"

"This pissant of a gangster named Domenic Carmona deals in guns."

"Got any pictures of him?"

"Whoa." Ollie leaned across the picnic table on his elbows. "I've shown you mine. You show some of yours."

Parr smiled at Ollie, pulled off his cowboy hat, and moved the tips of his fingers in circles around the leather band inside the crown. "You're right. It is hot."

Ollie smiled back. "Cooling off, though."

Parr took a sip of beer. "Could you just trust me on this one?"

"Trust ain't worth the effort it takes to spit."

Ollie didn't enjoy dickering the way he used to, maybe because he was aging, maybe dying. He went to the doctor regularly to see about his blood pressure, but he never told Parr how good or bad a shape he was in. Parr looked at Ollie's sagging, tired face and knew that he could have lied to him and gotten some kind of answer, but because he was a good friend, and tired, and deserving of the dignity he no longer got in his profession, Parr told him whom he suspected. "You remember Fuentes?"

"What is it gives you a hard-on about that Mexican?" Ollie asked, and stared back at the tree limbs. He lowered his head, spread out his arms, and said, "Gulf breeze is here. Be dark soon. Breathe deep. You can almost smell the Gulf."

"Fuentes is going to be back in town," Parr said.

"I read the papers," Ollie said, and dropped his arms, making the saggy flesh on his chest quiver. "And so you think the guns are going to meet him here." Parr knew that Ollie's heart wasn't in this. It was taking him too long to put the pieces together. Used to be, if Parr could interest him, Ollie would make some calls and get several FBI computers whirring and spitting out all kinds of facts.

"Yeah," Parr said.

Ollie folded his hands across his belly and looked at Parr. "He's too tough to catch even if he is doing something criminal, and he's probably just on vacation."

"That could be. Could be I'm just a limp-dick old man, like you say," Parr said.

"Could be," Ollie said. He gently lowered his face into his hands and rubbed it, then looked up at Parr. "I'll see if I can't find you a picture of Carmona."

Parr felt himself smile. "Thank you, Ollie."

Ollie, his eyes red from rubbing, said, "Joe, you never were like me."

"What?"

Ollie leaned on both elbows to put his face closer to Joe's. The drops of sweat on Ollie's face splattered on a wooden slat of the table just under his chin. Ollie, a goddamn Yankee, honest-to-God liked to sweat. "You want to run the whole fucking thing, see the whole picture. I just work with what they give me. Put the facts together with bank accounts and ledger sheets and telephone calls to Omaha, Nebraska. I never did this hard-dick cowboy shit you always want to do. Somebody calls me. I call somebody else. And a computer in Washington comes up with some hard facts." Ollie wiped his face with an open palm and, even though he was sweating, shivered just a bit from some chill that ran up his spine. "Henry Esparza's bank account shows only four thousand dollars' worth of deposits for an entire year, and suddenly this Mexican democrat donates just under the federal limit to a Republican congressman. I don't have to figure it all out. I don't have to make it make sense."

"That's easy," Joe Parr interrupted his friend. "The congressman is probably on the take or got business interests in Mexico, and Esparza's got business interests on both sides of the border, and one of those interests is a little shady."

Ollie smiled at his friend and said, "Shit, Joe Parr. You goddamn, silly-ass, out-of-date cowboy." The Gulf breeze picked up, and the sun sank that fraction of a degree so that the trees and building kept its rays off Joe and Ollie. Suddenly the world was cooler. "Relax, Joe. Just do the little trivial shit they tell you to do."

"I was the man that arrested Bud Harrelson. You were the man figured out where he was," Joe said.

Ollie smiled. "Time to start thinking about other things, Joe."

For a moment Parr thought his friend would tell him about the pressure in his veins or in his head, but Ollie just kept smiling at Parr and reached across the table to pat Parr's shoulder. "Wish I'd have taken up golf," Ollie said.

"It's a silly goddamn game. You wouldn't enjoy it," Joe said.

They drank beer until the sun went down and the south Texas dusk surrounded them. It was the nice time of day when the San Antonio heat finally let up and the mosquitoes and lightning bugs came out. It was a quiet time of day. The rush hour traffic was over, and people were out watering their lawns and walking instead of zooming around town in cars. Suddenly a man was cool for the first time since noon. He could drink beer and build up an appetite for a good supper. Joe Parr would have rather been somewhere with Jerri, but Ollie Nordmarken was good to have around every so often.

❧ A week later, after a bunch of dinners and smoky bars, a Sunday drive, and some country-western dancing, Parr stepped into Jerri's apartment for the second time. Parr would have had her over, but he wasn't sure what the Melba in his head would think of a woman in her house. Goddamn, though, why should he give a damn? Hell, Melba would probably be encouraging. But then again, when on a case, a law officer is never supposed to actually bed a suspect. Makes for a nasty trial. Not that it didn't go on, anyway. The old cops always said a little nookie in the line of duty never hurt nobody and would probably help their marriages. Back when he was a younger, handsome man, with blue eyes and a hard dick and a reputation for coaxing information out of female informers, Joe Parr himself had violated the rules about not bedding an informer.

As Parr sat on her overstuffed sofa, Jerri offered him a beer or wine. He winked. "I only drink wine at weddings and dinners I'm made to go to." Jerri walked into her kitchen, and Parr had a look around.

In the living room hung a very large portrait of Jerri. Parr liked it, but not the other painting of an obscenely shaped fat woman. Parr knew, though, that the painting of the fat lady was "artistic" because Melba would have liked it and wanted to buy it or donate it to a museum. Parr sniffed the furniture, which still smelled new, and looked at the shelves crammed with books. He stood and edged toward the bookcase, cocked back his head to see through the bottom frames of his glasses, and saw that most of what she read was novels. He recognized only the names Updike, Bellow, and Fuentes. Jerri crept up on him as he was staring at the books. "Do you read any of those people?" she asked. He jumped inside himself, his heart pounding into his throat. Goddamn getting old and senile, he said to himself. He didn't even hear her coming.

Parr stepped away from the bookcase, and Jerri motioned for him to sit beside her on the sofa. She set an opened, sweating can of beer with a napkin pasted to it in front of Parr. She had a glass of white wine.

"When I read a book, it's nonfiction. I feel like I'm cheating when I read something that didn't really happen."

"I used to want to draw, then sculpt, then write," Jerri said, then looked at him with a wry smile. "I got involved with the teacher." She chuckled. "Twice."

"You don't regret anything, do you?" Parr suddenly said to Jerri, turning to her. "Do you?"

"Most of us do what we have to or want to."

"What about getting involved with your teacher?"

Jerri stared into her wineglass, then set it down on the coffee table. "Not for a moment."

Parr scooted closer to Jerri to set down his beer. "I guess we both know why I'm here."

Jerri smiled, but before she could giggle, Parr leaned toward her, kissed her, and slid one arm behind her neck. When he pulled away from her, she giggled again. "You are direct."

"Don't have much time," Parr said, and gently kissed her neck and cheek, then felt himself slowly fall into her and both of them slide down the back of the sofa. They rolled so that they were lying on their sides facing each other. Parr was careful not to let the soles of his boots touch Jerri's sofa. When they pulled apart from kissing, Parr felt her breath on his face. She kissed him again, and Parr felt his hand slowly rise up her inner thigh. His hand hit her crotch, and she and his hand quivered. Goddamn, he thought, it's like riding a bicycle. Flushed, warm, Parr concentrated on his hand and where it was but also tried to feel every bit of his skin that touched hers. Then he pulled his hand away and sat upright. He had to take a time-out to wonder about his investigation, his motives, a possible trial.

Jerri pushed her hair into shape and sat up beside him. She stood, then she held out a hand for Parr. He took it. She pulled him up and led him toward her bedroom.

"I can't," Parr said on the way to the bedroom.

"After all the dinners and all the flirting?"

"You don't understand," Parr said, but didn't let go of her hand. He stood looking at her, and as he saw her eyes flashing with light and filled with own reflection, he said to himself that he had two choices. He could go ahead and tell her what he was up to, what was going on, and hope for forgiveness and then hope to be led into her bedroom anyway. Or he could just shut up, follow her into her bedroom, and forget the whole investigation, meaning that he would have to forgive her and forget Fuentes. But his mind got cloudy trying to decide. "Aw, the hell, I can't go in there."

Parr circled his arm around her and tightened it on her back. He felt her breath mingle with his and, as she tipped back her head to look at him, he kissed her. And, when she slowly stepped backward into her bedroom, Parr followed her.

The rest was even easier. He had his shirt off with no effort, then his boots, then his pants around his ankles. And he was thrilled by the feel, the smell, the touch, and the breath of a woman.

Afterward Parr lay on his back and looked at the shadows on Jerri's wall. He could concentrate now, so he worried about what he had done and what he didn't admit, but mostly he just felt proud of himself. Jerri rolled over to him and gently kissed him on the neck; then she wrapped an arm around him and kissed him harder. "Jerri, darling, I'm an old man. Those young guys may have rapid-fire weapons, but I've got a black powder, smooth bore muzzle loader. Once it's fired, it takes a while to reload." Jerri's gentle kiss turned into a giggle whispered into his ear.

"Would you like a beer, then?"

"No."

Parr felt her hand on his shoulder. "You can spend the night."

He didn't dare spend the night. He had to think, and he couldn't think lying next to her. "I really can't stay," he told her. "I'm used to my own bed."

"Then please forgive me if I don't show you out," she said. "I'd rather not put on clothes. And I'd rather you not see my body in the light."

"You got nothing to be ashamed about with your body. It works real well," Parr said, and kissed her good night. And though Jerri made the good-bye kiss a good one, Parr felt only clumsy at it. He slowly got dressed and kept an eye on her to see if she was watching him dress. He felt like her now, embarrassed about his body, a little like a dog that doesn't want anyone to watch while he eats or pisses. All dressed, he waved in sideways fashion, like a cartoon character, then turned to leave. On the way through the living room, he spotted two rings left by the wineglasses on the glass top coffee table. He rubbed at the moisture with his open palm and smeared the tabletop. He looked back into the bedroom and walked to the door to see Jerri lying on her back still. She waved her white arm from the dark bedroom and said, "AMF, Joe Parr."

Parr peered into the dark and said, "What the hell does that mean?"

"Adios, motherfucker," Jerri said with a giggle. "We'll have to try this again and see if we can get it right."

Deep down inside his mind and chest, Joe Parr felt himself smile yet cringe. "You bet," he said.

Parr turned from her, walked back through the living room, and turned out the light. When he had pulled the door closed behind him, he said, "Holy good goddamn!"

On his way home Joe passed the East Side Club at the east end of Commerce and saw Ollie Nordmarken's pickup. The East Side was the old "nigger bar" just on the edge of the freeway that would take him north to his own white part of town. Ollie Nordmarken liked even cruder bars than Joe did. Joe pulled the Continental up to the front of the bar and went in to have a drink with Ollie. It was just as well to go to a bar; he had too much to remember and think about to go home. The black folks stared at him as he walked inside, but he paid no mind to them. He felt like he could whip all of them. He stopped for a moment and searched for Ollie. He thought he heard a voice whisper, "Another goddamn white ass lawman."

Parr ignored the remark he only thought he had heard and spotted Ollie across the room in a corner between the bar and the wall. Joe walked past the few drinkers and pool players and planted his elbows on the bar beside Ollie. "Good ol' Joe," Ollie said, and reached to pat Joe's shoulder. He missed. Ollie was drunk, and Joe realized that it was Ollie who had made the comment about the white lawman. Joe ordered a beer from the bartender and, when the bartender turned to get the beer, Joe looked at Ollie's red eyes and said, "Maybe you ought to get home."

The bartender set the beer beside Joe's hand, and Joe laid two dollars on the bar. Ollie cocked his head and stared at Parr. He grinned when Parr looked at him. "You smiling like you just got some pussy," Ollie said.

Parr sipped his beer and smiled way down inside of himself. "I did," he said, and let the smile come out from inside of him and stretch his face.

Ollie laughed, slapped the bar with his open hand, and said, "Here's to Joe pussyhound Parr."

"Maybe you ought to go home," Parr said.

"No, let's drink to your dick!" Ollie said.

Parr heard some stuttered breathing behind him and turned to see a black man just barely standing up, his body revolving in tiny circles. "I'll drink to that man's dick," the black man said. "And to the pussy what he got." So Joe and Ollie had a few beers with the black men who would join them and drink to Joe's good fortune.

❍ After Parr left, Jerri lay in her bed and stared up at the ceiling, her fingers folded together behind her head, and thought about what she had done. Finally pulled the old man into her bedroom. Old man! Hell, he didn't look, act, or fuck that old. More important, she enjoyed his company and admired the sharp creases in his starched shirts, pants, and cowboy hats, the ironed handkerchiefs he pulled out of his pockets, then neatly folded after he used them, the white hair that folded behind his ears, then made all sorts of contorted curls on the back of his head.

Parr was like those men who were too old or too conservative to have fully enjoyed the sexual revolution and so were trying to catch up. Like them, he never seemed to press any sexual issue. He constantly flirted with her, made the usual innuendos, and kissed her before and after their nights out, yet he had never invited her to his house. So when he walked her upstairs to her door and she invited him in, she knew it would be a short time until she pulled him into her bed. After that, he figured things out for himself.

Sex had been clumsy, like most first times. They fumbled and groped, wondering what was too much and what was not enough. Then he calmed down. If she continued with him, sex would certainly get better. She could tell that his belly was once tight and muscled up. He had kept in shape and now had only some loose-hanging flab. His belly didn't rub against hers as Fuentes's had.

But she had used him. Parr was a well-mannered, well-dressed man with some intellect and money, but like the few others she had drunk wine with and gone to bed with in the last five years, he couldn't make her forget the charged particles that filled the air, making it so thick that she could push against it. He couldn't make her forget the *it* she had had with Royce and then with Fuentes. Of course, the memory of them and her anticipation that she could indeed be content with this man also made her remember the stinging acid that formed in her stomach and spread throughout her body when those other men left. The air between her and Joe Parr hadn't become thick with anticipation, just lightly scented. It wasn't love or lust that was in the scent of the air between her and Joe Parr. It wasn't the feeling that she could settle with or for this man. The scent in the air suggested that whether she lived with him or not, loved him or not, she could trust Joe Parr.

He talked about morals and right and wrong. With the memory of Fuentes now floating in and out of her mind, with her past, right, wrong, trust, and love were strings so tightly tangled together that she could never separate them. Her attitude about right and wrong was like Palo's. The only sure right and wrong was bounded by

89

your own backyard. For anything deeper, fuller, more complex, she would have to trust Vincent Fuentes and his ideas. That thought suddenly pulled Jerri's hands from behind her head. Her head banged against the headboard. She sat up in her bed. No, no, she was wrong. She might *want* to trust Vincent Fuentes, but she *could* trust Joe Parr.

Jerri wrapped and twisted the sheet and pillows around her. She felt like crying, not out of regret or sadness but out of confusion. But she didn't let herself cry, for despite her confusion, she ultimately knew what she would do. Fuentes was coming back, at least for a while. You had to play some things out. In the morning, regrettably, she would have to call the cowboy and tell him an old boyfriend was back in town.

CHAPTER SIX

Fuentes kept a mechanical smile on his face as he read his story and looked out at the audience. He didn't see the people, though. Sometime, somewhere, way back, he'd stopped seeing them. He had gone through the story so many times that he could almost recite it. The same was true of his speeches before and after the story: a continual revolution was the only guard against the political stagnation and corruption in Latin America; the priests, the intellectuals, the politicians were just illusionists who lacked the guts for real political action; something along the lines of a Nicaragua without its anti-U.S. hysteria was the answer; Cuba blundered; and so on, all the things he used to believe at one time or another.

He even had answers, the partial truths he was told to tell, to the Americans' questions: He spent most of a year in jail, comfortably writing; he was released for lack of evidence; he wasn't censored. He told them about writing. He tried, like all writers, to capture the human soul in struggle against all that would deny that soul's autonomy. He liked to write at night. Writing was a terribly hard job, but one that he felt compelled to do. He did try to write something every day. Yes, he paid attention to the rhythm in his sentences. Yes, it got easier. In truth, his writing was so easy and automatic that it was boring. Anymore, he really wrote only at long stretches, forcing himself to sit for a whole month and just take the dictation that his mind rambled off.

Since he had switched to political nonfiction, he didn't even have to bother with characters, mainly just political anecdotes that he thought of during his tours. He got lucky and had a best-seller in Latin America and in the United States. Some academics and some politicians liked the babble that he wrote, so he became a minor celebrity in the New World. The Americans liked him because they could feel good about their literary taste for Latin American fiction and their political awareness. In Mexico he was in no real danger because he was at his government's disposal. In the rest of Latin America he was a road show exhibit, kind of like a Las-Vegas-inspired circus show. The PRI had an interest in keeping him popular.

He looked down at his text, and his eyes followed the words across the page. His mouth moved and words came out of his mouth, but his mind was on telephone books, luxury hotels, and his headache. In jail he had learned how to put his mind somewhere else.

If your body hurt enough, your mind had the strange ability to leave it. Now he was escaping this morning's dull throb behind his forehead. The next step was to let his mind leave itself. He could let his consciousness forget the mechanics of thinking. He remembered when he thought.

Because he had been beaten in the face with the Saltillo telephone book and spent time in prison, he now got to enjoy the best hotels that American, Mexican, Guatemalan, Argentinean, Chilean, and Colombian cities offered. Staying in hotels, not writing, was what he really enjoyed. When his old blood made itself known in his veins, he wanted to pamper that blood. And these hotels with bathrobes and thick towels in their rooms, room service from fine kitchens, valets, maid service, shoe shines, and bars seemed to muster everything in their power to please his old selfish blood, to cater to his being. And hotels weren't homes. He was through with homes, whether they were houses, families, or countries. And for all they did for him, all the hotels wanted was money. Rich Yanqui universities and his government supplied him with the money. He could live most of the year flying on the first-class flights, staying at the better hotels, eating the best food, and drinking the best liquor. All he had to do was be the symbol they wanted him to be. No one seemed to care that he was already washed up, that he no longer wrote clearly or well, no longer researched. The work that he had done before he went to jail simply became more popular when his name became more noted. He could live comfortably on his name and his work for some time and not have to write or think. Until the smarter academics and politicians found him out, he would enjoy his undeserved glory.

He felt ashamed that he had taken so long to give in to his corruption. First there was school, then that silly business about being a priest, then writing, then the revolutionary thing. Now he was liberated. The youngest of Palo's children, the pride of the family, the pretty boy, he had taken the longest to accept Palo's bloodline but had accepted it more thoroughly than the rest. His brothers and sisters hid in Europe. He need not hide. He was protected. The PRI made him a VIP, a prima donna. He wished he had a drink.

"As Georgie Chavez set his first foot into Texas mud, he said to himself that Ignacio was a Mexican name. His first name would be George, after the president. He grabbed weeds and the limb of a mesquite to pull himself onto the dry, hard bank, then looked behind him," he read to the audience. He allowed his mind to participate in what he was doing. His head ached, and his throat was dry. He looked out at the people who silently listened to him. The freshmen who had been required to come in order to fill the auditorium looked at him with their mouths open. Sometimes they looked at their friends who sat next to them to see if the friends could figure any of this out. Some of the people smugly smiled to show him and those around them that they appreciated good literature. Hardly any Hispanics or blacks were in the audience. They were too busy earning low wages to be in school. Fuentes read, "Georgie reached into the muddy water but could feel nothing. He saw the suitcase floating farther downriver. He dove into the river and felt himself pulled. When he came up, he saw Alicia bob up ahead of him, then go under."

Fuentes raised his hand and waved it across the podium and over the audience as though he were a magician (no, an "illusionist," he said to himself). And he paused at the blank space in the book. Leave them hanging on a cataclysm, and they wouldn't notice how he manipulated them with sentimentality. This story always worked: a touch of symbolism, never very close, some immoral characters. It was all a very carefully brewed stew. He pushed his glasses farther up his nose toward his eyebrows. The sensitive sore spot behind his skull felt a thud when the bridge of the glasses hit his brow. He reached for the glass of water on the podium and took a long drink. The water didn't help his headache or the dryness in his throat.

He looked back up at the audience and saw the blue-haired Yanqui lady from the rich Alamo Heights suburb, the one whose party Jerri had taken him to, the one who had invited him to a dinner party in his honor on his return. He would like to eat her expensive food and drink her tasteful but not too expensive wines. Maybe Jerri would go with him. He pulled his head down from the old lady and tried to look at other members of the audience; he noticed other rich people from the Alamo Heights area. Their money wasn't important to him, he used other people's money, but he could use their regard. He wondered who won the battle between the chugholes and the symphony.

He continued reading, then looked at the front row and saw Jerri Johnson sitting with her son. J. J. was the boy's name, he remembered. J. J. had his elbow on the arm of the auditorium chair and his head resting on his outstretched palm. He eyes were shut, then they flickered open. He pulled up his head, shook it, then sat up straight. The boy was the only honest person in the auditorium.

Jerri's eyes smiled—lovely Jerri. Sex, he thought suddenly. He could have sex again tonight, another pleasure, like drinking and eating and luxury hotels. She could make a good life for him. His mind went backward, and he thought he remembered reading the story to her before, when he taught at the other university in town, when he had taken her to Puerto Peñasco; it would have to have been a time when he believed his story. Then heeding his blood, considering his best interest, he looked down at her, paused where he didn't need to, and smiled at her. She had grown more sophisticated since he had left her. She was wiser, tougher. But in the way she looked listening to him, Fuentes saw that ideas were still seductive to her. He could overlook that in her character, and he could use it. He had learned that an idea can lead out of one box, then along a twisted trail leading to another box. When he returned to the words on the page and read the first two, because of the headache and the parched throat and the audience, he let his mind go where it wished.

☯ Jerri stopped at the entrance to the Four Seasons Hotel and let Domenic Carmona walk in through the stone arch. The thickset man stopped and lightly bounced on the balls of his feet. He dabbed at the glistening drops of sweat on his forehead, then looked at the sweat smeared across his fingers. As Jerri stepped up to him, she thought that he deserved to sweat because his dark nylon shirt and silver polyester pants must trap the sunlight. And his ivory-colored Italian shoes, gold earring, matching necklace, and neatly trimmed and seemingly sculpted hair and beard made him look finicky. He looked like some of the poorer *cholos* would have liked to have looked, maybe like an Italian version of Palo's assistant coyote, Medina, if he had more money. But unlike *cholos,* he couldn't take the heat. He flicked his fingers to get rid of the sweat on them. "It's hot here," he said to Jerri, smiled, bounced on the toes of his Italian shoes, and added, "hot but beautiful."

"Yeah," Jerri said to him. Fuentes had to make the deal, so she didn't need to like Domenic or talk to him; all she was supposed to do was pick him up. Jerri had suggested that they meet at the pool of the Four Seasons because, from observing people involved in illicit activities, she knew that these affairs were best conducted out in the open where people could see but not record. For instance, no one could bug the courtyard at the Four Seasons. While Domenic bounced on the balls of his feet, Jerri looked for Fuentes but saw an empty courtyard. One person was doing laps in the pool. As the man in the pool curled at one end and swam away from her, Jerri could see, from the way his brown shoulders moved through the water, that he was Fuentes.

"What room's this Fuentes friend of yours in?" Domenic asked.

"We're going to meet him in the courtyard," Jerri said, and looked at the umbrella-shaded tables by the pool.

"Here?" Domenic said just as a waiter with what looked like a gin and tonic on a tray passed by. She followed the waiter, guessing that the drink was Fuentes's, a cure for that gigantic thirst he had gotten since he had left her. Jerri knew, though, that he wasn't yet a drunk. He certainly wasn't like the winos, and he wasn't like the judges and lawyers she knew who had to take off early because they got the shakes, who had to dry out before they worked a big case with a lot of media coverage. Fuentes drank mostly, it seemed to Jerri, in order to satisfy his appetite. He had come back less intellectual but far more sensual. His appetite for her even seemed to have increased.

The waiter put the drink down at a shaded table by a chair with a cloth beach bag, a cotton T-shirt, and a towel in its seat. Just as they walked to the table, Fuentes bounded out of the swimming pool. Jerri smiled and noticed Fuentes's shiny, swollen brown belly pushing out over his bikini swimming trunks. *"Quiero agua, por favor,"* Fuentes said to the Mexican waiter who had brought the drink. Jerri noticed now that Fuentes had a tan that he had obviously worked on. Before, he was indifferent to his looks. But now that he was conscious of his looks, he was losing them. "And whatever this gentleman and lady will have."

"Iced tea," Jerri said, looking at Fuentes's belly, which spoiled his tan. When out of proportion, human bodies looked obscene, like Royce's painting hanging in her living room, she thought. It was one of his best, and he was trying to show how one got one's sense of obscenity or sexuality from proportion. It hung next to the sentimental portrait that Royce had done of Jerri. Young people in good shape, Royce once said, could take their clothes off anywhere and really not embarrass anyone. Naked old men and old ladies would embarrass everyone. In his bikini Fuentes was close to embarrassing himself and Jerri.

"Yeah, yeah, iced tea," Domenic said, and bounced in place. "Yeah, tea. I'm on the job."

Jerri looked at Fuentes and said, "Vincent, this is Domenic Carmona."

"How you doing there?" Domenic stuck out his hand. Fuentes shook the man's hand with his own wet one, and Domenic shot a quick glance at his now damp hand. "I was saying to Ms. Johnson, you got a beautiful city here. So green."

"I'm from Mexico," Fuentes said.

"Oh, hey." Domenic caught himself. "Beautiful country."

Fuentes looked at Jerri and smiled at her with his eyes, like he had done at the reading. She felt one corner of her mouth creep up into a half smile. "Please, let's sit in the shade," Fuentes said. Domenic sat, and when Fuentes pulled out a lawn chair for Jerri, Domenic rose slightly. Fuentes then sat, dabbed at himself with his towel, and put on his T-shirt. Without his growing gut showing, he looked handsome. At his reading, where he read the story that Jerri had heard six years before in the creative-writing class at the University of Texas at San Antonio, he was the pretty, beautiful man she remembered. His slender fingers still moved gracefully in the air, his voice rose and dropped with the trace of that accent and created a slightly sprung rhythm. But he had added more drama to his presentation. He was more of a showman than he was when he first got his fame.

Jerri glanced at Domenic. His puffy hair style had gone flat. The sprayed pompadour on his forehead was now a series of thin strands of hair pasted to his forehead. The waiter brought the two iced teas. Jerri took her glass and rubbed its cool side against her forehead and cheek. Domenic copied her and wiped some of the sweat from his own face. Then, while she took a small sip, Domenic took a gulp. He pulled his glass from his mouth but left a chunk of ice there.

"Beautiful city," he said, "but hot," and the chunk of ice rattled against his teeth. "So what's the tune, Vincent?"

Fuentes's brows wrinkled. Jerri raised her hand to her mouth to keep from giggling at the idiom that Fuentes didn't understand.

Domenic rested his elbows on the wrought iron table and tried again to communicate with a literate man. "Hey, I mean this is an uptown place for a guerrilla schoolteacher." Domenic looked at Jerri. "You saw my digs." He then turned to Fuentes. "Me, I'm staying at a Motel 6 by the airport."

"I manage," Fuentes said, as though he cared as little about this meeting as he did about his reading.

Domenic looked at both of them, then leaned across the table toward Fuentes. Sweat dripped from his forehead. "So get down to business, that's what I always say."

"Yes, Domenic," Fuentes said, and lifted his beach bag onto the table.

Jerri wanted to say, My God, at Fuentes's nonchalance. "In there?" she asked.

Domenic looked at her, not understanding what she meant. Fuentes smiled at both of them. "The money you want is in my bag."

Domenic looked shocked, and Jerri leaned back to chuckle. She had been right. He was now a showman, but this P. T. Barnum had a lot of charm and style. Domenic made a quick move to grab the bag, then backed away. "All of it?"

"Yes," Fuentes said.

Domenic looked around him, then at the bag. He couldn't restrain himself. He reached slowly for the bag and carefully pulled back an edge to peer inside. "I won't count it," he said. "I trust you."

"And I understand that you have the shipment all worked out with Ms. Johnson?" Fuentes asked.

"Yeah, they can stop us, frisk us, throw us in jail. But they can't fuck with our mail." Domenic chuckled, looked at Fuentes, looked again in the bag, then looked over at Jerri.

"As long as you mail them in *parts*," Jerri said, took a drink out of her ice tea, and patted Fuentes on the back. She left her hand on Fuentes's back for longer than she might have, and when she turned her head to face Domenic, she saw him stare at her hand; then she felt Fuentes's hand patting her own.

"You two are boyfriend and girlfriend," Domenic said.

Jerri ducked her head and laughed a bit. "I'd prefer to be called lovers."

"Whatever rings your chimes, I always say," Domenic said.

Fuentes stood and stretched his hand across the table for Domenic to shake. "Thank you, Mr. Domenic. Ms. Johnson will now be able to take you where you need to be."

"That's it?" Domenic asked.

"What else is there?" Fuentes asked.

"Well, on a personal note . . ." Domenic pulled his portfolio closer to him, reached in it, and brought out a color brochure. "Could I interest either one of you in this handy-dandy little weapon? On sale this month." He flipped open the brochure and pointed into it.

"No, no," Fuentes said. "I know nothing about guns. I don't own one."

"I could give you a further discount after your purchase."

"Please," Fuentes said, and held up his hand.

Domenic turned to Jerri, who also stood up. "You, Ms. Johnson?" Before Jerri could say anything, Domenic flipped to another page. "Before you say no, just take a look at this little baby—.38 caliber, silver plated, the size of a stapler." Jerri saw no brand name or price. She was thinking, though, that when she was carrying a brick in her purse, a gun this size would make her load a lot lighter.

Jerri looked at Fuentes a moment, then took the brochure. "What would you take?" Jerri knew that Domenic was small time enough to bargain.

"Well, I'll leave you," Fuentes said, then looked at Jerri. "Ms. Johnson may have all my discounts." He turned and walked toward the lobby. Jerri looked at him, then at the picture of gun, then dropped the brochure on the table and ran to him. She caught him just as he entered the door to the lobby, took his hand, and walked into the lobby with him. Once they got inside the lobby doors, she kissed him, then said, "See you later."

"We lead good lives," Fuentes said to her.

After buying the gun, Jerri took the charmless Domenic, who

wouldn't know what a good life was, back to his room at a Motel 6 out by the airport. After dropping him off, making her way through the traffic on McAllister Freeway, Jerri thought about the old-style charm of Joe Parr. She wanted to see him. Then her thoughts shifted to Fuentes. He had seemed bored. Jerri adjusted the vent of her air conditioner to get a blast of cool air in her face. She needed a chill. And she had promised to meet J. J. for dinner.

At the reading at Trinity, Jerri had shoved an elbow into J. J.'s ribs to wake him up. He looked at her as though to say, *Aw, Mom.* She grimaced. J. J. had grown and denied all of her and his father's interest in art and instead focused on the measurable world.

Jerri squirmed in her car seat as her mind bumped from thought to memory. Jerri had squirmed in her seat and listened to Fuentes at Trinity. She had recognized most everything she heard and so was sent back to the time when she first met him, when the air between them was charged. And at Trinity's auditorium, despite the people, she had felt alone with Fuentes. She felt the air become charged. She felt the aphrodisiac of sentiment, of art, of a mind challenging her own. Jerri felt what she had on occasion during her second attempt at college. Listening to the lecture or the reading, or sometimes just discussing a point, Jerri felt an escape from self that came with the bright spark of understanding, then the return to a better, richer, and wiser self. Fuentes could do this for her.

How could her own son doze off? She knew that she could live with Fuentes, knew that she could be content with him. And then she had looked at J. J. and gotten scared. His real name was Jay. She and Royce had a lapse of imagination when they named him. They thought that Jay Johnson sounded cute yet snazzy. Over the years his schoolmates started calling him J. J., and the name stuck.

She adjusted the vent of the air conditioner again and turned it on high. Maybe what she could settle for or with in Fuentes, maybe the *it* that she saw in Fuentes, wasn't Fuentes himself but the ideas, the feeling he created around her, the deep sentiment. So okay, Fuentes or the notion of him, what's the difference? She could be content with whichever one it was. After Fuentes's speech, Jerri had glanced over at her son, and she had thought that she could live with Fuentes, but what she *had lived with* was this goofy kid.

⊘ Parr watched through a slat in a venetian blind as Jerri kissed Fuentes. Parr let go of his slat, heard its ping, dropped his binoculars, and heard them bang against his camera. "Goddamn it," Parr said out loud, and fumbled on his chest for the camera. He grabbed what he thought was the camera and raised it to his face. The thongs of the binoculars caught in the thongs of the camera so, while he had the camera in front of his face, the binoculars dangled beneath it. "Goddamn it, hell, piss, shit, fuck fire," Parr said as he poked the camera lens through a slat of the venetian blinds while another slat fit perfectly into a wrinkle on his forehead.

"Goddamn it," Parr said through his teeth. "If I'd of had a bug, I could fry that little wop's ass, too. Or one of those sound amplification things." He pulled away from the window. Even if he had had a sound amplification dish, he couldn't have poked it through the sealed window, and he didn't dare step out onto the balcony. So Parr thought for a moment about reality: up to now, U.S. attorneys and federal judges had never listened to him, and he didn't like bugs and high-tech shit and court orders.

Parr dropped the camera, which made a thud against his chest, grabbed his binoculars and raised them, their strap twisting up with the camera's strap, and looked back at the three of them. He dropped the binoculars, curled a finger over a venetian blind slat, and peeked at them with a naked eye. "Shit," he said, and grabbed his camera and took some more pictures. Suddenly, even though he could still see them, he felt that he had had enough. He let the camera drop, stepped back from the window, and as he thought about what he had done, tried to get the twisted mess of leather straps, binoculars, and camera off of him. Giving up on the twisted mess, he just let the goddamn things drop around his neck. Until now Jerri could have been innocent.

Parr walked to the other side of his room, the camera and binoculars bouncing off his chest, and sat in a chair by the dining table. Jerri was too smart, so he had followed Fuentes. The clerk thought he was some kind of old pervert when he came in early this morning and asked for a day rate for this room across from Fuentes and with a view of the street and the courtyard. After all, with no official approval, he was spending his own goddamn money, and even if he had money from selling Melba's shop, he didn't like spending it for an investigation.

Parr let his head fall back and rest on the top of the chair. He let his eyelids go shut and felt them scraping over his tired, bloodshot, swollen eyes. Somebody was going to get a hell of a bill if this case worked out. The night before, he went into Melba's bathroom, the one on the other side of their master bedroom, and found one of her "little pills." He thought about taking the tranquilizers but stayed up sipping scotch and thinking about Jerri.

Two days before, he got the call he knew he would get, the one where Jerri told him about the old boyfriend coming back to town. Hell, it was right there in the papers that Fuentes was coming back to town. But Jerri said that she would like to see him again, perhaps in three or four weeks. "Goddamn it all to hell, any fucking way," Parr said, stood, and walked across the room, his binoculars and camera clicking together with the rhythm of his gait. "Shit," Parr said, and tugged and pulled until he got the binoculars and camera off his chest and the straps from around his neck. He threw the goddamn things on his bed. He paced some more. He pulled his half-frame glasses out of his shirt pocket and put them on. "They're all sure as hell guilty now," he said to himself, and wished that he were at home late at night so that maybe the Melba in his head would talk to him. "Well, maybe they're all just on vacation and reliving old times?" Parr asked himself since Melba wasn't around. "Bullshit," he said. He didn't want to insult his own intelligence. "They just happened to meet that little shit ass with the guns."

Parr flopped on the bed and stared up at the ceiling. He reached over to shut the blinds to make the room dark. No more following people today. He took off his glasses and laid them on the lamp stand next to the bed. "Goddamn, boy," he said to himself. "What you bitching about? You got laid. You got a good case. Maybe you'll even get real cowboy stuff like a shoot-out and a high-speed car chase."

Then again, Parr thought, he could just forget it all. He was no goddamn Baptist Sunday school teacher. Don't take the pictures to Chief of Police Hoestadter. Apologize to the bastard for taking up his time. Tell him that he, Joe Parr, was getting old and foolish. He didn't need the case. He was the man who caught Bud Harrelson and shot it out with Fred Carrasco. He could indeed rest on old-timey laurels. What's it matter if some ignorant, powerless Mexicans who don't know how to use them get guns?

Then again, he didn't like the idea of Fuentes and that little Italian turd getting away with a crime. They didn't have more balls than a good ol' all-American good guy Texas Ranger like Joe Parr. Joe's sight disrupted his thought, and he looked at the flowered wallpaper. Then he let his eye lids drop over his hurting eyes and got a little sleep.

⊘ While Jerri took Carmona back to his own hotel, Fuentes got another drink from the bar, this time a margarita, and took it with him back to his room. With his headache and dry throat gone, liquor would again taste good. He would stop drinking just before Jerri returned to pick him up for the night. Even though his bathing suit was still wet, he lay back on the bed and stared up at the ceiling, letting the air-conditioning blow on him from the vents above him. When he tried to sip from the margarita, some of the wetness and the ice flowed over the lip of his glass and rolled down his cheeks. The ice felt as cool as the air-conditioning. He wiped at the coldness on his cheeks with the tail of his open shirt and heard a knock at the door. From the sound, Fuentes knew the knock belonged to the knuckle-dragging Neanderthal brute Natividad.

Fuentes got up, his drink still in hand, and opened the door. Trujillo and Natividad were both outside the door. "Come in, gentlemen," he said to them.

Trujillo came in first, as always, and Natividad followed him in. They both stared at his naked legs. "You got no pants?" Natividad asked. Colonel Trujillo made no comment but smirked. Since Fuentes first stared at his face, highlighted by the aura of a naked light-bulb in a Saltillo jail, he had learned that Trujillo was a refined man from wealthy Mexico City people. But he was small, with dark features and an effeminate manner. Giving up the Lenin beard he wore when Fuentes first saw him, he took time every day to keep his mustache pencil thin and used mousse to keep his hair straight back. He had a taste for expensive suits but never seemed able to find one to fit his small body. The sleeves were always too long and the shoulders too wide. Fuentes wondered what he would look like in his uniform; probably like a cadet in a boys' military school. In San Antonio the esteemed colonel settled on an open collar and a cotton sport coat. He tried to appear dashing, a ladies' man, but his small, feminine stature and mannerisms kept him from succeeding with ladies. He had probably grown up being called a *joto* or *maricón.*

As usual Natividad wore a short-sleeved white shirt, navy blue slacks, and cheap black oxfords. Fuentes noticed a long tear between the leather shank of the Neanderthal's shoe and the vinyl sole. "How about drinks all around?" he said to the two men in English, and took a sip from his. The worst part about his hotel life was that he had to keep company with the men assigned to watch him. He had grown accustomed to Trujillo and even welcomed his conversation sometimes. It seemed strange but almost fated that the man who first coaxed him into listening to his selfish blood now escorted him around the New World. Even if he didn't like Trujillo, he enjoyed the irony wrapped around Trujillo.

But Fuentes hated to be in the same room with Natividad. Natividad was a thug whom some Defense Ministry official found in Mexico City. He was just what a thug should be: big, brutal, without the intelligence to know when he was being paid too little. The PRI used him as one of the paramilitary goons they sent to do dirty jobs with other borderline psychopaths.

"Gracias, no." Trujillo sat in a chair. He looked at his nails the way a woman does, with palm out and his fingers tipped back toward him. Fuentes could see that he had just gotten a manicure. Natividad had to survive just on what the PRI paid him. Trujillo had his colonel's salary, family money, and an expense account.

"Do you care for a drink, Mr. Natividad?" Fuentes asked the other man. Being on a trip to San Antonio should have been the highlight of this simple man's life, but he didn't seem to enjoy anything in San Antonio or his own life.

"No," Natividad said.

"I think I'll have another," Fuentes said, and shivered as he walked toward the telephone.

"Please, Professor Fuentes," Trujillo said in Spanish. "Let us first talk, then you may have your drinks."

Natividad looked at him and said in Spanish, "Eat, drink, swim, run with the *gringa putas*."

Natividad looked at him to see if he had pressed a nerve. Fuentes got an admittedly perverse pleasure from teasing the crude, uncomplicated man. "I'm so glad you decided to come to my room," he said to Natividad in English. "When I last went to your room, something bit me. A mouse, I think. It's such a shabby place." He looked at the refined Trujillo and saw him suppress a giggle. The two secret policemen hired by the minister of defense, the Saltillo police, and the Coahuila Military District had far less money at their disposal than Fuentes did and, with the peso declining every day against the dollar, they had to stay in shabby downtown flophouses. The PRI figured that these two could watch him without staying at the expensive hotels. If the PRI really trusted him, if its politicians were getting their money's worth, if they really knew how to use him, they wouldn't send bargain rate keepers along on his trips to keep watch over him. It was all a part of the box that ideas made.

"Cura," Natividad said.

But Fuentes stopped him. "I'll give you whatever sacraments you want, but I'm no longer a priest."

"Priest," Natividad said, now switching into English, with a derogatory tone, "you are worse than that *puta*." He stood up. Trujillo got up and met him. "Please," he said in Spanish, "let's go if you are going to start another fight." Trujillo turned to Fuentes. "Excuse us, Professor Fuentes."

"We take money out of poor people's mouths," Natividad went

on in Spanish, "so you can eat caviar." Fuentes, from putting together Natividad's disdain for consumption and priests, guessed that he liked to think he was communist. Yet he was either not dedicated enough or not smart enough to quit his job for a corrupt democratic country that aligned itself with Yanqui imperialists and that sent him to smash up union or dissident meetings.

"I've had four drinks today," Fuentes said. "I wonder how many Mexican children have starved?" he said to Natividad.

"Someday the government will find out what you are," Natividad said in English. Fuentes smiled at him.

"Please, now." Trujillo walked to Fuentes and patted him gently on his shoulder. "Did you give the money to that Domenic man?" Trujillo spoke in English. Fuentes always liked to force their conversations into English because Natividad had to work harder at their second language and because Trujillo, who had studied at the Virginia Military Institute, delighted in Americans' double entendres and crude linguistic jokes.

"Yes," Fuentes said.

"Good, very well," Trujillo said.

"So why don't we get the money from this little man, Domenic?" Natividad asked Trujillo.

Fuentes answered, "This is America. You can't impede American businessmen." Natividad looked at Trujillo, who nodded in agreement with Fuentes.

"What do you care where the money went?" Fuentes said to Natividad. "It's not your precious PRI's. It's ill-gotten money from my people. It's American money. We got it by selling drugs to Americans. Now it's back in the American economy with American outlaws. And besides, the people plotting your overthrow are out nearly one hundred thousand American dollars. There goes the revolution. The PRI can now start the bulldozers and mow down the poor people who are starving because I eat caviar."

Fuentes paused. He looked at both men. "To hell with you," he said. "I want another drink." He walked to the telephone, picked it up, and ordered another margarita from room service. When he had hung up the telephone, he said to Natividad, "I pay for my own drinks. That comes from my salary at the university."

"You are a *cabrón*," Natividad said.

"You are right." Fuentes raised his glass as though to toast Natividad's deduction.

"Please, Professor," Trujillo said. "This *Angel* will arrive in three days?" Trujillo smiled at his simple joke.

"Doesn't the PRI tell you the plans? Do they rely upon me to let you know your jobs?"

Natividad sank deeper into his chair and tightened his fist. Fuentes could see that he also tightened his jaw. Trujillo, with a sense of humor and a greater understanding of his job—he often joked with Fuentes about duty—chuckled.

"Angel Martínez will be here in three days. He rents a truck, drives it to Mexico." Fuentes stopped. "Nobody bothers what goes into Mexico. Yanquis just worry what kind of drugs or diseases come out. Once he is in Nuevo Laredo and hoping to meet his contact, he meets you two. And you two kill him or whatever you are supposed to do with him. Great scenario. The bad-guy revolutionaries are out of money, and the leader of an urban movement is dead or in jail. I'm not a *cabrón*—I'm a hero. Someday Mexico will build a statue of me."

Trujillo chuckled again and looked at Natividad to see if he was amused. "Yes, Natividad, Señor Fuentes is almost right, except we kill Angel or do 'whatever' here in San Antonio. The American CIA gives its full consent." Trujillo stood with his arms spread out and his hands flopped back on his wrists. "And Señor Fuentes will help. He tells us when and where the pickup for the guns will be."

"And how am I supposed to know this?" Fuentes asked.

"Ask your friend Jerri Johnson," Trujillo said, and snapped his hands to the front of his wrists, then folded his arms.

Fuentes turned away from them. Part of the agreement was that he wouldn't actually catch or kill anyone and wouldn't be around to see them caught or killed. He hoped that Trujillo was just enjoying the game they played and wasn't serious. "Someday I'll get your ass," Fuentes heard Natividad say.

Fuentes just shrugged his shoulder to them, then turned to smile at Trujillo. Looking at Trujillo but talking to Natividad, Fuentes said, "Maybe Trujillo might like you to get his ass," just to let Trujillo know that he could play the cruel game, too. Trujillo frowned. Natividad smiled. And Fuentes was sorry that he had to hurt Trujillo.

"Or maybe," Natividad said, "I'll get your girlfriend's ass."

Fuentes turned to look at him and said almost as a warning, "She'd tear off your *huevos*." Natividad got up, and Trujillo grabbed his arm to lead him to the door. As he went to the door, he said to Fuentes, "*Mañana,* we will talk to you again. And try to wear some clothes."

"I'll look forward to it, and I'll try to wear some pants," Fuentes said as the American teenager appeared at his now open door with a margarita. Fuentes took it off the tray and tipped it toward his two colleagues. As he walked to the dresser for a tip, he said to Natividad so the American could hear, "Have you ever seen the American movie *King Kong*?"

"No," Natividad said.

Fuentes looked back at the young waiter and said to Natividad, "There's an actor in that movie who looks just like you." The waiter laughed. Trujillo pushed Natividad down the hall and told him in Spanish that he would join him in a moment. Fuentes smiled and gave the waiter a healthy tip.

"Professor Fuentes," Trujillo said after the waiter left, "I just want to let you know that Natividad wants to shoot you. You help us, but not too long ago you were ready to die for a cause. Remember your obligations."

"Oh, I do remember my promises. My cause days were before I got serious about life."

"And you will find when and where the exchange of guns will be."

"I will find out what I can," Fuentes said, and Trujillo smiled. Fuentes dropped his head. "In an odd, sad way, we three—you, me, and Natividad—symbolize the fate of Mexico and the nature of Mexicans." Fuentes sipped from his drink and looked at Trujillo.

Trujillo showed nothing. He rocked back and forth on his heels. "I'd like to hear a little more about this."

Fuentes raised his glass toward Trujillo. "Natividad is the peasant. You, you're the man of power, who keeps it—the power, the government, the PRI—all together, for the sake of itself. And me, I'm the hope, the intellectual, the cultural historian." Fuentes wasn't sure if he was thinking or remembering something. "The peasant's fate is a descent into brutality. Mine is to admit my own obsolescence."

Trujillo now smiled. "And my fate?"

Fuentes felt his head wrinkle as he tried to think of the right insult or joke. But Trujillo didn't let him finish. "No, wait. I'll tell you mine." They stared a moment longer at each other. "My fate is to bear Natividad's brutality and your obsolescence. And for that reason my disillusionment is far greater than yours. And my choice is to deal with it, not to turn the world into a joke and float in a lake of whiskey."

"Do you think any of us really has a choice?" Fuentes wouldn't let himself show his surprise at and admiration for Trujillo's glibness. He raised his glass, though. "Here's to you."

Trujillo shook his head. "No, to us," he said, and raised an invisible glass toward Fuentes. "We could have both been better."

Fuentes swallowed his drink, and Trujillo gave a slight limp wave and left to join Natividad. Sometimes, by himself in a hotel room, Fuentes missed Trujillo. He was the only real company that Fuentes had.

Fuentes took a long drink of the frozen drink and concentrated on the coldness against his upper lip. He could trace the trajectory and velocity of his corruption as though it were plotted on a chart. A pretty boy, a rich boy in a poor country, a boy with every promise guaranteed if he remained savvy; the son of a gangster, who in turn was a descendant of bandits; a Mexican born in the midst of politics and crime and yet protected by his pedigree and upbringing from those realities. Fuentes saw the inevitability of the sale of his soul to the PRI.

Fuentes sucked at the frozen drink, hoping it would cut off his thoughts, but it only gave him a stabbing ice burn in his head. The pretty boy with his untested ideas never realized the delicacy and fragility of ideas. For how could ideas, wants, desires, or dreams sustain themselves when confronted with the hard realities of flesh, of soles burned by cigarettes, of telephone books breaking teeth and jaws? The burdens placed on the human psyche and the human body were just too heavy to be supported by something as light as an idea, a cause, a novel. To Fuentes, people were all animals, and that was no insult. They were just a part of the great barbaric, bloody universe that people could finally never know. It was all so inevitable.

Now Fuentes yearned not for insight but for oblivion. He took another sip and the icy burn eased, and his mind began to calm down. Since he wasn't meeting Jerri Johnson yet, he would drink enough to erase his memory of the part of day that had passed so far.

❷ Parr walked around the family plots in the old East Side cemetery. It had been a humid day, and with the sun setting, the cemetery was hazy. Big crosses and angels poked up over smaller tombstones. Wide tombstones with husband and wife underneath stretched the entire distance of some plots. A few dead folks from the 1920s and 1930s had mausoleums. The pink marble with silver speckles in it, quarried in the hill country, caught what sunlight there was and reflected it.

Parr looked at the names of mostly old Germans and noted the dates they died; hardly anybody in the last ten years. Even the cemeteries had moved north of town. The dead wanted to be buried in suburban cemeteries, the kinds with the small, uniform tombstones, just barely rising out of the ground, spaced in neat rows, shaded by trees, surrounded by trimmed bright green grass. People were too goddamn particular about where they were buried, Parr thought. Not Melba; her final resting place featured burned grass, no trees, and constant reflection of sun off marble.

Parr tried to figure why the staunch civic leaders in the early part of this century wanted to bunch up all their cemeteries. Several blocks off East Commerce were nothing but cemeteries with

World War I and II memorials. The cemetery he was in was what had become the black part of town. Parr didn't know where the blacks buried their dead. Not here. They treated the historical white cemeteries like playgrounds. They broke tombstones and sprayed painted hearts, initials, and obscenities on the tombstones of the past elite of San Antonio.

Melba's flat, circular tombstone had *Dukes* sprayed onto the stone. The plastic flowers that Parr had stuck by her grave just last week were gone. Parr knelt by the grave. Because Melba had been a little off center all her life, the Melba in his mind wouldn't talk to Parr at the most obvious place, her burial site. So Parr didn't try to talk with Melba. He wished that he had brought some new flowers. He had had a few beers at the Esquire after work, gotten some enchiladas at Casa Rio, then decided to stop at his wife's grave on his way home. Back in his Lincoln, in a manila folder, he had the photos of Jerri, Fuentes, and the Italian gun dealer.

He heard some voices behind him and turned to see two black boys drinking Big Red soda waters. They were talking about some motherfuckers. Parr reached into his back pocket and pulled out his badge. He stood up and let the two boys see the gun strapped to his side. "You tell your friends," he said, and flashed his badge at them, "if I catch any you sons of bitches marking up graves, I'll shoot 'em."

Both boys stopped. One boy took a step back. The other stood firm. "Who you to be talking shit?"

"Get your asses gone," Parr said. Both boys turned and ran.

Parr knelt back down by the grave and wished he didn't have to go home, where Melba would talk to him. He knew he wouldn't sleep again. He looked over at his tombstone. The kids had left his alone, no marks. Maybe because he wasn't dead yet. He looked at his birth date and wondered about his death date. He didn't think he'd mind being dead and having black kids scar his tombstone.

❷ Fuentes woke the next morning, blinking against the expected headache and trying to remember what he did the night before and where he was sleeping. Surprisingly, it was a good morning. His headache was gone but not all of his memory. He recalled the sex he'd had with Jerri the night before. Further, his nose and ears were working; he smelled coffee brewing and heard people talking. He rolled away from the puddle of slobber under his mouth and looked up at the ceiling. It wasn't the ceiling of his hotel room. He squinted and tried to remember more.

He put the evening together and remembered Jerri dining on the river with him at the Kangaroo Court. He remembered her saying that she would have to go to her apartment because J. J. came by early on Thursday mornings for a chat and a cup of coffee. Other than the beer at the Kangaroo Court, he'd had no drinks at the river, just some gin at Jerri's apartment. Then he remembered her thighs running along the sides of his thighs and her legs stretching over him. He looked around him and saw Jerri's slacks lying in a bundle next to the bed. Through the bedroom door, he saw the edge of a painting of an ill-proportioned fat lady on the living room wall. His mind sent a pulse of memory and expectation to him and he knew, without seeing, that an inferior painting, a sentimental portrait of Jerri, hung next to the painting of the fat lady. He relaxed and laid his head back down on his pillow and smiled inside, only to himself. Then he remembered that they hadn't talked about Angel and the delivery.

He rolled over and stuck one leg over the side of the bed and looked through the doorway to see Jerri in the kitchen, leaning over the breakfast counter. She had a glass of orange juice in her hand. She wore the flimsy nylon robe, now tattered a bit, that he remembered her wearing five years before. He could see a sunbeam coming into the kitchen at a certain slant and, if he looked at the sunbeam and cocked his head just right, he could see through the translucent cloth of the robe and make out the curves of Jerri's thighs. Jerri always looked good in the light that she always seemed to attract. She was golden.

He heard a voice that wasn't Jerri's. He quickly rolled out of bed, crawled to the bedroom wall, and listened for the voice.

"Look, Mom," the voice said. "The school does have computers, but you have to wait in line to get to them. Mostly it's professors using them. Most kids have their own." It was the son. "For two thousand dollars I can have an IBM with the capabilities and the memory expansion."

"I don't know what you mean. You're talking a strange language," he heard Jerri say. Fuentes thought word processors were wonderful. They were more automatic than a typewriter. They could store and move and almost write the stuff for him. God bless America for the computer.

"Mom, come on," J. J. said. Fuentes backed up from the wall and snuck a look into the kitchen. J. J. sat across from Jerri and took a bite of toast. "Look, Mom, if I got my own computer, I'd have more time to study. Then I'd have a better grade point average. Then I'd have a better chance of getting into medical school."

Jerri reached up into a cabinet and pulled out two coffee cups. She poured a cup for herself and one for J. J. from the automatic drip coffeemaker. "Have you ever considered anything besides medical school?" Jerri asked as she put a cup of coffee in front of J. J. "Have you ever taken a course just because you thought it might be a kick?"

"What would I major in? English, I suppose?"

"God forbid you do something that stupid, just take something fun." Jerri leaned toward him.

"You took courses just for fun."

"Okay, I see your point. I'm a cynical old bitch. Get your father to pay for it."

"You forget. He majored in art. He's got no money."

Fuentes stood up and looked around from the corner of the door. Jerri laughed and reached across the breakfast counter to pull her son's forehead close to hers. "I've got a special job. I think that I can swing it in a month or two."

J. J. pulled back from his mother. "Mom, it's legal, isn't it? I mean, don't smuggle some drugs or something."

"Chill out, J. J.," Jerri said. Fuentes giggled at the way Jerri used the vernacular to ridicule her son. He was proud of Jerri for raising a son to be quick-witted and fun. He stepped back from the door, felt a current of air on his legs, and looked down, only then noticing that he had on just his underwear and his socks.

"Mom," J. J. said, "have you got somebody in there?"

Fuentes ran quickly for the bathroom to hide from J. J. He wasn't sure what he would say to him or if the boy would remember him. He knew that he didn't want to meet him again with only his socks and underwear on. Then he heard Jerri's voice. "Vincent, put something on and come into the living room. I want you to re-meet my son." Fuentes opened the door of the bathroom and tiptoed to the pile of clothes that he thought were his. As he slid into one pants leg, then the other, he knew that he couldn't really love Jerri, or anybody else, not when he didn't know how far the trajectory of his life had taken him, not when he couldn't see when he would reach the height of that trajectory and then fall back to earth and explode. But he liked her. That was enough for his purposes. And what's more, Fuentes thought, she somehow kept him fairly sober. "God, Mom," he heard J. J. say in a barely hushed whisper. He lowered his voice some more. "Haven't you heard about AIDS? Don't you have some discretion?" Then he heard Jerri's marvelous laugh fill the house. Fuentes smiled, zipped up his pants, and walked into the kitchen to re-meet J. J. It would be fun.

❂ Joe Parr paused to knock on San Antonio Chief of Police Charlie Hoestadter's office door. After the rap, he heard smilin' Charlie say, "Come in." Parr pushed open the door, stepped in, and felt his boots sink into the thick carpet. He looked across the long room at Charlie's enormous desk. Windows running the length of the wall gave Police Chief Hoestadter a panoramic view of the city jail. Charlie pushed himself up out of his tall swivel chair. He rounded the corner of his desk, pulled at the corners of his lapels, and met Parr halfway across the room. He stuck out his hand and said, "Joe, Joe, Joe, good to see you," just like their last tense goddamn meeting had never happened.

Parr grabbed Charlie's outstretched hand and let his arm be pumped. "Come on, sit," Charlie said, and motioned toward the chair in front of his desk. He went back behind his desk and sat. In back of Charlie was a drooping SAPD flag, a San Antonio Kiwanis flag, a Lions Club flag, a Texas flag, and a U.S. flag. "Now, what can I do for you or your people?" Charlie asked.

"I got no people," Parr said. "This is just for me." Parr would have had an easier time taking the civilities if the son of bitch would just quit smiling. Hoping to get on with business, Parr pulled the manila envelope out from under his arm and plopped it on Charlie's desk. "Those pictures are good enough to get me a federal court order."

Hoestadter reached across the desk and pulled the envelope closer to him. He smiled at Parr as he stuck his hand into the envelope and pulled his brows together to look serious when he pulled the pictures out; then his eyebrows straightened, the ever present, silly goddamn smile replaced the serious look, and he looked up at Parr for the explanation. "So?" he asked, still smiling.

Parr hesitated; he needed to think some more. Charlie Hoestadter's face and his act cracked. "Come on, Joe. What does all this mean?"

Parr forced his mind to stop running two steps ahead of his ears. "The Mexican with no shirt is Fuentes. The wop with the silver and gold is Domenic Carmona. He sells guns."

"Who's the woman?" Hoestadter shuffled through the pictures. "You got a picture of her face?"

"I think she's a friend of Fuentes's." Parr's mind stopped.

"What's her name?" Parr leaned back in his chair and stared out the window to look at Hoestadter's view of the jail. Charlie would think he was being difficult or senile. "Joe?" Charlie said firmly.

"I haven't gotten that far yet," Joe said, forcing the wind out through the knot in his chest. "She might have just been a friend."

Charlie cocked an eyebrow and finally dropped his TV preacher's smile. "Look, Joe, you really don't have much here." Charlie's smile returned.

"I've got enough to interest the FBI."

Hoestadter's smile dropped as he thought. "If we arrested somebody, we'd get news coverage. And if we did, even if the case went sour, we'd look good. I can see the theme: SAPD is always on the job, covering all the angles."

"Charlie, I'm not in this for politics."

"What are you in it for?"

"I take this to a U.S. Attorney or the FBI unless I get to run this."

"The feds would probably laugh at you."

"They've also got more money to waste than you do." Joe Parr squirmed in his chair. He didn't like this bargaining.

"We've got our own people. We'll handle it, but I guarantee you'll get credit."

"I don't want credit. I just want to do it."

"What the hell do you get out of it?" Charlie could get down to horse trading if he wanted. But like most smiling, bureaucratic bastards, you couldn't trust him during the trading, not like you could trust a stand-up, square trader like Ollie Nordmarken, who'd give you something, even if you couldn't use it.

"Some work. I just want to do something. Look, it works, you bow in front of some cameras and have to eat less chicken and kiss less babies next election. It doesn't work, a crazy old Ranger fucked up." Charlie stared at him without a smile. The veins in his forehead stood out. "All I want is to work," Parr said again.

Hoestadter nodded like he understood. "What do you need?"

"Some bugs on Fuentes?"

"That'll be too hard, but I'll ask."

"Some backup. Some undercover guys to help me follow Fuentes and some support when I need it."

"What about Jerri Johnson?"

Parr had just started to relax, but now his stomach knotted up and the muscles between his shoulders tightened. "What about her?"

"I asked around. She's a private eye, and she's something like Fuentes's girlfriend. Maybe that's her in the picture. She might be useful."

Goddamn, Parr said to himself. Old Charlie had some cop in him after all. But then his thoughts turned back to poor Jerri.

"I'll check her out," Parr said.

116

Charlie Hoestadter stood up and smiled, and the preacher's demeanor returned. Business was over. He extended his hand across the desk. "I'll get you some good people."

Parr shook his hand, then said, "I run it. You get the credit."

Charlie walked Parr to the door and patted him on the back. Once outside, Parr turned back to see Charlie wave bye-bye, so he immediately turned away again and heard the door slam behind. What a thickheaded son of a bitch Charlie Hoestadter was. With the pictures of a gun dealer, with Ollie's help, along with some favors owed him, Parr could have shopped around at different agencies over in the federal building and gotten federal help. He wouldn't have lost a wink of what little sleep he got over breaking his promise to bring the case to Hoestadter and the city, but if he had gone with the feds, the FBI would have come in. They did good work and had lots of computers behind them, but they would want to run the show. San Antonio was ruled under a crumbling good ol' boy system and a new, powerful *el patrón* system. It was more corrupt than any federal office bound by red tape, codes, and laws. Friends counted in San Antonio. With city cops, Jerri might be able to get a deal.

CHAPTER SEVEN

When Joe Parr opened the door to Jerri Johnson's office and slowly walked inside, his eyes hung on the wooden and cardboard crates piled behind the desk. Parr half wished that he didn't know what was in the crates.

Standing behind her desk, facing away from it, Jerri revealed her short blond hair and nice butt, a middle-aged butt, but one that pleased Joe Parr. She was talking to Vincent Fuentes. Joe stared down at his feet, crossed his arms, turned from the two of them, and faced the door to look back out of her front window and consider walking back out the door. Gut it out, he said to himself, so he turned back around. Automatically, without thought, he pulled off his hat, held it in front of him, and couldn't keep his head from dropping so that he again stared at his toes.

Jerri came from behind her desk and walked toward him. She cocked her head to see him better. "Joe." Parr hesitated but forced the muscles in his neck to raise his head.

"I've got to talk to you," Parr said, then caught Fuentes's green eyes that were too light for his black hair, making him look mean to Parr. That bastard, Parr heard a voice inside his head mumble. He was to blame.

"Fine," Jerri said. "I didn't expect to see you." She smiled and jerked her head toward Fuentes.

"Maybe I could come back when you're not busy," Parr said, and looked Fuentes in his flashing, evil green eyes. Go ahead, Parr said in his mind to Fuentes, do something so I can shoot you and be done with it here. Fuentes turned his head away, and Parr wondered what Jerri saw in the son of a bitch's eyes. He quickly pulled his stare back to Jerri.

"No," Fuentes said, "I'm here on a personal call. If you have business, stay." Fuentes took a step toward Jerri and bent like he was going to kiss her good-bye, but she pulled away and looked at Parr.

"Joe Parr, this is Vincent Fuentes. Joe is a Texas Ranger and helps me with some investigations."

"Well, what do you do, Mr. Fuentes?" Parr asked.

"I write, lately very poorly," Fuentes added, and artificially smiled.

"What about?"

"He's good, Joe," Jerri broke in. "He's Mexican. He knows the politics there and here."

Parr looked at Jerri. "Could we just take a walk?"

"To tell you the truth, Joe, sometime a little later, lunch maybe, would be better for me."

"Could we do it now, Jerri?" Parr said, and circled his hat in his hands.

"Go ahead, Jerri." Fuentes stooped to kiss her. "I've got to get back to school."

Jerri jerked quickly away from the kiss and looked at Parr. "Sure, Vincent," she said, though she looked at Parr. And Parr saw something like a plea in her eyes.

Parr walked to her office door and held it open for her while Jerri pulled her large purse out from behind her desk and slung the straps over her shoulder. Jerri, then Fuentes walked out. Fuentes stopped to shake Parr's hand and to say, without a smile, "I'll leave you with lovely Ms. Johnson, you lucky man." The statement was pleasant enough, but Parr thought that it sounded like a warning, except he couldn't figure if the warning was for him or Jerri. Fuentes then smiled at Jerri, turned, and walked west down Dolorosa. He turned once more and waved good-bye to them.

As Jerri watched him walk away, Parr took her elbow, gently tugged, and walked her across the street to city hall. "Joe, listen, I'm sorry," Jerri said. "I really did want to see you some more. But Vincent and I have this thing from way back. And I haven't seen him in five years. If I could just have a few days off, I'll be glad to . . ." Parr held up his hand to stop her explanation. He felt his face drooping and his eyes watering up. Don't be a fool for pussy, Parr told himself.

"Just walk with me." Parr walked appropriately next to Jerri's outside shoulder.

Jerri punctured the silence of their stroll and said gently, "Well?" once, then, "Joe?" She touched Parr's elbow, and he felt her slightly sweaty fingers on his skin.

Parr took her hand and pulled her under the shade of a tree on the far side of city hall. He looked back toward city hall and dropped her hand. He tried to return his eyes to her, but instead he had to drop his head to stare at his feet. "I want to see you again." Parr lifted his eyes just enough to see Jerri smile. "But I'm really after Fuentes." Slowly, through will and the muscles in his neck, Joe Parr looked up from his feet and into Jerri's face. Now her eyes darted around in her head, going from side to side, anything but settling on Joe Parr's face.

Jerri crossed her arms and grabbed her elbows. She twisted sideways and rocked on her heels, making her purse twist and bounce against her thigh. "So tell me the rest. Go on, tell me," she said, and took a step toward him and slapped the side of his arm with her open palm. Then she centered her gaze on him, and because he couldn't stand that gaze, Parr looked up at the steps of city hall and rubbed the spot on his arm where Jerri hit him. "Tell me. I was part of the investigation, right?" Parr looked back at Jerri and put his open palm on her shoulder. "Okay, so you don't have to draw me any pictures." Jerri shrugged so that his hand dropped off her shoulder. She looked toward Commerce Street, then down it; she squinted, like she was looking for Fuentes. Turning her head just enough toward Parr so that he could hear, she said, "I guess you've got some business you want to talk about now?"

Parr again took her elbow, but now she led him: across Commerce and to a flight of stairs that led down to the river. Just as they stepped down to the first step, Jerri stopped and looked back over her shoulder. "Anybody following us? Who else?"

"Nobody. This is small time. Just me, really."

Jerri stopped walking and looked at him. Parr stiffened his neck, stayed tough, and didn't drop or turn his head. He saw her mouth hanging at an angle and her eyes tearing but flashing just the same, as if she was all at once confused, mad, and hurt. "Well, then, call it off. Just quit."

"Can't do that," Parr said. Jerri turned away and rapidly skipped down the steps, Parr tangling his feet, trying to keep up with her.

When they got to the river walk, Parr said, "I know that you are involved in a gun deal with Vincent Fuentes. Right now, nobody else knows."

"You don't know shit," she said.

"I know, Jerri."

"How?" Parr didn't answer because he knew that tactically he shouldn't and because he was ashamed. "How, goddamn it?" she yelled again. Her eyes had quit watering; the sadness was gone, replaced completely by anger.

"I got pictures," Parr said, overcoming tactics and shame because he thought he owed her. He even hung his head, but not before he saw every line in Jerri's face wrinkle up.

He raised his head to see Jerri bite her bottom lip; then he heard her gather her breath to say, "Go on, tell me the rest."

Parr stepped in front of her and held her by her shoulders. "Tell me where the guns are, when they're going to be delivered, where they're going to go, who bought them, who sold them."

Jerri stared for a long moment at Parr and cocked her head. "I can't help you."

"You could go up on criminal charges if I have to go farther." Parr hesitated.

"That's a hell of a lot of information. Maybe your price isn't high enough. All I get is to go free. How about throwing in some sex. Some money. Some dope. Huh? Huh?" Jerri said as her eyes grew wild, almost like Fuentes's. Parr dropped his arms from Jerri's shoulders and walked away from her because he felt his eyes begin to water up. When he got some distance from her, he heard her tennis shoes squeak on the concrete as she ran up to him. She craned her neck to look at his face, but he couldn't bear to look at her, so he turned away from her. "Maybe you were just doing your job," she said to him.

He walked, and she followed. They passed a man selling *raspas.* "I'd like a *raspa,*" Jerri said.

Parr stopped and turned to her. "What flavor?" he asked.

"Cherry," Jerri said.

"Let the San Antonio Police Department buy you a snow cone."

"Are they the ones doing the investigation?" Parr didn't answer. Instead he paid the Mexican and gave the *raspa* to Jerri. She smiled as she took it, and Parr, hoping the worst was over, felt himself smile. She licked at her *raspa,* then walked to a bench and sat. Parr sat beside her and leaned forward to put his elbows on his knees. "I can beat the SA police." She turned to look at Parr. "I can beat you."

Parr gritted his teeth and looked at the river. "I want Fuentes and Domenic, not you." Maybe now they could be logical, work this out, and not hurt each other anymore.

"So I set up Vincent?"

Parr pulled his elbows and his weight off his knees and dared to reach across and pat Jerri's knee. He was surprised when she laid her hand on top of his. "You got no choice. You have to help me." Parr pulled his hand off her knee and let himself say what he felt about Fuentes: "The son of a bitch is a goddamn gun dealer. What the hell you doing with him anyway?"

Jerri turned to him. "Did you ever check to see why he was shipping the guns? Who he was shipping them to? You ever think about the people he's helped?"

"That doesn't mean shit. What he does is illegal." Parr slammed his hand on the arm of the bench.

"Legal. It's cops and robbers, cowboys and Indians to you fuckers."

"Okay, so it is." Parr rolled his butt so he could face Jerri. "But you're smarter than to get caught in something like this. You can't win. It'll mean your license, your job. Why don't you talk to me?"

Jerri's eyes got watery, and she dumped the *raspa* to splatter red ice over the hot sidewalk. She balled the paper cone in her hand and threw it in the river. "Maybe I love him."

Parr closed his eyes, turned away from her, and tried to think of something to say, but finally he couldn't resist being a foolish pussy-whipped old man, so he said, "What about me?"

Jerri smiled at him and leaned close to him. She placed her right hand, sticky from the dripping *raspa,* against Parr's cheek, then kissed him on the mouth. When she pulled away from him, she said, "You're a son of bitch. That's just what you did to me."

As she started to cry, Parr scooted closer to her and put his arm around her. But she wriggled out from Parr's arm and put her hands up to her face. She sat up and started walking away. Parr yelled after her, "If I have to, I'll close Palo down."

She stopped, turned to look at him even though her hands were over her face, and yelled, "You go straight to hell." Then she continued running down the river walk, her purse swinging on its straps and bouncing off her butt. Then she stopped again and turned around. "And you leave Palo alone." She turned and ran to the stairs leading back up to the streets.

Shit, Parr said to himself. He could get a heart attack chasing her. So he sat back down and tried to think of his next move. Most women would have told him everything. In the old days, he would have gotten a woman to talk. But this was Jerri, and he was old and making mistakes. The summer heat and humidity and his own sweat pasted his starched powder blue Western shirt to his chest and back, and he felt like a foolish old man who could just barely keep himself from crying.

❤ Vincent Fuentes drove the rented car from Trinity University back downtown to pick up Jerri for lunch. He hadn't had a drink all day. He had no headache to squint through or to drown in more liquor. The night before, he'd had only the two drinks at dinner. It had been the second night he'd seen her, and he'd stayed sober. She was working out quite well for him. He parked his car by a meter and walked to her office. When he stopped to peek in her window, he couldn't see her behind her desk. When he checked the door, he found it was open, and he went in and saw only her back as she bent over the wooden and cardboard crates stacked in back of her desk and Sam Ford looking on and saying, "It's about time you got that stuff out of the way." Fuentes walked into the office and around her desk. The fat man who started her in this business turned to look at Fuentes. "You're back?"

Jerri straightened up and turned to look at Fuentes. "Oh, good, you're here." She grabbed one of the crates and dragged it by a handle, the other end of the wooden crate screeching and scratching the linoleum floor.

"You were getting so much of this junk. It was starting to overflow into my office," Sam said, and waddled behind the crates. Fuentes stared for a moment, then ran to the dragging end of the crate and tried to pick it up. After he dropped it once, he grunted as he straightened up with the one end of the crate in his hands and looked across the crate at Jerri, who had a drop of sweat running down the bridge of her nose. The bead of sweat dripped from the point of her nose and splattered on the top of the crate. "What the hell is in here?" Sam asked.

"The door, Sam, the door," Jerri said, and Sam, waddling faster, opened the back door, held it open with one hand, and tried to step out of the way. Jerri stepped into the door frame, and Fuentes heaved his shoulders as the corner of the crate bit into his cramping fingers. He realized that Jerri must be stronger than he. Of course she was, he thought, in every way. She would be his salvation.

Fuentes looked at her and smiled. She didn't return the smile but looked straight at him with an anxious look on her face. As Fuentes went through the door frame, he had to cheat to one side to get past the part of Sam that stuck into the opening of the door and smelled the sweat from the fat man as he maneuvered the crate past him. With Jerri guiding him, they walked down the alley a couple of yards, then hefted the crate into the back of Jerri's Suburban. As Jerri pushed the crate farther back into the Suburban, Fuentes sat on the tailgate and brushed his hands together. "It's time for lunch. I thought seafood and a couple of drinks."

"These are your guns," she said.

"Sure, they are, but let's not look at the ugly things."

Jerri ran her open hand up the side of her face and through her hair. "The San Antonio police know about this."

Fuentes laughed because he now appreciated Trujillo and Natividad. They and the prestige of the Mexican government protected him. "Let them," he said.

"What the hell," Jerri said, and shook her head. "I've got to hide these."

"They were hidden in your office. Let's just get a drink." Fuentes looked at his watch. "I have a class this afternoon."

Fuentes thought, going over who knew what and who could not know what and what was best for him. These affairs got so convoluted once they started. He wanted to tell Jerri what was really happening but knew such honesty rarely worked, at least not yet. He decided for now to worry along with Jerri. "Yes, yes, let's hide them." He got off the tailgate and walked quickly back toward the office. Jerri was almost immediately by his side and racing ahead of him. "Where are we going to hide them?"

Jerri said, "There's a city warehouse down past the SP depot. I've got a key to it."

Thirty minutes later, Fuentes was wet with sweat, and his shoulder muscles ached after loading the heavy crates filled with gun parts into Jerri's Suburban. He rubbed at his shoulder with his open hand. Since his stay in jail, he liked to feel as little pain as possible. So, as he sat in the passenger side of the Suburban and waited for Jerri to start the car, he put his mind elsewhere. He was in Puerto Peñasco with Jerri. He remembered the smell of fish mingling with the smell of salt air, the ocean breeze mixing with the desert dryness, the small but still luxurious condominium Palo had owned. His mind stopped on Palo for just a moment. He wondered if he should see his father while he was in town. Then his mind returned to Peñasco and Jerri. Then the memory turned sour because, as he remembered the trip, he had been too consumed with art and politics to appreciate Jerri's thighs during sex or her company during their walks on the beach. Unselfish then, he had been a fool. When the time was right, he would escape everything but his own desires. He would ask Jerri to jump into the Suburban with him and drive away to a new life, anywhere in the world, just as she had done for Palo. So he returned his mind to where he was and saw Jerri driving the Suburban dangerously fast down the narrow alley.

When she reached a street, she slowed and drove carefully down it. Fuentes thought to find another place to put his mind, but before he could, Jerri said, "Look in back of us, real close. See if anybody is following us."

"How will I know?"

"Look at the drivers, see who pulls on the freeway with us. They stuck a bug up under the car."

This might be fun, Fuentes told himself, and kept his mind in Jerri's Suburban as he twisted in the seat to see who might be following. He wished that he had a drink to go along with the ride.

☯ Jerri pulled down a side street and headed the opposite way, down one-way Dolorosa, then she cut down another side street and turned down one-way Commerce back toward I-10. She knew downtown well. She could tell by sight where she was, even if she didn't know the exact street, since their names changed as often as they curled and changed direction. Every organ, all the tissue in her body seemed to have turned to acid. That sting was just shock. All that she could do was what she had learned in the private detective business. Nothing she had read, written, sculpted, or heard from Fuentes kept her from curling up into a ball, paralyzed from the sting. Only habit, the discipline of her job, the instincts she had had to develop, then train, gave her the ability to move, to do something, to force the sting into some kind of feeling that she could take action against. Strangely, she could work up no anger against Parr, even with the bug that somebody stuck under her axle. He had gotten her away from the office so some cop could put a tracking device on her car. But Parr was doing his job, consistent with what he was. He was doing only what she would have expected him to do. But while she had no anger, she felt some sorrow. She would probably never see him again. Fuentes was another matter. "Did you see anybody on either Dolorosa or Commerce?" she asked Fuentes.

"So many cars," he said.

"Watch closer," she said, and checked in the rearview mirror and spotted a dirty white Dodge Intrepid. Joe should have had an unmarked police car tailing her. But then, with a second to think, she realized that just he was tailing her, not the police, in order to keep the police away from her. She looked over at Fuentes. "Did you notice that dirty white Dodge?"

She returned her attention to the traffic in front of her and twisted her neck to see her lover looking back over the seat. "Yeah, I think I saw it back on Dolorosa."

"So did I," Jerri said. "Concentrate, Vincent, please."

With her body doing the habitual, her mind started its habitual analysis. The sting faded. She found her mind shifting from Joe Parr to Vincent Fuentes. She had been with him for two nights and most of two days. As she had expected, he had changed. She had feared that he might have become even more of an idealist and hence embittered. But he was looser, the exact opposite of someone embittered. He joked more than he ever had and seemed constantly distracted, like he was confused by what was going on before him; he was more careful to please her, to entertain her; and he was better in bed, taking the time to caress her and to read her movements and notice what she liked.

Jerri twisted her neck to stare at him to see if she could spot a physical sign of the change in him. He had turned into a man whom she, as well as most other women, should have adored. But she missed the long political talks, not so much for what he said but for the way the talk animated him. Since the first night, when he begged for her help, he hadn't mentioned the guns, as though he didn't know or didn't care about the illegal crates piling up in her office. In Puerto Peñasco, when he talked about privilege and poverty, his green eyes shone. Even in the dark, in bed or on the beach,

Jerri remembered she had sensed the shine in his eyes. Now his eyes, at times, were glassy and often bloodshot. Even Palo now seemed more full of conviction and passion than Fuentes.

Jerri pulled into the entrance ramp for I-10 and immediately checked the rearview mirror. The interstate this close to town was always crowded, and she couldn't see far behind her. She pressed on the accelerator hard and pulled into the far left lane. "I can't see a damn thing. It's too crowded."

"You do this often?" Fuentes asked.

"Look for a white Dodge."

"Maybe if I put on my glasses." Fuentes dug into his shirt pocket, pulled out his round scholar's glasses, and smiled at Jerri as he put them on. Jerri didn't return his smile. He looked somehow like a fake with the round glasses mixed with this broad grin that she hadn't seen before. Jerri almost wished that he wasn't with her. It was time for business. Her sense of business, not a cause or mission, would get her through this, and he was interfering. He pushed the glasses farther up the bridge of his nose and looked back through the back window of the Suburban.

Jerri quickly looked in the rearview mirror. "I can't tell with all those cars," she said. "That . . . that . . . that pinche cabrón."

Fuentes took off his seat belt now, twisting and folding his legs under him so that his chest was against the back of the seat. Jerri slowed down. He looked at her. "Where did you learn those words?"

Jerri shot a quick glance at Fuentes. "Everybody says it."

"Who are you cussing?"

Jerri looked ahead of her but said, "Now's a hell of a time to discuss my vocabulary and mood."

"Okay, when does the chase start?"

"There's never a chase. Just following." She slowed down to forty. A car behind her honked. Then it, then another, and another swung around from behind her, and Fuentes looked at the angry drivers who peered at him and cussed Jerri.

Jerri looked in her rearview mirror and felt herself smile as one truck swung to her right to go around her. Behind the truck was a dirty, white Dodge Intrepid. Jerri saw a clearing all the way to the far right lane. She jerked the wheel to the right and pulled the Suburban over. She closed her mind to the screech and honking horns from behind her and checked in the rearview mirror to see the white Dodge pulling across the same lanes as she had. A man in a large white hat was driving, and another man sitting next to him nervously pushed against the dash. Now, with movement and tactics, Jerri's mind could help her deal with Joe Parr. She even smiled to congratulate herself for her savvy but still wondered who the other man was. Then she looked at her passenger.

Fuentes, when she had jerked the wheel, had slammed against the passenger door and come away from it rubbing his shoulder. He turned back around to the proper position in his seat and strapped on his seat belt. As soon as he got on his seat belt and settled into the front seat, facing the right direction, Jerri pulled right again and got off the freeway.

From the small businesses—paint stores, hardware, mom-and-pop Mexican food, small liquor stores—most crumbling and going broke, Jerri, who hadn't paid attention to her exit, decided that she was on Fresno. Checking in the rearview mirror to see the Intrepid still behind her, she caught a glimpse of a 7-Eleven sign. A plan suddenly sprouted in her mind, and she again turned right: into the 7-Eleven store. Pulling up to the front of the store, turning to watch as Parr and his passenger sped past her, she said to Fuentes, "Go inside and buy some gum or something. Then . . ."

"Gum," Fuentes said. "How about some M&M's, too?"

Jerri breathed deeply, then started again. "Buy something. Pay for it. Go to the back of the building. There's an alley behind the building. I'll pick you up there."

"Are you sure?" Fuentes asked.

"Do it. These are your goddamn guns." She felt almost like leaving him at the store, but as he got out of the car, Jerri quickly strained against her seat belt to touch Fuentes's hand. He smiled at her, and she undid her seat belt, stretched the length of the front seat, and kissed him, hoping that Joe Parr would see the kiss. As he went into the 7-Eleven, she decided that for now she could overlook Fuentes's changes; she also knew that when she had time, she would cry about what Parr had really been doing.

✪ As Parr pulled off the busy thoroughfare into the driveway of a do-it-yourself dry cleaners and laundry, he saw Ollie Nordmarken sling his arm over the back of the seat of the Ranger's standard issue Dodge Intrepid and look at the 7-Eleven. "What are we going to do now, slick?" Ollie asked. Parr had thought that Ollie would enjoy getting out of the office and playing a little cowboy, but now, even though he could think of nobody he'd have rather have had for backup, he wished that he had followed Jerri alone.

Parr now saw Fuentes get out and duck his head back in while Jerri leaned across the front seat. She kissed him full on the lips in the middle of a car chase, and Joe Parr first cussed her, then admired her for her coolness and guts.

"Goddamn, holy shit," Parr said. "She's good. Drives that Suburban like a Ferrari. And the ass end is loaded down with what I bet is those guns." On Ollie's lap was an open notebook computer, seeming to Parr like some Amazon snake that would swallow them both. On the screen of the notebook was a miniature map of downtown, and a little dot was flashing from the downtown alley where Jerri had thrown the transmitter. The decoder/receiver that received the satellite signals was on Parr's dashboard. As Joe had watched Jerri pull out of the alley from a parking space on Commerce, Ollie had stared into the screen and said, "She hasn't gone anywhere yet."

"So what are we going to do?" Ollie asked.

Parr pounded his free hand against the steering wheel. "Goddamn, I need two cars." He knew that he should have let the undercover cops in unmarked cars, who had followed Fuentes to Jerri's office, follow Jerri. The bastard, just as Parr figured, led them right to her. They just sat in their cars and waited. As he sat figuring what to do, fighting all that was going on his head except for following Jerri, Parr thought that like a softhearted and softheaded old fool, he had followed Jerri in a car she could recognize. He reached for his radio to call for the other two cops but pulled his hand away.

"Goddamn it," Parr said, opened the door of the Dodge, and stepped outside.

"I say we give up," he heard Ollie say from inside the car. "Let's surrender to him." Ollie's door opened, and Parr saw Ollie poke his head over the roof of the Intrepid.

"Not yet, by God," Joe said. "You walk down to the 7-Eleven and see what Fuentes is up to." Parr knew, even before he said anything to Ollie, that it was Jerri confounding them, not Fuentes.

"Shit." Ollie slammed his door. "And meanwhile you get the air-conditioned car."

"They don't know you," Parr said.

"Real goddamn convenient," Ollie said, and started walking, then jogging, very slowly, like the old man he was, toward the 7-Eleven. Despite the fat that shook underneath his sport coat that hid his gun, despite his now piss-poor attitude, Ollie was a good man. Joe wanted to give him something to do besides book work, and he knew, or thought fairly certainly, that since this was just a favor and nothing official, Ollie would keep his mouth shut if Joe asked him to.

Joe was still watching Ollie half walking and half jogging down the street when Jerri started backing up the Suburban. Fuentes wasn't in the car. Ollie turned and looked back at the Dodge. Poor, fat, tired-looking Ollie gave a long elaborate shrug. "Goddamn it to hell," Joe said. "Stay with Fuentes," he yelled to Ollie, and ducked into his Dodge. This time he did reach for his radio and he told the two cops where Fuentes was.

Jerri's Suburban zoomed past him. Parr checked in his rear-view mirror to see Ollie running (more like scooting) toward the 7-Eleven; he zoomed after Jerri.

❷ Jerri pulled right again (God bless right turns) as soon as she saw the Dodge follow her. She quickly turned right down a gravel alley and pressed the accelerator. She hoped no dog or kid ran out of a backyard. She hit a bump, and the back end of the loaded Suburban felt like it hit ground. It would be hard for Joe to see far down this

131

alley, especially if he was going fast. As she looked in her rearview mirror, she saw Parr go right past the alley.

Now she would have to retrieve Fuentes. Kissing him had been a good idea. She had seen more of his graciousness and now easy charm. Not only in hiding from cops but in ordering dinner, going out for the night, screwing, or contacting a gun smuggler; he deferred to her. She stopped in back of the 7-Eleven and stared at the picket fence between it and the Suburban.

❂ Fuentes, unaccustomed to American convenience stores, hunted until he found a pack of Juicy Fruit. He started walking back to the cashier but thought that he'd like something to drink, so he walked to the back of the store and opened one of the frosty glass doors, reached into the refrigeration, and pulled out a six-pack of beer. When he turned around, he saw a Mexican man come into the store. He smiled and walked toward the man. The man, with sweat dripping down his face and staining his shirt, stared hesitantly at Fuentes. This man was either a cop or a construction worker buying a few Cokes for a hot day. Fuentes stopped. The man smiled.

"Hello," Fuentes said, and walked toward the counter. Without looking, Fuentes almost knew that the man behind his exposed back was nervously fingering the butt of a gun. He paid for the gum and the beer and turned around, smiling again, to see the man standing behind his back. "Good-bye," Fuentes said, and walked out the front door. When he got outside, Fuentes saw an older man, sweating into his sport coat, panting, and leaning against the glass of the 7-Eleven convenience store. The man stuck his hand inside his sport coat.

Fuentes turned to his left, rounded the corner of the convenience store, and turned to see the Mexican man leave the convenience store and walk across its parking lot. Then Fuentes started running and stopped abruptly when he came to the picket fence, as though it had jumped out in front of him. He turned and saw the man in the sport coat staring at him from the corner of the store.

He looked at the fence and then saw through it Jerri's Suburban screech to a halt in the alley behind the store. He choked on the dust that the car raised and saw Jerri leaning across the seat of the Suburban and yelling at him through the open passenger side window. "Jump the fence," she said.

"Hell, no," he yelled at Jerri. Before the words were out of his mouth, the man in the sport coat walked slowly toward him. Fuentes stuck the toe of his soft-soled shoe into one of the pickets and grabbed another picket with his fingers. As he climbed, he tried to balance his six-pack in his other hand. "Throw away the package," he heard Jerri say, but he continued to inch up the picket fence. He knew that the man might shoot him, but he also knew that if the cop was any good at his job, he wouldn't dare risk shooting him now. In fact, he looked at the cop and saw him standing with his feet spread apart, staring at him and sweating.

Just as he got to the top of the fence and slung a leg over it, catching his pants on one of the pointed pickets, Fuentes saw the man step closer and reach deeper into his sport coat. Fuentes decided just to jump. He pushed himself away from the fence and heard his pants rip. When he hit the ground, he felt something like a crunch in one of his ankles and heard a thud as one of the bottles of beer fell out of the six-pack and broke against a rock. The door to the Suburban swung open, and he climbed in.

Jerri leaned across his lap and raised her fist up to the passenger window. Fuentes looked out the window at the cop, who stood up against the picket fence with his fingers sticking through it. "Son of a bitch," the man said, calmly pulled his hand out from his sport coat, then smiled. And then Fuentes looked down at Jerri's fist to see her middle finger extend.

Fuentes felt the sudden surge as Jerri hit the gas and looked at her. "What the hell were you doing?" she asked.

"I was thirsty," he said, and reached into the cardboard that kept the remaining five beers in place and pulled out a bottle of beer. "Want a beer?"

She looked at him, and one corner of her mouth dropped. "And here's your gum. I hope Juicy Fruit is okay." He reached into his pants pocket and pulled out the crumpled pack of gum. She snatched the pack from him, turned onto a main street, and started to open the pack. She folded a piece of gum with one hand and popped it into her mouth as though it were a pill. Fuentes felt the need to say more. "You're good at this," he said, and decided that he still needed to say more. He looked back over his shoulder at the 7-Eleven. "Do you think that man was a cop?" he asked.

"I don't know," Jerri said.

❷ By the time Parr got back to the 7-Eleven, Ollie Nordmarken was leaning against the side of the building in the shade and sipping from a beer. Parr pulled up beside his buddy, leaned across the front seat, and opened the door for him. After Ollie got in and wiped the sweat from his face with his open palm, a few drops of sweat splattering on the Dodge's interior, he told Parr what had happened. "Well, why didn't you do something?" Parr said to his friend.

"Like what?" Ollie said, and sipped from his beer. "I'm just here as a bipartisan observer, remember. I couldn't have arrested him and made it stick."

"Shit, Ollie," Parr said. He knew that Ollie was right. Parr could have stopped them and arrested them, but then they'd never have found out where the guns were going. It was too early yet to play his hand. A few bluffs were in order.

"I guess you think I should have climbed the fence like he did? Shoot him, maybe?"

"Goddamn right," Parr said. "You should have shot him."

"For what?" Ollie said, and held out his coat to let the air-conditioning hit his sweating body. "For transporting a six-pack of beer over a picket fence? Yeah, you're right, I should have shot him; then I should have shot the bitch for shooting the finger at me."

Parr turned to look at Ollie. "You didn't say that she shot the bird at you."

Ollie chuckled. "Feisty bitch." Parr chuckled, too, and then Ollie said, "That's the one you're sweet on. That's your new girl-friend." Parr didn't answer him. "Jesus Christ, Joe, you're in a bucket of shit. Damned if you do, damned if you don't." Ollie, cooled, dropped the ends of his sport coat and finished off the last of his beer. Ollie didn't look at Joe but said, "Was it because you're sweet on her that you warned her?"

Joe started talking even before he swung his head toward Ollie. "If she had any sense, she would have told us. She'd have informed on him. That's what I was doing. Giving her a chance to save her ass."

"We talking about the same woman?"

Parr couldn't find any more amusement in Ollie, so he said, "Shit," and hit the steering wheel with his fist.

"Just let him go," Ollie said. "We're too old to play this cowboy shit. We're lucky to get any pussy, and now you want to arrest what you got." Ollie shook his head. "He's got a stiffer dick than us. Let him go." Ollie turned to look at Joe to let him know he was serious.

"He ain't got a stiffer dick than me, Ollie. I'm going to get his ass. Besides, it's Jerri doing this, not him. She's the smart one." Ollie shrugged. And after Ollie went inside the 7-Eleven and bought a couple more beers, and as they sat in Joe's car and took their first sips, the Polack and the Mexican cop who were Joe's team, given to him by Charlie Hoestadter, each pulled up to the 7-Eleven in their unmarked police cars.

❷ Fuentes sat on top of one of the crates and coughed from the dust that swirled around in the vacuum of the decrepit and crumbling warehouse. His face seemed muddy from the sweat running in rivulets through the dust that settled on him. With the sun setting and the heat from a day of baking gathered up, the warehouse was like a sauna. Dust had even settled into the rip in his pants and stained his leg. His ankle hurt. He pulled the last bottle of warm beer out of the carton that had been the six-pack and wiped at his face with his open palm and smeared more sweat-wetted dust on his face. He twisted the top off the bottle and took a long sip of the tepid beer.

Jerri hadn't drunk any of the beer. After she had lost whoever was following them, she drove back downtown and up to a deserted row of warehouses. "Why didn't we come here in the first place?" Fuentes asked.

"You remember the guy chasing us?" she answered as though scolding him for not thinking.

"Just kidding," Fuentes said, and patted her leg.

After she had backed the Suburban up to the warehouse and they had unloaded all the crates, she sat with her back against another crate, her face turned away from Fuentes, and blinked against the sweat in her eyes. Fuentes had tried to make conversation with her, but she was trapped inside herself. Very well, Fuentes thought, he too could move his mind elsewhere. So he looked down the uneven aisles of the warehouse with the sunbeams shining through several vents and holes in the ceiling and noted the shapes of the monsters and madmen who stared back at him. Papier-mâché faces and figures, wilted and distorted from the rain that fell through the holes in the ceiling, looked at him with tortured expressions. A Yanqui version of a Mexican (some smiling loony with a wide-brimmed sombrero, chunks fallen out of the brim), a blue devil with a pitchfork (the fork still intact but the handle corroded and the forked devil's tail gone), Bugs Bunny with no ears, and an ape's face all smiled at him or taunted him. And the malignant smiles and taunts reminded him of what he saw or remembered seeing in the Saltillo jail. That whole episode was no longer real, not a nightmare, not even a dream. He knew it had taught him something, but it was something he couldn't really explain or understand. If he could truly understand it and what he had felt, he could better cope with what he now did, or he could more easily desert Trujillo and Natividad. Now his ankle hurt, and he crossed his legs and rubbed it. "What are these?" he said toward Jerri. She didn't answer. "Jerri, is something wrong?"

Jerri got up and walked toward him. Sweat pasted her shirt to her chest, so that he could see the outline of her bra and her breasts. Her hair was soaked with sweat all the way to its roots. It seemed wild and stringy. "Every year the city stores the old floats from all the Fiesta parades in here. People only come in here once a year."

"An excellent place to hide the guns. Angel Martínez will be proud of your selection," Fuentes said.

"Palo's got it all set up. Tomorrow I won't see much of you. I pick up Angel."

"Where?" Fuentes asked.

Jerri seemed careful as she answered. He could see her think as drops of sweat rolled off her nose and chin. "Palo's usual place."

"Where is that?"

Jerri turned away from him and walked back to where she had been sitting. "Come on. We better get out of here before someone sees us who shouldn't." Fuentes pushed himself up. He realized that he craved another beer or even something stronger. He wanted to be through with Trinity University and its students. He remembered that he had a group discussion tonight. "I need to get back," he suddenly said to himself as well as Jerri.

"I'm going to drop you off downtown. You can walk to your hotel. Then I'm going to Palo's. You go on with your business."

"What about dinner tonight? Or a drink after the discussion?"

"Vincent, this is serious. We're in deep shit here."

Fuentes wanted to tell her that Trujillo and Natividad would take care of everything but said, "Relax."

"I am relaxed. And I'm thinking well." She put her hands on her hips and breathed in deeply. "You'll be easy to find. You have to be at Trinity. That's good. We'll let them see you. And I'll hide. And then I'll hide Angel."

"Where?"

"Somewhere he'll be safe until he can pick the guns up."

"Fine."

Fuentes started limping toward the entry of the loading dock. As he got to it, Jerri asked, "Have you seen Palo yet?"

"No."

"You should."

"Perhaps, but I'd rather see you."

"When this is all through, I'll take you to see him."

"Perhaps I should see him on my own. I'm not sure we would have much to say to each other."

Fuentes walked out the loading dock door before she could ask another question. He jumped off the loading dock, clenched his teeth when his weight came down on his ankle, and got in on the passenger side of the Suburban. Soon Jerri came in through the driver's door. She started the car and drove down the rutted road toward the gate they had come in. "Is there anything you should tell me, Vincent?" she asked without smiling.

Fuentes thought for a moment, then chose to answer what he hoped she meant: "I want to be with you when we finish this."

"Vincent, I mean now, about this."

Fuentes thought about tactics and decided simply to smile and say, "No."

❧ Parr pushed at the hotel door, but it was locked. He knocked, and the door slowly opened. The young Mexican cop looked at him from the crack between the door and the wall, then pulled open the door, and Parr stepped in. The Polack cop lay on the bed and watched the evening news. "Goddamn Iraqis," he mumbled.

The young Mexican cop closed the door behind him. "Ranger Parr, hey, great to see you again, man." He patted Parr on the back. Parr thought he remembered that the Mexican cop's name was Carrillo. "What do we do now, jefe?"

The Polack cop sat up on the bed. "Why the hell do we let every goddamn Mideast country fuck around with us?" Parr tried to remember his name. It was a Polish name with a bunch of zs in it. He walked around to the TV and shut it off. "This hotel stakeout is a great idea. No dusty damn attics or trashy alleys to hide in. I once had to sit two days in a meat locker to catch some asshole stealing sides of beef."

"What's your name again?" Parr asked.

The white cop smiled. "Jarozombek. Nobody remembers bohunk names."

"Sit down, Mr. Parr," Carrillo said. But Parr walked farther into the room and leaned against the one large table.

"So, *qué pasó?*" Parr asked.

"He ain't been nowhere," Carrillo said. "He was walking when he got here. Wasn't with Jerri."

"Almost hate to take money for this shit." Jarozombek pointed around the room. "Air-conditioned, room service."

"Yeah, just like a vacation," Parr said.

"Say, Parr, I'm sorry you and your friend lost Fuentes and that Jerri Johnson, you know. But what the hell. What could you do? Gun him down? Tackle him, and blow the whole thing?" Jarozombek asked.

"Well, thanks," Parr said. The Polack, in a way, was taunting him. "She's good. We're not going to follow her if she doesn't want us to."

"We called her in. We got her address. We can get two more plainclothes over to her place the next day or so," Carrillo said.

Parr felt his neck get stiff. "We don't need it."

"Look, Mr. Parr, excuse me, but you don't got to work this hard. SAPD can take care of all this. You still run the show, so why don't you go home or go to your office, let us do the hard stuff and give you a call when we got something?" Carrillo smiled and patted Parr's shoulder.

"My dick may not get as hard as y'all's. But I can keep up with you."

"See, taco bender," Jarozombek said to Carrillo, "you pissed him off." Jarozombek turned to Parr. "Carrillo wants to be a Ranger. He's the right minority, but you tell him how tough the competition is."

Joe Parr looked at Carrillo. The little Mexican was better off taking notes on Charlie Hoestadter and glad handing and smiling his way through police politics. "The competition is tough, Carrillo. You even got to have some advanced college on top of the police training." Carrillo looked at Parr, then shrugged at Jarozombek.

"Hey, Joe," Jarozombek said, and dug in his shirt pocket for his pack of cigarettes. "Jerri's okay by me." He pulled a cigarette out of the pack. "So if we're trying to keep her ass out of the chili, man, you just say so." Jarozombek put the cigarette in his mouth and lit it.

Parr at first wanted to say that he wasn't keeping anybody's goddamn ass out of the chili, but he caught himself and said, "I'll take care of her." Parr knew that Jerri probably wouldn't stay at her apartment tonight. He would drive by to check for her Suburban, then go on to Palo's, where she would stay.

"I'd like to take care of her." Jarozombek giggled, then flipped the TV back on. Parr lifted one foot, then the other, and looked around the hotel room to keep from saying to Jarozombek, *Fuck you and the horse you rode in on.*

Parr looked around the luxury hotel room. "Fuentes will probably hit the river tonight and drink till he's shit faced."

"We drew straws," Jarozombek said. "I get to follow him."

"Well, I better get going." Parr turned toward the door.

"Say, man," Carrillo said. "You know if they know we're following them, our chances of catching them are pretty well shot to hell. We need all the help we can get. Why don't we call for some more people?"

"I'm working on an informer," Parr said.

"Who?" Carrillo asked. Jarozombek smiled. Carrillo turned to Jarozombek. "Who?"

"Dumb taco bender," Jarozombek said, and Parr didn't let the door hit his ass on the way out.

❷ Jerri sat in the padded, rocking lawn chair on Palo's screened-in back porch and watched the blinking fireflies in the gray shadows of his backyard. It was a still night, with little of the usually reliable Gulf breeze. Besides the cars from Commerce Street, Jerri could hear occasional buzzing from the cicadas, even though it was late at night. And again this night, she convinced herself that she could hear the mosquitoes and moths and other bugs that sought the faint light from the kitchen behind her slam into the screen and smash. Jerri turned when the light from the kitchen grew brighter and saw Palo coming out to the back porch with two bowls of ice cream. "Blue Bell Caramel Turtle flavor, this week's special at HEB's," Palo said.

Palo handed one bowl to Jerri, and she set the bowl in her lap. He didn't sit beside her. "Let's go inside into the air-conditioning. It is too hot here tonight," Palo said. Jerri heard or thought she heard the faint explosion of another bug slamming into the screen. Sam's joke came into her head: What's the last thing to go through a bug's mind when he hits a windshield? His asshole was the answer.

"I like it out here," she said to Palo.

"Very good," he said, sat beside her, put the bowl of ice cream in his lap, and looked into it. "See, the ice cream melts." He dipped his spoon into the soupy ice cream and sucked the melted stuff from the spoon. Jerri knew that he wanted to go inside. But Jerri wanted to sit outside because they usually did and because they usually had at his condominium in Puerto Peñasco. And she wanted some memory, some sentimentality, or some allegiance to anybody or anything to help her mind now that she had subdued the sting under her skin. Palo looked at her again from over his bowl of ice cream.

Jerri took her spoon and dipped some of the rapidly melting ice cream. She sucked up the fluid, then glanced at Palo. She handed the bowl to him and said, "You eat mine."

Palo took the bowl from her, seeming surprised that she wouldn't eat the ice cream. "Blue Bell Caramel Turtle," he said.

"I know. I'll eat two bowls later." Jerri crossed her arms and leaned her head back in her chair. She was, despite the day, sleepy. If she didn't let herself think or mull over what had happened today, she could get to sleep. And she needed sleep for what she had to do in the morning.

"You sleep in the front bedroom. It is made up for you," Palo said, sensing, as he had learned to do over the years since she brought him to San Antonio, just what Jerri felt. Perhaps, she thought, she should take a walk around Palo's house to look for any strange cars or people. She didn't want to be seen or followed. Her lids grew heavy and slowly started to close. "You are sleepy," Palo said, and Jerri again opened her eyes to see him slurp his last bit of ice cream and switch to her bowl. He sucked the ice cream off his spoon. "I shouldn't eat two bowls," he said. "Too much ice cream gives me the constipation."

Jerri reached across from her chair to the arm of his and patted his forearm. "Perhaps I should go in and get to bed."

Jerri rose to her feet and started to walk into the kitchen, and

Palo rested his spoon in the bowl of melting ice cream and grabbed her wrist. "You don't need to go tomorrow."

"I promised Vincent."

"Break the promise. It is not fair of him."

Palo grunted as he tried to get up but couldn't, so he pulled on Jerri's wrist, and Jerri let him guide her until she was sitting on the arm of his chair. She suddenly felt his arm around her waist. "It does you no good. It risks everything you have. He has no right to ask you to do anything like this."

Jerri put her open palms on either side of Palo's chin and pressed his cheeks. "Thank you. But I have to." Jerri looked at Palo and, even in the dark, could see his eyes shift away from her. His unsteady eyes, like Joe Parr's during his feeble confrontation, dodged away from her.

"Fuck him," he said. "Fuck him." Jerri dropped her hands from Palo's face. He let his chin fall to his chest. "You have become more a daughter to me than he is my son." Palo took a deep breath to continue. "He asks me to do this gun stuff. Has he seen me? No!" Palo looked up at Jerri. "Let him have his cause. But his cause has taken away all his care for his family."

Palo was more adamant than Joe Parr had been. Vincent and Palo both argued emotionally and well for their own purposes. But now Palo, like Fuentes five years before and now ever so often, argued for her sake too. Perhaps the blood and genes in these two men's bodies made them both love her. And suddenly she thought of the fantasy, the unthinkable luxury, of them all living together in San Antonio. The only way to have any hope of achieving this fantasy, of making it to any degree real, was to pick up Angel Martínez. She would pick up this poor Mexican and her part of the bargain would be over, and she could put her attention toward her love and concern for both men.

"I have to help him, Palo," Jerri said, straightened, then reached down to pat Palo's shoulder. Palo only nodded and scooped up some now completely melted Blue Bell Caramel Turtle ice cream. And as Jerri opened the kitchen door, she listened to the sound she might have only thought she could hear: the splatter of insects as they gutted themselves chasing after their mindless obsession.

✪ Parr heard the thud, then felt it as his head hit the dash of the ancient-looking Chevy with the big engine. He shook his head and focused his eyes and saw just dark. All the lights were off in Palo's house. Joe was beginning, just barely, to think how Jerri would think, and he knew she wasn't coming out of the house tonight. Tomorrow, sunup or later, she might lead him somewhere—if he could keep up with her. And if he caught her doing the crime red-handed, by following her himself, he'd again give himself the option and the torture of slapping cuffs on her or looking the other way. To hell, Parr said to himself, he'd slap the cuffs on her. He should have the balls to be the arresting officer; he owed it to himself and to her.

No breeze was blowing tonight, and the humidity covered everything with a film that made human skin sticky and dirty. Worse, he had heard several mósquitoes buzzing around his face. He scratched at the bites on his arms and hands, and he knew, from the way his face felt, that he had bites on his forehead and nose. Parr had tried to roll up his windows to keep the mosquitoes out, but the heat almost choked him. Goddamn should of just gone home like the Mexican kid cop said.

He cussed himself a little more, then the door on the passenger's side opened, and Melba, holding a cup and saucer, carefully got in. "Hello, Joe," Melba said. It was the first time his mind let her speak to him other than at his house. It was the first time that his mind let him see her.

"Goddamn it, Melba. What are you doing here?" Joe said. "This is a stakeout. I'm working."

"Please, dear," she said. "Don't cuss. I can read those words, but you know how I just don't like to hear them." She raised a teacup to her mouth and took a dainty sip of hot tea. Goddamn. Melba was the only person he knew in all of Texas who'd drink hot tea on a Texas summer night and be dead yet while she was doing it. As she raised the teacup to her lips, he heard the familiar sound of her lips sucking at the tea, the sound he never dared mention to her. She prided herself on her manners, so Joe let her die without ever saying to her that she made little tiny sounds when she ate.

Melba looked around her at the car. "Joe, why are you in this car? What did you do with the Lincoln?"

"Jerri Johnson will recognize my Lincoln. This is a police car."

"Smart of you, dear," Melba said.

"Forget the goddamn car. What are you doing here, Melba?" Joe didn't like cutesy, pet names. A man ought to call his wife by her given name.

"I just wanted to chat about what you are doing." She lowered her cup and smiled at Joe.

"It's my business. It's none of yours."

"Joe, don't get angry."

"Goddamn it."

"Please, darling."

"Okay," Joe said, and breathed in. "I never could understand why I couldn't cuss in my own goddamn house."

Melba smiled as she sipped her tea. "We're not at the house, dear."

Joe smiled a little bit to himself. Even dead, she liked to tease. "So what are you so goddamn worried about?"

"Joe, your language has really gotten worse since I died."

"Damn it, Melba. Let's forget my language." Joe tried to concentrate on something else besides Melba, but then he felt his mosquito bites itching. He scratched at his left arm with the fingernails on his right hand.

"Oh, my," Melba said, and leaned toward Joe. "Are those mosquito bites? I should have brought some Off! with me."

"I'm okay," Joe said.

Melba leaned back to her side of the car and casually sipped her tea. "Dear, why are you bothering that nice girl? I thought that you liked her." Parr looked away from her, then gasped when she touched his forearm. He turned in his seat to look at her. Now his mind was letting him feel the dead woman. "You better get some Campho-Phenique for those mosquito bites."

Joe pulled his arm away from Melba. "Why are you worried about Jerri?"

Melba sipped her tea, then set the saucer and the cup on the dashboard of the Chevy. "Because you like her so much. She means so much to you. You shouldn't be doing this to her."

"It's my job."

"Oh, come on, Joe. Let somebody else do your job. They're going to make you retire."

"But I'm still employed by the state of Texas."

"What are you trying to prove?"

"Nothing. I'm just doing what I'm good at."

"Why couldn't you have retired years ago and gotten good at something else?"

"Okay, okay. I see now. You're going to start that old argument." They had quit that argument before she died, but now Melba brought it up regular.

"No, I'm not," Melba said, and swiveled in her seat and stared, her nose up, out the windshield. Somewhere along the line, as she got older, she started getting that Baptist-Sunday-school-teacher-smelling-a-turd look, kind of like Charlie Hoestadter.

"Go on, Melba. Unless you say something, you're going to pout."

Melba jerked around, and she said in a smooth, tolerant voice, "If you had retired early, we would have had three years together before I died." Parr had heard this before, but every time Melba said it, he listened. "And this whole affair is the same thing, Joe." This was new, and Joe stared at the unreal Melba and waited for her to explain. "You could have such a beautiful time with Ms. Johnson. You're going to be very lonely when you retire. You should find a nice lady friend."

Joe forgot his anger at her and said, "Melba, darling, could you please go away . . . for now? Come back a little later and talk to me about it. But let me think. Okay?"

"Sure, dear," Melba said, and leaned toward Joe. And holy Jesus fucking Christ, Joe Parr felt her kiss on his cheek. Then Melba got her saucer and cup, climbed slowly out of the car, and walked down Palo's street toward brighter West Commerce. She waddled like an old lady. Generally she looked older than Parr remembered her. He watched her until she got to West Commerce.

CHAPTER EIGHT

Joe Parr slumped forward to follow his head, but as soon as he became aware of the movement, he was awake. Still, he could do nothing to stop his forehead from hitting the steering wheel of the Chevy. When he pulled his head off the greasy, black-stained steering wheel, he wished that he could still drive his roomy Lincoln. Nothing had moved at Palo's house.

He reached in the backseat to grab his thermos of coffee and started to pour some into the cup that served as a lid. In the dim, spreading first light, as he held the open thermos over the cup, he saw the door to Palo's garage open. He quickly poured what coffee was in his cup back into the thermos, sealed it, put it on the seat beside him, and reached into the backseat to grab his straw cowboy hat and put it on. A Ford truck with a camper pulled out of the driveway. Parr reached in his pocket, grabbed his half-frame glasses, stuck the arms behind his ears, then tilted back his head to see through the bottom lens. Jerri was in the driver's seat. Now, rather than the coffee, his adrenaline kept him awake. He started the old Chevy and slipped it into gear, and for safety he reached for his radio to tell Carrillo and Jarozombek where he was and what he was doing.

Parr stayed behind Jerri at a distance where she wouldn't notice him. As he followed her, he tried to work the radio and tell the two SAPD cops where he was. Finally, after seeing more landscape than cityscape, he knew that he was going south out of town on I-35.

After several miles Parr saw Jerri's blinker go on, almost as though to deliberately attract him. She turned her truck into a roadside café advertising itself as the Hungry Farmer. Parr pulled in after her, a white Toyota Corolla pulling in behind him. Jerri parked on the side of the building, and he parked down from her, pulled off his hat, and ducked down his head. With his head down, he heard another car, one with a tiny motor, pull up beside him, so he turned to his right and raised his head a bit to see the Toyota pull into a parking place. The two Mexican men sitting in the Toyota looked toward Jerri.

He turned off his Dodge just as the back end of Jerri's truck started rolling out of the parking space. As he fumbled to start the car, he jerked his head to his right and saw the big Mexican in the Toyota trying to start his car. When Joe Parr again looked for Jerri, he saw her behind him, stopped, looking at both him and the two Mexicans. She had goddamn pulled them both off the road to see who was following her. Suddenly, wheels spinning in the asphalt of the Hungry Farmer, Jerri's truck leapt forward. Parr quickly slammed his Chevy into reverse and pulled out of the parking space and damn near hit the front end of the Toyota. The Toyota immediately swerved around him and chased Jerri.

At the stop sign between the café parking lot and the frontage road of I-35, Jerri stopped and waited. The Toyota pulled up behind her, and Parr pulled up behind the Toyota. He pulled a pencil out of his shirt pocket and got the license of the Toyota, then reached quickly for the radio and got the katzenjammer cops. "Somebody else is following Jerri."

"Shit," Jarozombek voice crackled over the radio. "What'll we do?"

"Shit," Parr said.

Parr saw Jerri's arm come out of the window of the truck, saw her middle finger extend from her fist. Joe tried not to smile but couldn't keep from it; after all, Jerri's finger was as much for the two Mexicans in the Toyota as for him. "Hellfire, just wait for me," Parr said through the radio. Jerri's back tires grabbed more asphalt, and the truck slid around the corner and down the frontage road.

"You gonna follow her? You need some backup?" he heard over the radio.

Parr said to himself and to Jarozombek, "Hell, let's not make this a parade. She'll outrun those assholes or a DPS officer will stop her. Either way, I lost her." Parr was tempted to follow anyway, maybe even to try to signal her to stop and join her, just to see what she was up to. Instead Parr, the Texas Ranger, in the tradition of all tough, duty-minded Rangers, turned around and drove back to the Hungry Farmer for coffee and a big breakfast.

◑ Jerri lost the white Toyota by getting off I-35 at Dilley and driving down a ranch road. From the ranch road she cut off on a dirt road, took the Toyota cross-country, then circled behind to get back onto the ranch road, then to I-35. She kept a constant watch for them all the way to Palo's pickup point outside Laredo.

When she pulled onto blacktop, she relaxed and glanced out the window of the truck at the fields of prickly pear and mesquite trees. In this countryside everything stung, bit, or stuck, sort of like the countryside she had seen in Arizona with Palo and Fuentes. And she wondered who the Mexicans in the Toyota might be. Dodging them and Parr at the same time might be more than she could pull off by herself. She desperately wanted to trust Fuentes more than she did.

Once she pulled off paved road, Jerri turned off the air-conditioning. The truck used enough juice pulling in low gear down these country dirt roads. She opened both front windows and hoped to get air crisscrossing between the open windows, but she couldn't drive fast enough. Instead she got dust settling into the cab, and she heard the brush scratch at the truck as it bounced on the rutted dirt road.

Jerri drove into the clearing, which had a crumbling windmill and a three-room rancher's shack where the wetbacks stayed in cold or wet weather. If they had any sense—the wetbacks, the coyotes, even Palo—they wouldn't try to come up this time of year. The rain and cold might be uncomfortable, but the heat got more of them then the rain, cold, or *la migra*. Jerri stopped and honked her horn three quick times, waited, then honked twice more, Palo's signal. Mexicans started appearing out of the brush. All were cut and sliced from the thorns and stickers. In all, nine men and two women walked out. Then she noticed brush starting to move and saw three men carrying a large woman. A small boy walked alongside them and held the woman's hand. They laid the woman under a mesquite tree, and most of the people gathered and then squatted around her. They bent their knees and hunkered down, their butts not touching the ground, the way all poor people learn to rest, the way Jerri had seen the wetbacks coming up to San Antonio and the poor in Puerto Peñasco rest.

Najereda, Palo's coyote, looked up from the group and stood. He had become prosperous smuggling wetbacks, so he no longer squatted like them but sat on his butt. He stared, recognized her, waved, and walked toward her. Jerri grabbed her purse, opened the glove compartment, and pulled out her pistol. She looked around and finally reached under her seat, where she always kept her spare brick. After all, she was a woman, and she was unexpected. She put the pistol and the brick in her purse and slung it over her shoulder as she got out of the car. Gnats immediately surrounded her, so she puckered her lips and blew through them to keep the gnats out of her mouth.

Swishing gnats out of his face, Najereda walked toward her. He was a short, slight man with curly black hair combed off his forehead and a thin black mustache. He limped slightly from an old gunshot wound. She wouldn't be surprised if Najereda had the nerve and the smarts to start running dope across along with the Mexicans. If he was, he'd probably soon cross his stupid partner, Medina. "You not supposed to be here. Medina's supposed to make a pickup."

"I'm just here for one," Jerri said, and walked toward the crowd. "Angel Martínez," she shouted toward the group. A man from the middle of the group stood up, then looked down. He squatted again, then came up with a small duffel bag, which he gracefully slung over his shoulder. His white shirt was open, showing a hairless chest and an undershirt wet with sweat. His pants and thick-soled shoes were muddy. He was a medium-sized young man with wide shoulders that made him look as though he were either a manual laborer or a weight lifter. Jerri guessed the former. His thick chest made him look powerful but slow. He looked almost Indian with his squat build and stringy black hair.

As he got closer, Jerri pushed her thumb under the straps of her purse, grabbed the straps, and let the purse drop toward the ground. Straps in her hand, she dangled the purse by her calves. She whispered to Najereda, "Palo's worried that somebody is smuggling dope across."

Najereda shuffled his feet and looked at Angel, who walked toward them. "You here to see who does this terrible dope stuff?"

Jerri tightened her grip on the purse straps. "No. Just passing the word, hoping it might stop."

"What you do, it don't?"

Jerri stepped closer toward Angel, who glanced behind him at the group gathered around the woman. "Palo may hire me to find out who's doing it."

Najereda looked at her and smiled. "I don't know who is doing it."

"If you find out, maybe you ought to tell them to stop."

"Boss gots to understand, things changing, profits to be made. This dope makes him shit yellow, like a baby. He has no *cojones* for it."

"He's already lost one for it. He doesn't want to lose his ass." Jerri turned to look at Najereda.

"Maybe somebody needs to take his place."

"Maybe you ought to see nobody does." Jerri tightened her grip on the purse. Najereda knew she could shoot him right now, leave him out here, and probably get away with it. In his case, a Mexican national who hurt a white woman would probably get hanged on either side of the border, if not by the police, then by the people he worked for.

Angel walked toward her as Najereda glanced at Jerri out of the corners of his eyes. "Angel Martínez," Jerri said, and stuck out her hand for him to shake.

"You pick me up?" he asked.

"I pick you up," Jerri said, and released his hand. He immediately jerked his head back toward the others.

"What about the woman?" he asked.

He started walking back toward the group. Jerri and Najereda walked behind him. "A big woman got snake bit," Najereda said.

"Oh, no," Jerri said, then added, "shit."

"It happens," Najereda said.

"Why the hell do y'all bring them up this time of year?" Jerri asked, and looked at Najereda, then walked faster to get away from him.

"Ain't as bad as somebody bringing dope over," Najereda said, and Jerri felt the urge to take a good swing at him with her purse.

Angel pushed some people aside as he, Jerri, and Najereda gathered around the woman. Jerri immediately heard the buzz of the gnats and the horseflies feeding off the group. The small boy held the woman's head in his lap and shooed the flies from her face. Her teeth were clenched, her face beaded in sweat, one leg swollen. *"Ella pútrido,"* one of the men said, and cupped his hand over his mouth and nose. Jerri looked around at them and knew, from the bulges under their T-shirts, that two had bags of cocaine taped to their bellies. For a price they would bring it across, get caught, get deported, then bring some more across. Najereda could recruit them. Medina or some of Palo's other people would transport them to San Antonio, collect the dope between here and there, and then sell it to some connection in San Antonio. The dope would make his people greedy. They would run more dope. The police would stop a few, then shut Palo down.

Jerri took a step forward, then knelt to look at the woman's face. Angel knelt too. A wave of stink hit them. The woman had puke caked on her face and smelled as though she had shit her pants. *"Qué pasa?"* Jerri asked the little boy. He babbled quickly in Spanish and squeezed the woman's hand. Angel translated. The woman was his aunt; they were making the trip alone. A snake bit her early in the morning when she wandered off to pee in the brush. The boy begged them to take her to a hospital.

"A blessing of God, you have come," Angel said to Jerri.

"A saint she is," said Najereda.

Jerri stood up and pulled the straps of her purse over her shoulder and stuck her thumb under the straps. "Come on. Let's go," she said to Angel, and walked out of the group. She turned when Angel didn't follow her and saw him and the boy trying to lift the woman. "Come on," she said.

"We take her with us," Angel said.

Jerri felt herself wanting to open up with her gun on all of them and wanting to cry; worse, she felt the sting she had been fighting for the last couple of days start to form in her throat. "We can't," she said as though pleading, and thought she heard Najereda snickering. "I've got to get you back. I was followed." She looked around at Najereda, who took a step back and looked down the road.

"We leave her here, she dies," Angel said.

"What about your neighborhood people?"

Angel stood up and grabbed his duffel bag. He reached into the top part and pulled out an Uzi machine pistol. The Mexicans around the woman immediately stood up and scattered. And Najereda started backing away. "We take her with us."

"Okay, then, goddamn it," Jerri said. "Your choice. We take her with us. You get caught, you get deported. Your neighborhood has no guns. No revolution. You fail. You blow the money." Jerri hesitated. "You got to be smart. You got to be tough."

"You got to have *cojones,*" she heard Najereda purr.

"*Chinga tu madre,* we don't leave her here," Angel said.

"I wish we didn't, but we have to," Jerri said, and swooshed the gnats from out of her face so that she could see clearly to draw and shoot if she had to.

"*Estupido.* Tough *vato.* Think. You go to a hospital, you get arrested and sent back to Mexico," Najereda said.

"And people could do time for running dope." She looked at Najereda.

"Put down the gun," Najereda said. "She got no chance. You got no choice."

"*Chinga,*" Angel said, and put the Uzi back in the duffel bag. When he had shouldered the duffel bag and stepped away from the woman, the little boy grabbed Angel's hand and started crying. Angel looked at Jerri as if begging her to take the woman but knowing that she couldn't.

"People are suspicious. American policemen and FBI are following us. Somebody else is following us. I could do time. It's just too dangerous," she said to comfort Angel and not to threaten him.

Angel pulled his hand away from the boy's hand and walked away. The Mexicans who had backed off or run for cover gathered around the Mexican woman again. Jerri went to the truck and opened the back of it. Angel threw in his duffel bag, then walked straight to the passenger side, opened the door, and got in. Najereda walked to Jerri's side and walked her to the driver's door, even held her elbow and helped her in, but she still wanted to swing her purse at his smile.

As she started the truck, she again felt the heat; not yet noon and the temperature was probably in the midnineties. It would creep close to a hundred degrees today in this part of the country. And besides the heat, she felt the growing sting of her tissues and organs turning to acid, and she knew that she needed something to concentrate on to fight the sting. Looking over at Angel, she said, "Surely you have heard Fuentes's views. Think about what he would do." Angel simply turned his head to look back over his shoulder. "We did the right thing," Jerri told him, and swallowed hard.

As she pulled away toward the blacktop, toward I-35, and toward America, where such things didn't take place, Jerri thought about Palo's rules of selfishness and of family. She wondered if Palo would have seen the woman as family or as another chance to prove selfishness. She suddenly knew that for all that he had hurt people, Palo had never seen them hurt. The car bomb that killed his wife and brother left him unconscious; he saw their cleaned-up bodies, but he never saw them die or hurting. He never saw a simple, obscure human being in pain. Life, to him, was full of give-and-take, not morality. And for a moment Fuentes, or the way she remembered him to be, seemed to make so much more sense with his anger and causes that benefited simple, obscure human beings and imposed right and wrong on life. Then again, she thought, sitting next to her was another cause (who wanted guns to start some urban war) and, along with him, she had just deserted a simple, hurting human being. She didn't know whether Fuentes or Palo or both would have deserted the woman. Joe Parr wouldn't have deserted her. He would have even offered her a handkerchief. She looked in her rearview mirror and saw Najereda smiling and waving good-bye.

✪ Joe Parr, tired of the puny Chevy with the greasy interior, pulled in front of Palo's shaded front yard. He opened his door and yanked off his sunglasses in one move and walked up the sidewalk toward the house, scratching once at his nose and again at the mosquito bites on his arms. As he passed under the giant pecan trees that kept the yard cool, Parr could remember the time before air-conditioning when San Antonio contractors built high-roofed, roomy houses like Palo's and didn't dare cut down a shade tree. When he put his first foot on the front porch steps, Parr noticed an old Mexican sitting on the front porch, cracking some pecans. Inside his mind Parr gasped, for the Mexican could have gotten a drop on him. His goddamn mind and instincts were turning to shit.

Parr's boot made a hollow thud when he stepped on the next step's wooden slats. When the Mexican looked up at the creak on his stairs, Parr tipped his hat. The old Mexican didn't reach up for his Panama hat but tipped his head, then he let go of the hammer at the end of the long tube, and Parr heard a snap and saw bits of pecan shells fly around the man's face. "You're Palo Fuentes, I bet?"

"You bet right," Palo said, and, with one finger and a thumb, pulled a cracked pecan out of the nutcracker. He started prying bits of pecan shell from the meat with his thumbnail. "Just got this," Palo said. "Cracks the pecans almost by itself."

Parr reached into his back pocket, brought out his wallet, and flipped it open to show Palo his badge. "If you ain't guessed from this gun I wear, I'm a policeman."

Palo didn't bother to look but kept prying at his pecan. "What's a matter now? What you mad at? I got no dope."

"Palo," Parr said, "I'm not a San Antonio cop. I'm a Texas Ranger. And this is federal business," he lied.

"Serious shit, huh?" Palo asked.

"Yeah," Parr said, his lie working. Palo set the bowl of pecans down beside him and the pecan cracker down beside it. Parr stuck his wallet back in his pocket and leaned against the wooden railing that fenced in the large front porch. "Your son's doing something with some stolen guns." Parr waited for a response, but Palo just kept looking attentively at him. "I want you to tell me what he's doing."

"I wish he tells me what he's doing," Palo said, and reached down for his pecans. "You been to dinner with Jerri, huh? She said something about this Ranger guy."

"I've seen her."

"Why you chasing her, then?"

Parr stood up and stamped a boot heel on the wooden porch. "Hold on. You pay attention to me." Palo looked up at him. "You got a real nice nest here. But you piss me off, I could raise up a real strong wind and blow your nest out of here."

"So you want me to tell you something." Palo didn't ask a question or wait for Parr to say anything. "But I got nothing I can tell you."

"Where's Jerri Johnson?"

"You tried where she works?"

"She stayed here last night."

"We eat our suppers together. Sometimes she stays."

"What's your son up to?"

"He don't tell me."

"You don't seem to know how close I am to *la migra*."

Palo looked up at him, not mad, almost tickled. He shrugged. "Mexican *federales* once say they going to kill me. You can't kill me. This is America." Palo shrugged again. "Fuck it. I got a savings account." Parr chuckled a little bit inside his head, but the old man wasn't finished. "What you going to do, shoot them? That's what you going to have to do to stop them. But American don't got the *cojones* to shoot some poor illegal Mexicans. Poor Mexico, so far from God and so close to the United States."

Parr got tired of listening to the old man preach like he was giving a lecture to a Lions Club. "Mind if I use your bathroom?"

"You got to pee?"

"Yeah," Parr said.

"It's open." Palo motioned toward the front door. "On the left of the living room."

Joe Parr walked through the front door and quickly looked around the living room. He walked through it and came to a hallway. He opened the first door he saw and stepped into a bedroom. Bending over the unmade bad, he sniffed just a faint scent of Jerri's perfume. As he turned to go, he caught sight of himself in the mirror and saw the red, swelling mosquito bite on his nose. He whispered, "Shit," to himself, scratched at the mosquito bite, then stepped up to the dresser. He jerked open a drawer and saw that it had some of Jerri's lingerie in it. Shit, shit, he said to himself.

He walked out of the room and then walked to the next door and yanked it open. This was the bathroom. He opened two more doors and saw Palo's bedroom and an empty bedroom. He followed the hallway to its end and ended up in a kitchen. The sink was filled with dishes caked with and smelling of old chili. Then Parr heard a tapping sound. Like a fool, he listened hard to the taps and got surprised when Palo, leaning on a cane, walked into the kitchen. "This ain't the bathroom," Palo said. "Don't pee in my kitchen."

"Where's Jerri?" Parr said.

"I told you, I don't know."

"You tell me what you know, goddamn it! I can't help your son, but I can help Jerri. Now, from what I understand, you owe her."

Palo nodded. "You find her, and you tell her fuck Vincent. Tell her to help you. Tell her to save her ass." Palo pounded his cane to emphasize the words.

"You already tell her this?" Parr asked.

"Last night," Palo said.

"Okay, Palo, but you find out anything, you let me know. Huh?"

Palo smiled, but Parr didn't know what the smile meant. What he did know was that Palo had been a successful criminal on both sides of the border for far too long to ever help any cop without some kind of a deal.

Palo tapped his cane to the refrigerator. "You want some lunch, maybe? I got some leftovers. Chicken, I think." He pulled open the refrigerator door and looked in. "I can make you a sandwich."

Parr looked at the old man's scrawny shoulders and wondered if the old man had ever had broad shoulders, if he had ever been anything but small and curled over. Palo turned back around to look at Parr. "I want you to find Jerri and tell her to stop all this shit. To hell with Vincent."

"He's your son, right?"

Palo grimaced as he tapped his way toward the hall. "No matter. Now I want Jerri safe."

Parr followed him. Palo turned toward Parr and smiled. "Why you so concerned? You after Vincent or Jerri?"

"It's my job."

Palo waved a hand at Parr. "An old man has a lot of problems with dignity. Just getting by without pissing your pants or falling down is hard enough. An old man just tries to get by and takes dignity where he can find it." He looked at Joe. "That's me."

Parr tipped his hat to the old Mexican, then shook his hand. "I'll help you with Jerri," the Mexican said as Parr shook his hand. Parr didn't let the door hit him on the ass on the way out.

☻ Only as they neared San Antonio did they start to talk and the sting inside Jerri ease. *"Deberíamos de haberla llevado,"* Angel said.

"Speak in English. It's less conspicuous," Jerri told him. "And I have a hard time with Spanish."

"We should take her. We cannot be forgiven."

"To hell with forgiven. You want those silly guns or not?" Jerri was angry at him for being a cause.

"It does not excuse us."

"You some kind of a saint?"

Jerri—with her mind on Fuentes, Parr, the white Toyota, Palo, the sting inside her, and Angel's safety—didn't want anything else to think about. Jerri wanted only to be through with this job, then she could sort through the details of what happened and figure out guilt and complicity. Right now the rules and the job said only to get Angel to El Mirador Hotel, a flophouse on the West Side, near Palo. And the next morning, before sunrise, she would drive one of Palo's pickups to El Mirador, take Angel to the warehouse, and help him load the truck. Then she would give him the keys, and he and this gun business would drive out of her life. Najereda and his Mexico people could arrange to get Palo's truck back to him. Parr would have nothing to pin on her. And Fuentes had two more weeks in San Antonio. "Forget it," she said.

"How? You so tough. You so smart. You tell me how." Angel slammed his hand, palm down, on the dash of the truck. "You say. You tell me."

"Okay, so you don't forget it. You live with it. You'd be surprised how much you can live with." Jerri looked over at Angel and saw him take his hand off the dash and cross his arms, his mouth working its way into a pout. "At first the feeling stings, and then it spreads all over your body, and you don't think you can move." He brushed a strand of his stringy black hair out of his face and along the side of his head, and with the sweat and dirt in his hair, the strand just stuck on the side of his head. "But then you do start to move."

Since the trip back from the pickup point, Jerri had had to smell the caked sweat and dirt on the young man. Underneath the dirt and the stink, he was a handsome man. He had an angular Roman nose and high cheekbones and, though squat, he wasn't fat. The muscles in his chest bulged out beyond his belly, and the veins inside his biceps swelled against his tight, dark brown skin. Angel was almost black.

Jerri looked to her left and saw the Hungry Farmer flashing by her window and, in the flash, she saw the white Toyota parked in the driveway. She stepped on the gas and looked in the rearview mirror. She saw the Toyota pulling onto the frontage road and then pressed harder on the gas. "Who do you think would be tailing you?"

"*Qué?*" Angel asked.

"Who would follow you? Who would want to stop you?"

"The *policía*."

"Whose police?"

"Saltillo, *federales?*"

Jerri looked in the rearview mirror and saw the Toyota enter the freeway behind her. She pushed the gas pedal to the floor and saw the speedometer pass eighty.

"Qué pasó?"

"Someone's following us. They aren't Americans." The ticks of thought in Jerri's brain seemed so loud to her that she thought Angel could hear them, but at least the sting was gone. She eased off the gas. "Wait." She turned to look at Angel. "Let's find out who they are. Enough of this chasing shit."

Jerri slowed down until the Toyota was behind her and then drove comfortably so that they could easily follow her. Angel looked out the back window of the truck and then at Jerri. "What do you do?"

"Changing plans and tactics," Jerri said. "You recognize those guys?"

Angel squinted, then said, "No."

Jerri drove to downtown and got off on Commerce Street. She drove past the hotels, the courthouse, and city hall, making sure that the Toyota was behind her. Just at the Commerce Street bridge that led to the West Side and Palo's house, Jerri turned left and crossed to Dolorosa. West of the Mercado, she stopped at a meter, in easy view of the Dolorosa Street traffic. "Get out," she told Angel.

"*Qué?*" Angel said.

"Come on. We're going to have a drink," Jerri said, and looking out her window saw the white Toyota pass by and quickly pull into a parking lot. She giggled to herself because they would have to pay the extra dollars to park in a lot. "Hand me my purse, please," she asked Angel, who reached for the purse by his feet and grunted, then looked at the heavy purse as he handed it to Jerri. Jerri got out of the truck, then pulled the purse out after her and slung it around her shoulder. She walked around the front of the truck to Angel, who stood gawking at the strange world around him, and dropped two quarters in the meter. "Welcome to America," Jerri said, and tugged on Angel's bicep to lead him down the street to Los Apaches Bar, a dive where she found information.

When they walked in, the bartender, Tomás, lifted up the towel he was wiping the bar with and waved. The old Mexican waitress got up from a bar stool and walked up behind Jerri. Both Jerri and Angel squinted and tried to adjust their eyes to the dark bar. Tomás kept the bar dark so that customers couldn't see the dirt. Jerri led Angel to a table toward the back of the bar, and they sat in the vinyl chairs around the lemon-colored vinyl-topped table, both chairs and tables refugees from the fifties. Jerri unslung her purse and laid it, with its mouth open, under her right hand.

Rosie walked up to her with her usual exaggerated swing. She was a terribly ugly woman who tried to hide some of the ugliness with layers of cheap base and powder. She dyed her gray hair but always got it so black that it had a satinlike sheen to it. Jerri suspected that fat Sam, even if he had had a male prostitution ring, might have bedded ol' Rosie. At any rate, she owed Sam and Jerri. "You want business or pleasure?" she asked Jerri.

"Two beers," Jerri said. "What's your flavor?" she asked Angel, who looked blankly at her.

"Two Coors' Lights," Jerri told Rosie.

When Rosie had left and walked back with her old hips swinging as though on a rusty ball bearing, Angel asked, "Why we here?" On the trip down Commerce, he had stared out both sides of the truck to look at what for him must have been affluence. Now, agitated and confused, he needed comforting.

Jerri patted Angel's forearm. "I'm hoping that whoever is following us will come in here. I can then see who they are. If they know what they're doing, they'll just keep an eye on my car. If they do, we go out the back and sneak you into a hotel. I'll spend the night in my office and get my car in the morning."

"Fuentes says I stay at a place called El Mirador," Angel said.

"No, it's too hot," Jerri said.

"Yes, it is hot," Angel said.

Jerri laughed and squeezed the man's arm. "No, no. It's too dangerous. Too many people are looking for you. They may know where you're going to stay."

As Jerri took her hand off Angel's forearm, two Mexicans walked in. They weren't locals—the laborers who came in after five or the crooks and dopers who came in during the day. They were dressed too well. The short man had on a fitted suit that was still to large for him. He had enough money for an expensive haircut and a manicure. The large man had on pleated navy blue pants. They both squinted and tried to adjust their eyes to the bar. When they could see, they sat at the first table that they saw. Jerri leaned toward Angel. "Those are the men who have been following us."

"I don't know them," Angel said.

Rosie came with the beers and set them down in front of Jerri and Angel. "Tomás says you get the first round on the house." Angel grabbed his beer, stuck the bottle in his mouth, tipped the bottle up, and began to suck out the beer. Jerri suddenly felt sorry that she hadn't offered Angel, who had probably walked for a day cross-country, any water. The shy, unassuming man, totally unfit to shoot an Uzi, hadn't even asked for a drink.

Jerri looked toward the bar at Tomás and nodded, then shifted her glance toward the two men sitting at the table by the front door. After Rosie went to the two men and took their order (the big one ogling her rusty swiveling hips), Jerri pushed herself up with the flats of her palms. Angel laid his hand over hers. "Don't worry yet," she whispered to him, and shouldered her purse.

Jerri stuck her hands in the tight pockets of her jeans and walked to the two men's table. Her purse bounced against her right hip. When she got to their table, Jerri nodded, first at the small man, then at the big one, who looked surprised and ducked his head. The little one smiled sweetly, stood, then pulled out a chair and waved his hand in front of it. Jerri sat in the chair, and the little man pushed the chair up under her. She kept her purse dangling from her shoulder. "You guys new in here?" The little man just nodded, and the big one stared at the table. "How about I buy you a beer?" Jerri asked. No sooner had she asked than Rosie brought two more Coors' Lights and set them in front of the two men.

"Perhaps we could buy you a beer?" the little man asked.

"No, thank you," Jerri said, and reached down toward the mouth of her purse. As the men took deliberately small sips of beer, Jerri asked, "You fellas have something you want to tell me?"

The little man leaned closer to her, and the big man now looked at his beer, grabbed it, set it down, then looked over its neck at Jerri. The little man said slowly, "We would like you to simply go to your car and leave. We will take care of Angel."

"I bet you would," Jerri said, and tensed the fingers on her right hand.

"You don't know what you are into," the little man said.

"We have no quarrel with you," the big man said from across the table, and tried to smile as sweetly as the dapper little man.

"Please," the little man said, and suddenly, while she looked at the big man, she felt the breath of the other man on the side of her face and his hand wrapped around her right wrist.

"Let go," Jerri said. "They know me here."

The little man let go, and Jerri looked toward the bar and yelled, "Rosie." Rosie came over, and Jerri stood to talk with her. She slowly led Rosie toward her table and Angel. "Rosie, is the back door unlocked?" Jerri whispered.

"Those guys bothering you, I throw them out." Rosie started to turn toward the thugs, but Jerri caught her elbow and kept her walking toward Angel.

"When we leave, those guys are going to follow us," Jerri said. "As soon as we get out the back door, lock it, and don't let those men out." She turned to Angel. "Let's go." Angel turned up the bottle of the beer and drank the last bit of it. Jerri opened the back door, held it open for Angel, then went through it herself and quickly shut it. Immediately she blinked in the sunlight and tried to see.

163

She realized that she was in an alley and quickly leaned against the door and put her ear against it and listened as Rosie turned the latch. She heard the two men asking Rosie to open the door, and she heard Rosie refuse. The two Mexicans were far more dangerous than Parr. They were too composed and deliberate. They had done this before. They could scare people.

Suddenly she heard rattling and turned quickly to her left and dipped her right hand into her purse to bring out her pistol and point it at the sound. A wino had his waist bent over a Dumpster and his head and arms inside. "No," she heard Angel scream.

The wino put his feet on the ground and pulled his torso out of the Dumpster. When he saw Jerri, he put his hands above him. Jerri dropped her head and put her gun away. "Go on," she said. She hunched her shoulders and grabbed the straps of her purse. "Run for the car," she told Angel. Angel took off to his right. "No, this way." Jerri turned to her left and ran past the wino.

Angel soon was running even with her, and as they ran, he deftly scooped the heavy purse off her shoulder, grabbed her hand, and pulled her after him. They were in the car and speeding down Dolorosa when they saw the two men coming out of Los Apaches.

❂ Jerri parked the truck three blocks down from the Aztec Hotel and walked with Angel to the hotel. Just in case it all came to shit, which it had, she had gotten Angel an overnight room with perverts, winos, and criminals all around him. His room was littered with beer, Sterno, and food cans; pigeon bones (the winos claimed pigeons were better than chicken and certainly cheaper); old newspapers; even a hypodermic needle. Angel sat on his bed. And Jerri pulled the one kitchen chair up beside the bed. "Go on, lie down," Jerri said to him. Angel stretched out on the bed. "Don't worry about getting the bed dirty. They have a sink in here and a toilet. There's a bathtub down the hall, but don't count on the plumbing in there working. This place is a health hazard, but it's the safest place that I can think of." Jerri wondered what Angel thought of his accommodations after staring at the upper floors of the expensive hotels off Commerce.

The sun was setting, and a sunbeam full of motes shone through the one window and across Angel's tight belly. "Those guys mean some serious harm to you. They're dangerous."

Angel rose up on his elbows, as though he had a final thought before he went to sleep. "I need to pick up the guns tomorrow. Where do I get this truck?"

"I'm supposed to pick you up before sunrise in a friend's truck and take you to the warehouse where I have the guns. You load them and take off for Mexico in my friend's truck."

"How do I get his truck back?" Jerri ducked her head. She wanted to giggle at Angel and cry for him. He was still too much the poor Mexican man to have any idea about what he was doing, or how he was to go about it, or whom he was involved with.

"It's all taken care of." Angel lay back down. But Jerri wanted to talk to him. "What do you do?"

Angel opened his eyes and smiled without straightening up. "I'm a carpenter, but for a year, I am out of work. Now I build"—he motioned with his hands—"*toiletas.*" He smiled at Jerri. "For my neighborhood's toilets."

"Latrines."

"Yeah, everything."

"Aren't you a leader? Didn't you organize these people into an urban movement?"

"A man came and said he was from an urban something and said we should prepare. I got elected to leader of the committee. We built a laundry and a . . ." He waved his hands above his face to find more words, "a center, a place to meet, play basketball."

"A civic center."

"I don't know how to call all the things."

"You speak English well," Jerri said to him, and he closed his eyes. "Why do you want these guns?" Jerri wasn't ready to let him sleep.

Angel patiently opened his eyes and tried to explain, but though his mouth was open, no words came out. Then he said, "We know that we will meet the bulldozers. We could lay our children in front of the bulldozers, but the police come and pick up the children. We get arrested when we go to pick our children up. So a man from another group comes and says he can get us guns. He talks *revolución*. Whatever happens, somebody dies." Angel raised up and looked at Jerri, so that she saw into his bloodshot eyes and believed that his stare was a question about what he should do or a plea for an affirmation of what he was about to do.

"Do you have any children?"

"Three," he said, smiled, and laid his head back down. "You?"

"Just one. Much older than yours, I'm sure, and probably twice the trouble." Angel giggled. "Why don't you just stay here in San Antonio?"

"What?"

"Just stay here."

"Mi familia."

"I could have them brought up. I could find you work. I've done this before."

"I made promises."

Jerri hung her head, then tried again. "Then go back, but leave the guns."

Angel smiled, slowly closed his eyes, and fell asleep. Jerri stood up, and as she did the sunbeam caught her eyes, and she blinked against it. She walked to the window and closed the shabby paper blind. She put her back to the wall and slowly slid down it until her butt was on the floor.

Angel was a lamb, the same as the snake-bitten woman whom she had sentenced to death earlier in the day. He had no business with guns, yet he had an Uzi in his duffel bag and a truckload of automatic weapons to drive to Mexico. He was just meat to the people who knew about such stuff. Jerri knew that he would never make it to Mexico. Just after the divorce, when J. J. was about eight or nine, he fell out of a tree in the front yard and broke his arm. Jerri had heard him scream as he fell, and she was running even as he screamed. She saw him lying with his misaligned arm at his side. He smiled and said, "Don't get mad, Mom." She scooped him up in her arms and started running. She had gotten to the end of the block when a neighbor pulled up alongside her in his truck, and she got in and let Mr. Shuler drive her to the hospital.

Without Royce, she had panicked, and that fact scared her. She swore that in another emergency she would never again be frightened or dependent on anyone else. This oath made her particularly aware of those people who needed sensible, practical help. This oath was why she helped Palo. This oath and her failures at keeping it, as with the snake-bit woman, made her look at Angel.

Then she realized that she loved people besides Fuentes or Royce. She loved people who really needed her love: J. J. and Palo, maybe even Sam Ford. She looked at poor Angel. His face and his dilemma showed the burden of his loyalties and humanity. It was like a photo, a poem, a painting. She closed her eyes. Fuentes had been adorable. His new appetites for the physical delighted her as much as his worthlessness in crises scared her. She trusted Joe Parr. Even now, he was doing nothing more than what he consistently was. She could settle with or for what Fuentes was. But she had lived with, she had helped Palo and J. J. Helping Angel was like that. Helping Angel was her way to write, paint, or sculpt something.

She stood up and walked to Angel's side; she gently shook him until he opened his eyes. She smiled when he rubbed them with the backs of his hands like a child. Here was one specific person with the elemental problem of his own survival—the simplicity of a poem, none of the complexity of loyalty or cause. "You're not going to drive the guns to Mexico. Just go to sleep. Sleep as long as you want. Wait in this room all day tomorrow. Don't you dare go out. I'll bring some food up for you from the store down the street. Then at midnight tomorrow I'll pick you up, and I'll drive you and the guns to Nuevo Laredo. After that, you're on your own."

"But they will expect me tomorrow."

"So they'll just have to wait a little later. You leave tomorrow, you'll never make it."

Angel looked around, then looked suspiciously at Jerri. "Why are you doing this?"

Jerri patted his arm. "I really don't know. I'm tired of all the shit whirling around you and me, and I want to see it end." Angel wrinkled his brows. "Go to sleep," Jerri said. "And remember, tomorrow at midnight."

Angel laid his head back down and went almost immediately to sleep. Jerri sat on the edge of the bed. She could smell the sweat and the stink the man was wrapped in. She would go home tonight, go to work in the morning, make herself obvious. They were watching Fuentes. Now they could watch her too. She would keep all of them away from Angel.

❷ Jerri walked to the convenience store down the street, bought food for Angel, went back to the Aztec, left the key on the table, and locked the door behind her. As she walked to the truck, Fuentes, then Parr, then Palo forced themselves into her mind. She walked with her head ducked down so a passerby wouldn't see her lip quivering. She dabbed at some tears with the back of her hand. If Palo asked, she would find out more about the dope ring. Dare she mention Najereda? If she did, Najereda would probably die. She half staggered to her truck and drove herself to Palo's. There, she reached under the rotten wood of the garage, right under the water meter, and tripped the burglar alarm. She let herself into the garage and exchanged the truck for her Suburban. She was glad to be back in it.

At her apartment, as she opened her front door, she could almost feel several pairs of eyes watching her. Parr might be out there, or he might have some help. But right now, it didn't matter.

A shower made her feel better at first. But then she leaned against the wet shower wall and slid down it. She laid her forehead on her knees and felt the spray from the shower hit the back of her head and her shoulders. A violent sob worked its way out of her chest and shook her shoulders. She had loved Fuentes, maybe. But she trusted Parr. She owed a lot to Palo. He owed her. She bit into the side of her palm to keep from crying out loud and blinked against the spray of the shower and tasted the soap and water on her hand. Then, just as quickly as she started crying, she hushed herself. She had killed a woman today. If she didn't help him, Angel would be dead or in jail. She liked this simple man's manner.

Right or not, efficient or not, safe or not, she would try to save Angel. Helping him made some ironic sense. Helping him eased the sting inside her. It was the only allegiance with any dignity.

She stood back up and finished her shower. In bed, she felt good enough and tired enough to sleep.

❷ Joe Parr sat in his backyard and watched the Gulf breeze ruffle the treetops above him, scratched his bare belly, and took a sip of his scotch. Feeling Jerri's thoughts as he did, he knew that tomorrow some of whatever "it" was would happen.

He was waiting to talk to Melba, but he was afraid that he would go to sleep before she got into his head. The neighbors' teenage kids had one of their loud rock-and-roll pool parties that kept Joe up, and Melba away, until late in the goddamn night. "Melba, where are you?" Joe said. "Ain't it about time?"

From out of the wall, Melba walked with her cup of tea. She sat beside Joe in the lawn chair that had been hers. She looked over at Joe and said, "I'd almost rather hear you cuss than say 'ain't' with that country accent you affect."

"Where've you been?" Joe asked.

"My, my, Joe Parr, put on some clothes."

"I like sitting out here in my underwear. It's cool."

"What if the neighbors should see?" She sipped her hot tea.

"Damn, quit bitching and talk to me."

Melba stared down into her cup of tea as though her feelings were hurt. Joe reached toward her to pat her shoulder, then jerked his hand away. Maybe he'd let himself feel a dead woman touch him, but he'd be damned if he'd let himself touch a dead woman. "I'm sorry," he said.

Melba turned to smile at him. "Joe, did I ever tell you how much I enjoyed my funeral? All your police friends were there, and they had on all those uniforms. Oh, Joe, and the courage you showed to stand in front of the congregation and say those words. Such lovely thoughts. I was proud of you, Joe."

"You've told me, Melba. I feel nothing bad about your funeral or even your death. It's about other things that I feel bad."

Melba looked away from him at her saucer. "You don't like me to touch you now. Do you?"

"No, I don't," Joe said.

"Very well," Melba said, and made a special effort to turn her head toward Joe and smile at him. "I won't."

"Melba, now I'm thinking of fucking with her family."

"Please don't use that language around me."

Joe let his head fall and caught it with his hands. When he raised his head, he saw Melba's powdered, pink face staring into his. "Oh, Joe, dear, you need to get some sleep. You look terrible." She pulled back her head, but Joe wanted to see her close again. "I'd better leave you and let you get to bed."

Melba slowly stood, and Joe Parr jumped up and begged, "No, Melba. Don't go. Not yet."

"Dear, it's late."

"Please sit back down. I'm old. Old people don't need much sleep." Joe sat as Melba did, and when she had settled her rump, which had gotten fatter than Joe remembered, in her lawn chair, he said, "I called her son and asked him to help me."

"Oh, Joe." Melba turned to look at him. "No, no, you didn't." Parr looked at her. She drew back from him and said, "You did. My sweet Jesus, you did, Joe."

"I had to. Now I can't live with myself."

Melba set down her cup and saucer and folded her hands in her lap in that Baptist-Sunday-school-teacher style. "No, Joe," she started, "I will tell you. You should get that girl out of this mess that you got her in. You should just let her go ahead with these guns that she has."

"Goddamn it. It's illegal. I'm a Ranger."

"That's right, Joe. You've always been a Ranger."

Parr started reaching for Melba, but she got up again. "Poor Joe. You do what you must." Then Melba walked back through the wall and into the house. Joe ran through the back door and yelled for her, but she didn't answer. "Goddamn it, Melba, now I want to talk and you shut up," he said, and cussed his mind, this time for letting her go.

CHAPTER NINE

Fuentes pushed the toothbrush back and forth in his mouth, and the bristles of the brush seemed to cut through his teeth and into the nerves, which in turn sent shock waves to his head to awaken the usual morning ache. As he looked in the mirror, he saw that his hair pointed at angles out from his head. He heard a knock but wasn't sure if the knock was in his head or at his door. He spat out the suds and moved toward the sound of the knock. As he walked through the bathroom door, the strong, urgent knock sounded again.

He looked around him and saw that he was in his hotel room, saw his pants lying crumpled in a corner with several dollar bills spread out around them. Seeing his pants, he looked down at his chest and saw that he had on a shirt, but, as he looked farther, he saw that he wore his jockey shorts but no pants. The knock sounded and, with the raps of the knock, his brain slammed into his skull. "Wait, please," he yelled toward the door. He wiped a wet hand on his shirt, then bunched up a wad of shirt and smelled it. It had the rancid, twelve-hour-old smell of stale cigarettes and dried liquor. At least he had gotten home. He couldn't remember if he had walked or driven. Tempted just to answer the knock in his underwear, Fuentes grabbed his crumpled pants and stuck one leg into them. As he pulled the pants up his leg, the knock again sounded, and he stumbled into the wall. As he tried to slip his other leg into his pants, he wavered on his stiff leg and again fell into the wall.

Snapping and zipping his pants, he walked to the door. When he opened it, he saw a smiling Trujillo. Without being asked, Trujillo stepped into Fuentes's room. Fuentes noticed that Trujillo's badly fitting suit was now very dusty. The little man folded his arms and walked around the room, strutting, Fuentes thought, like the tiny gamecocks he could remember as a boy, like the tiny roosters that got beat. "It is three hours past the time of the pickup of the guns," Trujillo said, and rocked back and forth on his heels like Mussolini.

Fuentes almost laughed at the little man who tried to act tough. "Well, how about a drink?"

"No," Trujillo said, and rocked back and forth on his heels.

"Breakfast? A cup of coffee?" Fuentes said, then backed up as Trujillo stepped toward him. "Where is your pet gorilla?" Fuentes mockingly looked around.

"Natividad is alone in the warehouse, eating some very bad *chorizo* and eggs. He wanted to come talk to you, but I convinced him to let me come. Where is Angel?"

"I don't know." Fuentes hadn't yet had a drink of water for his usually futile first attempt to wash away the dryness in his throat. He didn't want to talk and push words against that dryness.

"Where is Jerri?"

"I don't know. Isn't all of this supposed to be your job? I mean, aren't you supposed to be sitting in the hot, dusty warehouse eating bad *chorizo?*"

"Natividad wanted to break some part of you," Trujillo said, and held out a hand that immediately flopped back on its wrist. "Vincent, you know the deal. You know what could happen to you if you don't honor it."

"Thank you for coming, then. I do enjoy your company." Fuentes smiled and said to the little cock, who didn't smile back at him: "Now, excuse me, please." Fuentes turned to go back into the bathroom to finish brushing his teeth, to take his first big gulp of water, and to shave.

But then he felt an explosion inside his head. The explosion sent him into a counterclockwise half circle so that he was again facing Trujillo. He wanted to ask what was happening but saw the San Antonio yellow pages coming toward the side of his face. He couldn't duck, could say nothing, only grunt when the yellow pages hit him on the side of the face. Fuentes fell to one side and caught himself with his elbow. He got up, rubbing his elbow, and saw the yellow pages again swing toward his face. This time he could see the diminutive Trujillo behind the pages. He held up his sore elbow and took the next blow, which sent him into his bed. He rolled over, hoping to roll to the other side and then to run out the door before this mad little rooster could hit him again. But he felt some weight on top of him. Then he felt something pointed pressing into his head just behind his ear, as though about to puncture his skull.

He tried to shift his eyes to see what poked him but could only see Trujillo's hand around the handle of something long and pointed. Then he heard, "This is an ice pick. I push it down hard, and you never talk again." Fuentes, straining to push his eyes into the corners of their sockets, could see that the little man was indeed pressing an ice pick against his skull. Fuentes held his breath, then closed his eyes. He could feel the sweat beading out of his forehead. He closed his eyelids together and tried to get his mind to escape. No pain, no reconfiguration of his life up to this point, no feeling of his precious blood where it should be, in his veins—just numbness, oblivion, escape.

"I move it just a little," Trujillo said, and moved the ice pick, "and maybe you don't see. Some more and you are fucked. You know nothing, not even what you are. You understand?" Fuentes felt the ice pick farther behind his ear. Feeling it kept him from escaping.

Fuentes nodded and thought that the ice pick might puncture the swollen balloon inside his skull, thus relieving his headache and sending the balloon fizzling around inside his vacant skull. If the puncture could be fast and relatively painless, he would almost have welcomed it. "I wish that you would hurry with this." Fuentes felt the ice pick pierce his skin and could tell that a tiny rivulet of blood flowed out of the prick in his scalp.

"Don't fuck with me," Trujillo said, and Fuentes felt the backhanded slap of the little man. Then he felt the tight and burning sensation by his eye. He tried to reach for it, to touch his wound, but the little man pulled his hand away. "Where is Angel?"

"You were to follow Jerri. I haven't seen her or him."

"Where was she to take him?"

"The Mirador."

"He's not there."

"Is that my fault?" Fuentes was getting tired of the obviousness of this game.

"Where's Jerri?" Fuentes felt the pressure of the ice pick let up and the pressure of the tightness next to his eye increase.

"She stayed at Palo's. I don't know anymore." Fuentes felt the weight of the man leave. He slowly pushed himself up, rubbed the back of his neck, and touched the swollen lump of skin under his eye.

"You better not fuck with us," Trujillo said, and shook the ice pick in front of Fuentes.

"I have better things to fuck with," Fuentes said, and Trujillo giggled, then bent over and pulled up his pants leg. Trujillo pressed the ice pick against his calf and curled two strips of adhesive tape around it. Fuentes noticed that his legs were shaved. When he straightened, Fuentes said, "I know another place you could stick that ice pick." Trujillo again giggled. He stepped toward Fuentes, and Fuentes took a quick step back.

"I'm going back," Trujillo said, no longer smiling like a sweet, effeminate boy, and stepped toward the front door. "Clean yourself up, and find Jerri. I want to know when the pickup is going to be and where Angel is."

"Is that my job?"

Trujillo smiled widely and flipped his hand back on his wrist. "Your job is what I say it is." He took a step toward Fuentes, and Fuentes braced himself for a punch. But Trujillo only patted his shoulder. "Next time, I send Natividad. He's not as gentle as me."

"Okay," Fuentes said.

"No bad feelings," Trujillo said. "Vincent, Vincent, when do you think my sonar can't pick up your thoughts? You can't get out of this." He raised a finger in front of Fuentes's face. "Jerri Johnson cannot help you."

Fuentes reached up to brush his cowlick out of his face. "I plan to give a lecture and drink a lot."

Trujillo closed his eyes, then quickly opened them as though he suspected that Fuentes might try to hit him over the head. "Vincent, everything you say is a pretense."

"That's my job, isn't it? To pretend."

"And eventually these schools, these book clubs, these governments will discover your pretense at being a scholar. Then they will stop inviting you. Then they will forget about you." Fuentes could feel the little man's gaze. He prepared to be hit again. "Then the PRI will have no more use for you. Then you will be free of me and your deal."

"No more hotels?" Fuentes asked.

Trujillo smiled. "Then, with your career and reputation ruined, you will have to make an honest living."

"The horror," Fuentes said. His hand started to shake, not from the booze but from fright. For he knew, without Trujillo telling him, that he had no future.

"But now," Trujillo said, raised his finger, opened the front door, and backed toward it. He stopped. "Vincent, Vincent, you think you know, but you don't see. What is my given name?"

Fuentes played along. "*Henri* . . . you say."

"And yours is *Vincent.*" Trujillo raised his hand as though he was about to pat Fuentes's face. "Neither a Mexican name. Both of our sets of parents gave us European names to try to will us out of Mexico and its problems. And Henri and Vincent tried, but I'm still *Enrique,* and you are still . . . Palo's son. Names, manners, clothes, education; we can't hide. We're the same. That's why I'm going to miss you if I have to kill you. Now I'm going to leave before you make some silly comment." Trujillo backed slowly out of the room while he froze Fuentes with his stare.

When Trujillo left, Fuentes remained motionless, as though the little man had robbed him of all will. But after a few moments Fuentes rubbed the back of his neck and pushed his feet toward the bathroom. Once there, he reached into his medicine cabinet and pulled down the plastic bag full of white powder. He wanted a drink. He wanted his mind to be elsewhere. The white powder would help. But he also desperately needed to find Jerri, not to help his keepers but to get on with his own plan. He needed to stay clearheaded, but he also wanted to relieve his mind and his headache. As he snorted up the layer of white powder that was on his thumbnail, he knew he had made a mistake. Raised by privileged parents, sent to the best schools in Mexico and the United States, favored by the PRI and the army (one and the same, really) but grown up tiny and womanish, Colonel Henri Trujillo had a chip on his shoulder and something to prove. He was the dangerous one, the one Fuentes should have been careful of. With his intelligence, his position, and his ruthlessness, he might be president someday. He wasn't a pretty man, but he had followed the same path as Fuentes. His corruption, though, was in a different direction than Fuentes's. With another snort, Fuentes's mind was in the old familiar ruts: telephone books, luxury hotels, and Jerri Johnson's thighs.

❷ Parr scratched the mosquito bite on his forehead and the other one on his nose and looked around the corner from the lobby of the Four Seasons Hotel at the elevator. The doors opened, and a tiny Mexican in a dirty, too big suit stepped out. Parr straightened himself and stepped out from behind the corner to point his boots toward the elevator. He tilted back his head to see through his half-frame glasses and take another look at the pissant, then pulled off the glasses by grabbing them with his thumb and forefinger. He folded the glasses, palmed them, and stuffed them in his white shirt pocket.

As Parr got close, the little Mexican halted in his tracks, then started to step backward. "I think we need to have a drink there, fella," Parr said to the pissant.

The man looked up at him, then said, "No, thank you." He tried to step by Parr, but Parr stayed in front of him. When the little man reached down toward his ankle, Parr grabbed his wrist and wrapped his other big, bony hand around the squirt's other arm and started dragging him down the hallway. At the edge of the lobby Parr let go of the man's arm, and the Mexican tried to brush the wrinkles out of his suit. Parr stepped in front of the man. "Please," Parr said, "a cup of coffee," and flashed his badge in front of the man. "You see that says I'm a Texas Ranger, and it means you better not fuck around with me."

"I'm not an American," the little fart said, and tried to step away from Parr.

Parr grabbed the man's arm, then tested his grip on the skinny arm. "But you're in America. And unless you cooperate, I'm gonna arrest you. And you'll spend some time in a cell while I try to find out about you. That'll make your suit even dirtier."

The pissant smiled broadly. "Perhaps a cup of coffee."

Parr smiled just as broadly. "This way," he said, and motioned toward the Four Seasons' restaurant.

They went into the restaurant and sat at a table to one side with a view of the garden. As soon as they sat, the mosquito bite on Parr's nose started to itch, so he took a hard scratch at it. "Please," the little man said. He reached for his back pocket. Parr again grabbed for the man's arm. "Please," the little man said, like he was pissed.

"Okay," Parr said, and the little man slid his hand into his back pants pocket and brought out a wallet. He flipped it open and showed Parr a badge. When Parr peered toward the badge, the little man leaned slightly toward him as though he were staring at the red, swollen mosquito bites.

"That says I work for the Mexican Department of Defense under official orders from the state of Coahuila and the minister of defense. My name is Colonel Henri Trujillo." The little man emphasized the *colonel* as though pulling rank on Parr. "I'm here on official business from the PRI. You do not need to know this business." He extended his hand, but Parr wasn't about to shake it.

Parr put one elbow on the table, then leaned toward the little man, the table creaking under his weight. "I found out all about how proud you are of that colonel shit at the rental car office. I know who you work for. I know where your hotel is. That's not what I want to know. What I want to know is why you and some other Mexican fella are chasing Jerri Johnson and talking to Vincent Fuentes." The little man shifted his eyes, then on the second shift, Parr followed his eyes to see the waitress standing above them. "We just want coffee," Parr said to her.

"Wait, wait. Please," Trujillo said. "I'm hungry, please." The waitress smiled and handed the man a menu. Parr waited patiently but drummed his fingers on the table while the man looked at the menu. "How long, may I ask, do you poach the eggs?" Trujillo asked the waitress.

Parr snatched the menu away from Trujillo and handed it back to the waitress. "He'll take the eggs however long you poach them and a couple of pieces of toast." Trujillo leaned back in his chair and looked at Parr like he had just let a fart. "Enough of this fucking around, Mister Trujillo. I asked you a question."

"*Colonel* is the proper title," Trujillo said.

Parr leaned across the table. "Son of bitch is the proper title if I say so. Now, you tell me what you know, what you're doing here, and why you're hassling an American citizen."

"Believe me, Mr. Parr, we know what we are doing. You have nothing to worry about." Trujillo smiled at Parr, then turned to look for the waitress. "Now, I should like my eggs just barely poached, so if you don't mind . . ."

Parr reached toward him and quickly grabbed Trujillo's lapel and pulled his torso toward the other side of the table. "Look here, I'm the stud duck you gotta worry about here. I can run you in for attempted rape for following Jerri Johnson around. You'll beat that charge, but it won't do your career as 'Colonel Trujillo' no good. Now you tell me real quick about Vincent Fuentes, just for starters."

Trujillo grunted as though something were caught in his throat and looked up at Parr. Parr looked at the little turd's reddening face and let go. Then Parr caught a glimpse of the young waitress, who was inching away from them. "Honey, we're just a couple of old friends out whooping it up a little." The waitress smiled and took a couple of steps back. Then Trujillo leaned toward Parr and whispered, "You can no longer play Texas Ranger with a Mexican citizen."

"Used to I could. Back in the good ol' days," Parr said. "And I'm close enough to retirement where I don't give a shit what I do."

Trujillo straightened and rubbed his lapel to push out the wrinkles that Parr made. Parr looked ahead at the waitress, who stood watching with a hand over her mouth, obviously wondering if she should call the police. Parr smiled at her, got her attention, and shook his head to tell her to let things lie. When she turned back toward the kitchen, Parr looked back at Trujillo. "Let's try again, Colonel Trujillo. I have to know. I've been watching Vincent Fuentes, and I know he sees Ms. Johnson. Now." Parr hesitated, then said emphatically, "I need to know what you can tell me."

"You don't need to know shit," Trujillo said, and rubbed his lapels. Parr stood, put a palm down in the middle of the table, and leaned toward Trujillo, but the waitress brought coffee and water. She set a cup of coffee and a glass of water in front of each man. Parr smiled, then winked at her. "Have you talked to your own CIA?" Trujillo asked when the waitress left.

"This is my case. Not the goddamn CIA's," Parr said. "I don't trust those covert bastards."

"It is an international affair," Trujillo said, "and therefore not your case. You have no business harassing or molesting me or Vincent Fuentes. Perhaps, if you just put a quarter in a telephone and called them . . ." Trujillo mildly sipped from his cup of coffee like a Baptist Sunday school teacher. Parr leaned over so that he was close to Trujillo's face. Trujillo stuck up a hand connected to a weak wrist and motioned for Parr to back up. He sipped from his coffee, then said, "Please understand. It is not your case."

"I understand that you are impeding my criminal investigation. And that means if you or the other asshole spits the wrong way, I'll roast your ass. That means you get the hell out of here and leave Fuentes and Johnson alone. They're mine."

Trujillo raised his glass of water, took a long sip, then set the glass down. "We shall soon see. And you, sir, though you are a great Texas Ranger, are not above international law. You may go fuck yourself." Parr sprang up with his fist cocked, but before he could hit the little bastard, Trujillo ducked and reached for his ankle and

179

came up with an ice pick. Parr slowly sat and stared at the ice pick, thinking how he'd like to have a go at shoving it up the pissant's ass.

"Excuse me," Parr said through his teeth.

Trujillo smiled sweetly and said, "Of course. We are all gentlemen here."

"Then as one gentleman to another, what can you tell me?"

Trujillo took a sip from his coffee, set down his cup, and turned to study Parr's face. "I would put something on those nasty bumps on your face."

Parr slowly stood up and smiled at Trujillo. "I'm going to remember all your help." He walked past the waitress and to the lobby. Outside, he walked up to a banana tree in the courtyard, swung his fist at the soft trunk, putting a dent into it, and swore that the little bastard just wasn't going to get away with that shit.

❂ Jerri sat at her desk and looked out her office window, hoping to see somebody watching her, for she knew that if somebody watched her, his eyes and his attention were off Angel. Once she had gotten to bed the night before, she had slept well. She felt good but anxious and ignored the papers on her desk, the telephone, and Sam.

"You might as well take today off too for all you done." Sam casually pointed one of his Tootsie Roll fingers at Jerri.

"Leave me alone, Sam," Jerri said, and stared out her window.

"Hell, ever since that Mexican boyfriend of yours showed up, you've been worthless as tits to a boar hog around this place," Sam said.

Jerri held up a pencil at Sam. "Sam, leave me alone."

Sam blew air out his mouth or nose to make the sound of a wounded bull. "Should of just let you stay a Girl Scout smiling at Yankee tourists."

"Not now, Sam, just not now."

Sam snorted again. "Don't do it, Jerri. Whatever it is, just don't do it. Forget it. You're gonna fuck up." Jerri raised her head to meet Sam's gaze. They held each other in place for a few seconds, then

Sam snorted again and ducked his head to break the gaze. "Maybe we ought to go have lunch," he said. "Maybe after lunch you should take the day off, and maybe you could tell me what you're into."

Jerri looked at Sam's bowed head with his fine hair trying to cover his scalp. "Maybe I'll tell you at lunch."

They walked to Commerce, then decided to eat at the downtown Luby's cafeteria. They pushed their trays through the line and sat by a window with a view of Commerce Street, surrounded by secretaries, lawyers, bankers, and insurance men. The uniforms—the tasteful slacks and skirts of the women and the pinstripe or seersucker suits of the men—and the line made Luby's almost look like a mess hall for some civilian business army. Jerri forced Sam to sit with his back to the window so that she could sit across from him and look out at Commerce.

As Sam dangled a fork full of chicken fried steak in front of his mouth, he said, "Mrs. Townsend cried when the city council dropped the funds for the symphony." Sam chewed the chicken fried in the corner of his mouth.

"Can't stand in the way of progress," Jerri said.

Sam squinted as though trying to understand Jerri's comment, then said, "That's what I say." He chewed a bit longer, then asked, "So are you in some kind of trouble?"

Jerri ducked. "Believe me, right now, you don't want to know."

"Or is it you don't want to tell." Sam looked down at his plate. "Do you need some money?"

Jerri raised her head, and they gazed at each other. "No, Sam. Not now. But thanks."

Sam then broke the gaze to look up above Jerri. "Can I help you?" Sam asked.

Jerri dropped her fork and turned to look behind her. At first she saw just the silver belt buckle and the jeans, then she looked at the face above the baggy white shirt. "J. J.," she said, and stood up.

"Mom, can I talk to you?" J. J. asked.

Jerri turned back to look at Sam. He had food in one cheek but didn't chew. He started slowly chewing. "Excuse me, Sam," Jerri said, and led J. J. around and between several tables of business suits and tasteful slacks and skirts to a dish-covered table in the corner. They sat on either side of the dirty dishes.

"What's the problem?"

J. J. snaked his arm through the dirty dishes to touch Jerri's knuckles as she rested her crossed hands on the table. She looked down at his fingers on top of her hands. He had never touched her like that before. "Mom, I'm just worried about you. That's all."

"Why?" Jerri asked him. "Has your father told you something?" J. J. didn't say anything. "What's he said?"

"It's not Dad." J. J. hung his head and muttered, "Forget Fuentes. I knew he'd be trouble for you. Just forget him. Dump him."

Jerri pulled her hand away from her son. "How do you know about Fuentes?" Jerri looked quickly around but couldn't see Parr. She repeated herself. "How do you know about Fuentes? What do you know?"

"I just know," J. J. said.

"Where's Joe Parr?"

"I want you to dump Fuentes. But before you do, tell that cop what he wants to know. Give them what they want." Jerri turned back to look at J. J. He hung his head. "I'm begging you, please."

"Go back and tell Parr you're not going to be his stooge," Jerri said, and stood up. She turned from J. J. and walked away from him.

Before she got back to Sam, she felt a hand on her shoulder and felt the secretaries and businessmen staring at her. She turned to see J. J., his mouth drooping at one corner. "Mom, you don't know what you're getting into," he said.

"I know what I'm doing." She turned away and started walking again. "And you shouldn't interfere."

J. J.'s body went limp the way loose-limbed teenagers' bodies do. His jaw got slack. Jerri looked closely at her kid's expression, which showed her that he hadn't yet matured enough for her or anyone else to tell the difference between exasperation, hurt, and the urge to cry. Perhaps J. J. himself didn't know what he felt. Jerri felt herself start to smile. She had no reason to be angry with her son. "Don't worry, please." J. J. nodded, backed away from her, and walked off.

When she sat back down, Sam put down his fork, looked at her, and chewed. She felt his eyes on her. "You better go after him. That's what you want to do. I got the tab," Sam said.

Jerri pushed herself up, nodded to Sam, and walked briskly to the front door. Outside, Jerri looked down Commerce to her left, then back east to her right, and saw J. J. crossing the street at the first crosswalk. Cars were halted, so she ran across the street. Once she got across, she ran to catch up with J. J. She saw him walk into a parking lot stuck in between two tall buildings and ran to the parking lot just in time to see J. J. open the front passenger door of a Lincoln.

Jerri jerked to a stop and walked toward the Lincoln. She blocked out the sounds of traffic behind her as step after step brought her closer to the car. J. J. turned and saw her. She walked to the front of the Lincoln and looked straight at J. J. "Oh, honey, I'm sorry. I didn't mean to be so rude to you," Jerri said. Then she stepped toward the driver's side and tried to see through the tinted window of the Lincoln. She heard a faint whir as the window of the Lincoln rolled down, and she saw Parr. The door opened, and Parr pushed one long leg out, then the other.

The old cowboy tipped his hat and said, "Jerri." She took a step back, and J. J. got to her first and simply uttered, "Mom."

Jerri turned to face Parr. "So who's next? My ex-husband? My mother?"

"Palo says to forget Fuentes and tell me what I need to know," Parr said, then dropped his eyes and dug at the asphalt with the pointed toe of his boot. Then the old Ranger put his weight on both feet and looked Jerri in the eye. She didn't drop her eyes, didn't feel the sting; this was professional for both of them, not personal.

"I'm sorry, Mom," J. J. said. "He said you could go to jail."

"She could," Parr said, then hesitated. "Jerri, you're just gonna have to tell me what's going on."

"Tell him what he needs to know." J. J. patted her back.

Jerri put her hands over her face and looked at the pink undersides of her fingers. When she pulled her hands away, she said, "There's a city warehouse." She hesitated and looked at her son and would-be boyfriend. "Tonight at midnight we'll pick up the guns there." She hesitated again. "It's on Judson Road, just off of I-35. I don't know the address, but you can find it."

"Thank you," Parr said. "I'm sorry, Jerri. And I swear, I'll protect you as much as I can."

"Oh, you've done a good job of protecting me so far."

"You did the right thing," J. J. said.

"Do you want to come with me?" Jerri asked J. J.

"I'll take him back to school," Parr said.

"It's okay, Mom," J. J. said, "I'll go with Mr. Parr."

Jerri smiled, turned her back to them, and trotted away from them with her hands over her mouth. Parr had been easy to hurt and fool, but so had J. J.

☺ Parr lifted a taco up to his mouth and bit into it, and as he shifted his eyes away from his taco and looked across the people sitting at the iron tables in front of Casa Rio, he saw Vincent Fuentes staring down at a plate of enchiladas. Parr had taken J. J. back to school and felt slightly good because, even if Jerri had lied to protect all the bastards swirling around her, he knew the whole goddamn case was at least going to end. So he decided to buy himself a lunch at Casa Rio. But he realized that he had never even talked to the pivotal character. So he lowered his taco, stood, and walked to Vincent Fuentes's table.

Parr stopped in front of Fuentes's iron table and watched the nearly handsome Mexican raise a fork full of enchiladas to his face. Parr sized up the younger man, who could probably attract a woman like Jerri, and watched him chew. "Mr. Fuentes," Parr said.

Fuentes looked up at Parr. His head seemed to wobble. He squinted and said, "Sir." In trying to stand and shake Parr's hand, Fuentes pushed his left hand down for balance. It landed in his plate of enchiladas. Parr leaned back his head to squint at Fuentes's hand resting in the enchiladas. Fuentes sat, picked up a cloth napkin with his right hand, and wiped at his enchilada-stained left hand.

Parr sat across the table from Fuentes and pulled out his badge.

"That says I'm a Texas Ranger. I've been watching you. I want to know what you're up to."

Fuentes raised his eyes and, from the wrinkled look on his face, it seemed whatever was going on behind his skull hurt him. Parr hoped that he would say nothing to hurt Jerri. "Early today I had an ice pick in my ear. Unless you do that, I don't cooperate," Fuentes said. He leaned across the table toward Parr, and Parr was able to get a whiff of the liquor on his breath. "Arrest me, shoot me, I just don't care."

"Jesus," Parr said, just loud enough so that only Fuentes could hear. The fancy-ass Mexican was shitfaced. Parr stood up. "Sorry to have bothered you," he said, and started to turn.

"Wait," Fuentes said, watched for a spot to put his hand, planted it, then stood up.

"Maybe you ought to stay sitting down," Parr said. Fuentes dropped into his chair. He motioned for Parr to come toward him. Parr stepped toward the table and bent his head over the Mexican's enchiladas.

"I want to stay in this country," Fuentes said. "I can do the time in prison here if I have to. But I must stay here. Can you help me?"

"I'll look into it," Parr said, and started to go.

"Fine, fine. I'm at the Four Seasons Hotel," Fuentes said, then chuckled. "But I bet you know that if you have watched me."

"Yeah," Parr said, and stepped backward. "What can you tell me about what's going on?"

"Nothing. I'm trying to surrender. I'll admit to whatever it is that's going to happen."

"I'll be in touch," Parr said. Fuentes managed a wink and looked back down at his enchiladas.

Parr turned away from Fuentes and walked back to his taco plate. Liquor alone didn't make a man's eyes all dilated and red like Fuentes's. Parr sat and took another bite out of his taco as he looked across the tables at the drunk Mexican shoving enchiladas in his mouth. Fuentes was too fucked up to plan anything. Somebody else was behind this. And Parr worried that perhaps Jerri was in some kind of danger.

CHAPTER TEN

Fuentes looked at the faces of his students, all serious, all with pencils in hand, ready to take down what they assumed was inside his mind, what his witty reply would be to the pretty girl's question. He couldn't remember the question. He let his head drop into his open hands. As his head hit his palms, he thought that if he had not caught his head, it would have rolled off his neck, across the top of his desk, dropped to the floor, then rolled up under the feet of the rich, pretty, and studious girl who had asked the unremembered question.

He opened his eyes and looked at the pinkish brown insides of his palms and tried to remember what the girl had asked about the short story they were discussing. Fuentes couldn't remember the short story. Instead he thought about the students in the state-supported school on the other side of town where he used to work. He tried to remember the name of that school. Those students wanted and got a no-frills education. They wanted practical facts, not theories. These students, the sons and daughters of people rich enough to pay the outlandish tuition, had the luxury to discuss theory and idea. Bread was on the table for them, always had been, always would be, probably. They didn't know how their luxurious world of ideas, a world most people in most countries would never have the leisure and the opportunity to even consider, could suddenly turn against them, lead them into an inner labyrinth twisting in on itself like a conch shell. They didn't know that you had to let the mind escape itself. That was a thing no school would allow him to teach. That was a thing he didn't know if he could teach.

Then mixed with his thought was pain. His palm had pressed against the swollen lump at the corner of his eye. He had triggered the throbbing again. He pulled his head out of his hands and felt the round frame of the glass over his left eye resting just against the pain. Sliding his hand under the lens, he touched the cut along the peak of what Americans call a mouse. The cut burned. He looked at the dried blood and the thin, watery, pink blood on his fingers. He looked back at the class. "Professor Fuentes?" the girl asked. "Did you hear me?" Two boys giggled. He looked quickly to find them, but his eyes moved too slowly to catch the giggles that had frozen back into serious, scholarly looks. That is good, he told himself. Go ahead, giggle, he wanted to tell them. This is funny. Instead he got up and tilted back his head to better see the students. He stepped with his left foot, then let his right follow, then his left foot followed that step until he was in the door frame. Wavering for a moment, he let his left shoulder catch his fall against the door frame, then rolled so that his back leaned against the frame. His head rolled toward the class. Thought was gone. Good riddance. "Class dismissed," he said.

Outside, in the hot afternoon sun, he broke a sweat. The sweat made him come back from his mind to Trinity University's shaded and flowered campus. He lifted his hand to greet the people he met and let foot follow foot until he was in a parking lot. He looked for his rented car, but he couldn't find it. Besides, he knew he could no longer drive. "Professor Fuentes," he heard from behind him, and turned to see the girl who had asked him the questions in class. She held her books pressed to her chest by crossed arms. She had to be flat chested to do that, Fuentes thought, not like Jerri Johnson. "Can I help you?" she asked.

"Sweet young lady," Fuentes said, "call a taxi."

Leaning back, he hit something, and turning, he saw that it was the rear end of a Mercedes. He let the Mercedes absorb his weight, then slid down the fender until he sat on the asphalt. "Go," he said to the girl, and waved his hand in the direction he thought a telephone might be in. She backed up, then turned and hurried off. He put his hand into his pocket and brought out the plastic bag with the powder. He licked his pinkie, stuck it into the bag, brought it out, then stuck it in his mouth. He rolled the plastic bag back up and stuck it in his pocket. What he needed was a drink. Gin or vodka would be best.

The sun was bouncing off the asphalt of the parking lot and hitting him in the face. He needed to get to some shade, but if he left, the taxi, if the girl called one, wouldn't know where to pick him up. So he took off his shirt, sweated, and tried not to think about the heat. Students came by and looked at him; some snickered. A faculty member who taught some kind of science thing helped him up. Wayne was all he could remember about the man's name, and he thanked him. And then he let Wayne lead him to some shade where he could lie back and watch the spot by the Mercedes for the taxi. Waiting and cooled, he put his sweaty shirt back on.

When the taxi showed up and he stood and pushed himself toward it, he allowed his mind to drift into the present and the rational. He had to tell the taxi driver where to go. As he could best remember, he now had options. The tall man in the cowboy hat who even had a sheriff's badge might be able to help him. Trujillo had ordered him to find Angel. His plan from the beginning was to escape with Jerri. Jerri could keep him from drinking. Now, if he were to escape with her, if he were to find Angel, if he were to barter with the tall sheriff, he needed Jerri, whom he remembered was last at Palo's house. "Palo's house," he told the taxi driver. Fuentes realized that he had not given enough information and tried to remember the address he wrote on envelopes of his letters to Palo. But the Mexican taxi driver said, *"Sí,"* and took him straight to Palo's house.

❷ Fuentes listened to the crunch of his feet stepping in the gravel of Palo's driveway. Mixed with the crunch was the incessant, loud buzz of the cicadas. And mixed too were the sounds of the mockingbirds and grackles, probably up in the pecan trees, eating the cicadas. The shade, though, was cool and helped the headache that the sounds gave him. His white powder was gone. It had spilled out of the plastic bag when he dropped it in Palo's front yard while trying to get a little of the powder. His feet were still following each other. And though he had never been to Palo's house, he knew Palo would live in a big house like this. He came up to a gate for the picket fence and scratched his hand on a picket trying to get the gate open. A friendly Mexican appeared and opened the gate for him. Then he walked through the gate into the backyard, which was cooler than the front.

Fuentes was proud of his mind, for he knew, from what he could remember of all that Jerri had told him and from what Palo had written to him, that Palo would be sitting in the backyard. Fuentes looked down at the deep green grass and could almost feel its coolness through the soles of his shoes. He sat and took off his shoes and socks. Then he lay down in the grass and felt its coolness on his back.

When he woke up, the long, late afternoon shadows stretched all the way across the backyard, and Palo was sitting in a padded lawn chair in front of him with his feet in a plastic tub filled with water, and he was cracking pecans by putting them in a long metal tube, then pulling back a hammer on one end of the tube. Fuentes heard the pop of a cracking pecan. He pushed himself up with his elbows to look at Palo and, from the way his head hurt, he knew he was getting sober. "Have you eaten?" Palo said in English. Fuentes thought whether he should talk to his father in Spanish or English. Spanish was the language he had learned to write in. It was the language he had used to think in. It was the language he had used to incite people. English was the language his father forced himself to learn once he decided to come to America. English was the language he now used for his deceptions. English was the second language, the language that had rescued and could still rescue their selfish blood. English was the language for selfishness. They should speak to each other in English.

"I only want to find Jerri."

"Lili fixes the enchiladas tonight. A good night to eat here."

189

"All I want to do is find Jerri."

"You need a meal." Palo pushed himself up and made holes in the grass with his cane as he walked into his house, and Fuentes followed the trail of cane holes.

Later, Fuentes sat in Palo's dining room and picked at his enchiladas. He remembered that he had had cheese enchiladas for lunch at Casa Rio and watched the barges full of tourists and talked to the sheriff. Palo urged him to eat more.

Later still, they sat on the padded lawn furniture on the back porch and ate ice cream, which Fuentes liked better than the enchiladas because it coated his stomach and made him feel less sick from the white powder and the margaritas. He was enjoying his father's house and his meal, but he needed a drink, and he needed to find Jerri. "Palo, I have to find Jerri," he said.

"Then go find her."

"Where is she, Palo?"

"Where else should she be?"

The old man ate his ice cream with deliberate moves while he spoke, never breaking the rhythm of dipping the spoon, hoisting the spoon to his mouth, and mushing the ice cream in his mouth. So this was where he came from, Fuentes thought. His father's outward manner had turned kindly, grandfatherly, sweet. It was all a lie. It denied the bribes, the murders, the plots. "Is she at home?" Fuentes asked.

"You going to eat that ice cream?" Palo jerked his chin toward the bowl Fuentes had rested on his lap.

"Palo, I have no more time to waste. Why do you always start this with me? I have to find Jerri. I am in trouble."

Palo slowly stood, and Fuentes heard his bones pop. "Palo," Fuentes said as he took the bowl of ice cream off his lap and got up, too. His father pushed himself along as he walked through the door and into the dark kitchen, his cane tapping the linoleum. Fuentes followed him into the kitchen and shut the door behind him. It was dark, and Fuentes's eyes couldn't yet see in this dark. This was the man who had convinced him that he was a pretty boy. But beneath his father's demeanor and encouragement were the

190

dark means he used to acquire his power and confidence and Fuentes's birthright. Fuentes tried to see if his father, now this kindly old man in his house in America, could see how the long terrible history of Mexico and his part in it had destined him to this pretense. But Palo showed him nothing. "Palo, take me to her house. This is important."

"Important. Shit," Palo said. "Who you are to give me orders?" Fuentes heard the taps of Palo's cane against the linoleum of the kitchen floor.

"Palo, I have to find her. I am going to ask her to help me. Not you. I am going to answer to her."

"You don't need me, you mean," Palo said, and walked away from him. Then as he was about to go into his living room, he halted, and Fuentes could see the form that was his father point a long, bony finger at him. "I know you."

"You just remember me. You don't know me anymore," Fuentes said. "Now, please."

"I know you. You live in fancy hotels all over the country. You dress like a real *pachuco*. No rebel ever dressed like you. No rebel ever lived like you. I know what you are doing. You don't even got to tell me."

"You don't know. You don't know. You were never in prison."

"You never got blown up. And you don't fool me." Fuentes heard Palo sob. He still couldn't see him clearly in the dark kitchen but saw his form and heard the taps of his cane as he moved toward the kitchen table. "I figure you out. I know you. You hurt me because I am your father. Okay. I am still your father, but you don't come see me. Weeks you are here and just now I see you. And look at you. What kind of Mexican are you?" Palo hesitated and then pounded his fist on the table.

Fuentes didn't come to see his father because he couldn't bear to be reminded of all the notions, hopes, and ideas that used to prop them both up. But he felt ideas burning their way back into his brain. His knees bent and his shoulders drooped from the weight of his family and Mexico. He wanted to defend Mexico to and from his father. The pretty boy spoke: "America, with its luck, its history and wealth, with its crude, greedy, simple Anglo, Scotch-Irish pioneers, could afford ideas. But poor Mexico, with its bad luck, with an agreeable, accommodating, persistent people, with its leaders who recognized that it could only get worse before it got better, knows reality. All Mexico can afford is its peculiar, corrupt republicanism."

Fuentes's mind raced backward. He remembered writing somewhere, sometime ago, what he had said. So he said more: "Uncouth Americans were too simpleminded to see any superiors, so they bullied and bartered their way into prominence. And they pushed their popular culture into the minds of the third world. Mexicans were still like the Aztecs who met Cortés, so fascinated with these golden strangers and their shiny toys and ideas that they saw them as potential gods."

Fuentes stopped when he realized he wasn't even making the right argument for this occasion. He knew that his father remembered all of their old arguments. They blinked, as though to clear their heads, and stared at each other. "You still talk shit," Palo said.

Fuentes dropped his head and saw his father do the same. Evidently, without an argument about blood or Mexico, they had nothing to talk about. "Palo, do you have something to drink here?" Fuentes asked so that he might have the option of a free-floating mind.

"Damn you to hell." Palo slammed his old fist on his rickety kitchen table. Fuentes reached for the table and held it because he thought that it would either shatter or fall. "But Jerri. For whatever it is that you would do to her, I shit on you."

"Palo, I want to help. That is why I want to see her," Fuentes said, and knew he wasn't really lying. It was she who could save Fuentes, could keep his blood from spilling.

"Before you can save your soul. No, no, *soul* sounds too much like the priest shit you used to talk. Before you can have any *cojones,* you going to have to help her."

"I am," Fuentes said. "I'm going to warn her. Now take me there."

He heard Palo's cane start to tap as he moved back across the kitchen and toward the back door. "Come on," Palo said.

"Do you have something to drink?" Fuentes asked.

"Borrachón," he heard Palo mumble in their native language.

❷ When Palo pulled the truck into Jerri's parking lot, Fuentes recognized the Suburban that was parked under her second-floor apartment and was grateful to have found her. He thanked Palo, who only grunted, and ran, as best he could, up the iron stairs to Jerri's front door. Fuentes knocked on Jerri's door and, over his shoulder, watched Palo drive away. He wondered if the sheriff was watching him. He looked at the large window in front of her apartment and saw that she had no light on in the living room. He knocked harder and hoped that she was home. Finally Jerri opened the door and peeked around it from out of the darkness of her living room.

"Vincent," she said, and looked at him as though surprised. Fuentes immediately stepped in and shut the door behind him. He squinted in the dark to see her and felt for a light switch but couldn't find it. Unable to see, he grabbed for her and got his arms around her. She steadied him by holding him with her hands, and suddenly he felt as if the air between them had grown more dense, had been compacted by the force of his need.

"Where have you been? I've missed you," Fuentes said, and pulled her closer and felt her breasts mash and seemingly spread into his chest. He thought of her thighs and sex with her. "Let's go to bed, right now," he said. She let him drag her toward the bedroom but pulled back against him at the lighted bedroom door. He could use the delight he found in her rather than the vodka or gin. Right now, before escaping, he needed to be as close to her as possible. He wanted to compact the air some more. But Jerri forced her hands in between them and pushed him away with the heels of her palms.

"God, what is wrong with you?" Jerri asked, and leaned against her wall as if protecting herself from him.

"I love you," Fuentes said, then smiled. He saw her face cut in half by the beam of light coming out of the lit bedroom. She was dressed in tight jeans. The side of her face that he saw had no makeup. Her hair was pulled back into a ponytail, the way he remembered her. He couldn't resist the desperation in his mind and grabbed her again. She pushed him away again.

"Vincent," Jerri said, "listen to me." She turned and walked back into the dark living room. Fuentes tried to follow her but only bumped into an end table. Then he saw a tiny streak of light coming in through the living room drapes. She had pulled one drape slightly to one side and peeked out the large window at the front of her apartment. "Did anybody follow you?"

"No, Jerri," Fuentes said.

"Are you sure?"

"Jerri," Vincent said, and stepped toward her.

She let the drape go, and he could see nothing more of her. "Vincent, I have to go."

Fuentes squinted until his headache came back and his brain seemed to pound into his skull. The lump under his eye began to hurt. "Right, you have to go with me. You have to go with me."

Then he felt her take his hand and pull him toward the shaft of light coming from the bedroom door. Stopped just short of the light and pulling his head down to hers, she hugged him, then let him go. "No, I have to go get the guns. I'm going to get Angel, and then I'm going to take the guns to Nuevo Laredo."

Fuentes circled her waist with his arms. "Why . . . why do you want to do that?"

"He'd never make it on his own," Jerri whispered to him.

"What do you owe him?"

"I owe him a chance, same as you do."

"Don't go."

"Why? Tell me why."

"So you can leave with me. Leave right now. Go anywhere we want. Anywhere on earth."

"Leave it all?"

"Like Puerto Peñasco."

"I've got to take him."

"You don't have to do anything."

Jerri turned away from him but still stayed within his arms. Fuentes tightened his arms around her and pulled her to his chest. Resting his chin on her shoulder, his cheek next to hers, he muttered, "No." He could then tell by the salty taste in his mouth, by the slight burn in his eyes, and by the sting on the swelling cut under his eye that he was crying. "Please. You just don't understand. You don't know what you are getting into." And he knew what he hadn't understood. She couldn't help him, but he had just wanted her. Now he knew. He had hurt her, and he was sorry. She had been very important to him. He desperately needed something important.

Jerri pulled away from him and said in a tone that started as a suppressed shout and turned into an anxious whisper: "Tell me. Tell me. Tell me what I don't know." She waited. And Fuentes could hear a few snivels. She was crying.

"Don't go. We can run away."

"What about your plans for a liberated Mexico?" Jerri's voice shook.

"Forget about it."

"I think I have," Jerri said, and stepped again into the light and his arms. She hung her head, then raised it to look at Fuentes. "Just like you. I'm just taking care of some poor *pelado*."

She pulled away from him and stepped backward into the dark. Fuentes saw her form open the front door and the night's reflections from outside catch in her blond hair and turn it golden. "Don't turn on the lights for another thirty minutes." From the light outside, he saw her pick up her heavy purse lying beside the front door.

Fuentes knew that Natividad and Trujillo, armed and waiting, were in the warehouse. They would probably try to shoot Angel. They might not take care to miss her. He *wanted* to tell her. But so far, technically, he had done his job. "Come back. Whatever happens, come back tonight," was the best that he could force out of his throat when he saw the door start to close.

"I'll be back from Nuevo Laredo as soon as I can."

195

"Come back tonight," Fuentes said. But the door closed, and he was in darkness.

With Jerri gone, Fuentes allowed tears to run down his cheeks. They burned into the crack of skin on the lump under his eye. He tried to force his mind to think about expensive hotels and Jerri's thighs. But along with hotels and thighs, telephone books came into his mind. With both hands against the wall he felt his way into the kitchen, past the refrigerator, along the kitchen counter, up to the cabinet, to the last door of the cabinet. He opened the door, reached into the cabinet, and brought out a bottle. He carried the bottle into the light. It was bourbon.

Fuentes took the bottle into Jerri's bedroom, sat in the one chair, and took a healthy drink of bourbon out of the bottle. He took another drink and tried to swallow as much as possible. Even if he had told her, she might not have gone with him. He took another drink. He had done the best he could have done. He had followed the right tactics. His mind had done its best rational job. But then, this again was proof of the danger of rationality.

He took another drink and tasted the bite that the cheap bourbon left on the back of his throat. But his mind lingered on Jerri and on Trujillo's threat. His mind held on to the here and now but longed to be someplace else, perhaps in Puerto Peñasco or Jerri's house from five years before or in class with the students from the state university across town, or perhaps five years in the future, somewhere that wasn't a prison or a luxury hotel. In the constant transition that had been his life, he had made one mistake that was greater than all the rest. He had not fallen in love with Jerri until now. And he realized, just as his mind skirted around the edges of oblivion, that his sojourns in his mind weren't from a simple wish to put his mind elsewhere but to escape from his fright. No *cojones,* he thought as he took the sip that pushed him into the peaceful and luxurious disorientation that kept his fright away.

❷ Jerri walked out her door and strained against the weight of her purse. She could tell by the strap's bite into her shoulder that her brick and her pistol were in the purse. She stepped gently on each

196

of the steps coming down from her apartment and looked ahead of her. With her living room light out, anyone who might be watching would have a hard time seeing her leave. Perhaps it was best that Fuentes came over and stayed. Whoever watched would think that they were both inside screwing and accounted for. She reached the bottom step and walked between her Suburban and the pickup parked next to it. Unlike the bugs that swirled around the streetlights, trying to get into light, she avoided it as she trotted across the lighted parking lot, trying to get into darkness.

Once in the street, she crossed to the dark side and stayed in the shadows. She looked over her shoulder continuously and kept one hand over the opening of the purse and the other squeezing the straps. Not only were cops on this dark downtown street but so were muggers and thieves. As she walked, she checked her watch. She looked up and saw the bus, right on schedule, pulling up toward the bus stop. Fuentes had thrown her off. She ran for the lighted bus stop and caught the bus. She went to the back and sat on the last seat and looked behind her to see who might be following her. This time, she thought, she had chosen to desert Fuentes. She didn't know how that made her feel. She didn't have time to think about it.

The bus took her to within a block of the U-Haul rental on Durango just on the other side of the freeway overpass. She took a chance and walked down a dark alley. The owner of the U-Haul had left the big truck sitting out under the awning. She pulled the keys out of her purse and opened the truck's door. She would have preferred to have been driving her Suburban, but too many people now recognized it. Joe Parr was old but one of the sharpest lawmen she had ever met. It was as though he could get into her mind.

With the start of the motor, her stomach felt uneasy. She could, if she wished, drive back and belligerently, defiantly, and guiltlessly walk out of her apartment with Fuentes and drive off into the sunset or wherever Fuentes wanted to go. It would of course hurt Angel. She could give him the truck and let him drive alone as planned, but he would never make it.

Jerri shifted the truck into gear and turned into the street. Five years before, Fuentes wouldn't have stumbled into her apartment and begged her to desert Angel. Three days before, she had known that she could settle with and for Fuentes. Now, if she had to, she would give up a lover to adopt, for a moment, a helpless child like Angel or the poor snake-bitten woman she had already killed. She gained speed in the truck and had a little trouble shifting, ground the gears. And she jerked back into the seat of the truck when a large bug splattered itself across the windshield.

❷ Jerri opened the lock to the fence around the warehouse, walked back to the cab of the truck, and drove through the gate. Then she got out and closed but didn't lock the gate behind her. Back in the truck, Jerri drove toward the warehouse on a rutted road. She pulled off the ruts and backed the truck up to the loading dock. Angel grabbed the Uzi sitting on the seat in between them and slung the strap around his head and over his shoulder. "Be careful with that," she said.

Angel looked over at her. "You think maybe I am *estupido, pendejo.*"

Jerri shook her head. "You are desperate." Angel opened the door, but Jerri grabbed his arm. "In your neighborhood, do you have lots of dogs?"

Angel looked at her as though she were *pendejo* or loco, but he answered, *"Sí."*

"Do they sleep in the streets during the day?"

"Always," Angel said. Jerri smiled. Vincent Fuentes was no longer a Mexican; Palo was somewhere in between a Mexican and an American. Angel was a real Mexican, one who would drive around the mangy, tired dogs and give even them their dignity. He could probably point to a stack of rusty cans and not call it trash but cans.

Angel's smile turned into a grimace of confusion that made him look stupid. As he shoved the door and the dome light lit them both, Jerri squeezed his arm. "Are you sure you want to do this? We go now, there's no turning back." Angel pushed open the door and got out. Jerri watched as he jumped up on the loading dock with one bound, then steadied the Uzi. Jerri grabbed her purse, which lay on the floor of the truck, thought a moment, then laid it back on the floor. She reached into it and pulled out only a large flashlight. When she walked to the loading dock, Angel stuck out his hand. She grabbed it, and he helped pull her up on the dock. She slipped the key into the padlock, turned the key, removed the lock, and slid open the door. Before he stepped in front of her to go into the dark warehouse, he smiled at her and said, "*Gracias,* not for the guns, *para mi.*" Jerri could think of nothing to say to him.

As Jerri rounded the corner, light, bright as the headlights of an oncoming truck, hit them both in the eyes, paralyzing them and their ability to step out of the beam. Like deer hypnotized by a poacher's spotlight, like the bugs flying at night, they stared into the light. All Jerri could do was raise her hand to shield her eyes. Then Jerri heard a voice disrupt the silent beam: "*Alto,* Angel." Jerri looked at Angel, who tried desperately to see into the bright light. She reached for him and wound up with his hand in hers. "I have a gun on you," the Hispanic voice said.

Jerri looked at Angel and whispered, "Don't do anything."

"Don't talk. *Silencio,*" she heard. Then she heard, "Jerri Johnson, go away." She knew who it was. She wished she knew how good the two men in the white Toyota really were. "Go away, Johnson. Run away."

As she looked at Angel again, she saw him step out of the beam of light and reach for the Uzi. She heard gunfire and the zoom of bullets in the air and the ping they made when they hit wood. Jerri threw her flashlight toward the people firing and dove for the ground. On her way down, she heard Angel's Uzi. Flat on her belly, sucking the dust on the floor into her mouth and throat, Jerri looked for the open door. She could tell where it was only by the few stars she could see through it, and by pretending to grab at those stars, she crawled through the door. Once through, she got up on her knees, crawled to the edge of the dock, jumped off, and ran to the driver's side of the U-Haul. She started the truck, then honked the horn and reached into her purse and pulled out her pistol. She spun the cylinder and could tell from the sound that the gun was loaded.

Jerri scooted to the passenger side of the truck, swiveled in the seat, and pointed her gun out the open window at the opening of the warehouse. She heard several shots, then she yelled, "I'm okay, Angel. I'm in the truck." She saw a squat figure appear in the doorway and wrapped her finger around the trigger. Several shots rang, and the squat figure fell backward, toward the truck, but Angel hit the ground rolling and rolled off the loading dock. Jerri fired at the opening until her gun was empty. She then slid into the driver's seat and slipped the truck into gear. "Get in, Angel," she yelled, and the passenger door opened. She heard heavy breathing and saw Angel's head appear over the seat as she pressed on the gas. Angel clawed at the vinyl seat of the truck to try to pull himself inside.

Jerri reached across the seat, grabbed Angel by the collar, and heaved to pull him into the cab. Then, by the sound of the metallic zing, she could tell that a bullet hit the cab. She pressed hard on the gas and sped toward the gate. "Dumb bitch," she said as she got close to the gate because she had closed it behind her. Holding her foot steady, she crashed into the gate. The picket fence wrapped itself around the cab and scraped the asphalt behind her.

As Jerri turned into the street, she looked behind her and saw the white Toyota speeding toward the exit she had just made. She looked at Angel. "You okay?"

He swung the Uzi toward her. *"Puta,"* he said.

"What the hell?" Jerri said, and turned the truck down an alley. The fence trailing behind her dragged trash cans and tore bricks and boards loose. *"Pinche,"* she said. "Everybody in town can hear this fucking racket."

"Me chingaron," Angel said. "You fucked me."

"Think, goddamn it." She looked at Angel. "Think. I didn't screw you over. I couldn't have." Angel slowly lowered the gun.

"You think I'm stupid, huh?" he said.

Jerri turned, stopped at the end of the alley, and looked in the rearview mirror. She saw the lights of the small Toyota coming. She turned out her own lights and started backing up slowly. "Hold on," she told Angel. "My insurance rates are going to go sky-high for this shit." She saw the headlights in her rearview mirror and heard the brakes of the Toyota screech and felt the truck surge forward when the Toyota rear-ended it. "Ouch, you motherfuckers," Jerri said, and quickly shifted into first gear. The U-Haul dragged the Toyota and the fence a bit but then released the Toyota. Jerri drove away with the fence again cutting grooves in the asphalt.

She looked at Angel, who had slumped down in the seat. "We're going to a hospital."

"No," he said, and again pointed the Uzi at her.

Jerri slapped the Uzi away from her and said, "We're going to a hospital."

"Mexico," Angel said. "Just Mexico." Jerri looked over to see if she could see the wound. From a streetlight she saw the dark black blood on Angel's fingers.

"You'll probably die."

"Mexico," he said.

Jerri pulled the truck into an alley, got out, and cut her fingers trying to unwind the heavy picket fence from around the hood and cab of the truck. Then she drove for Santa Rosa Hospital, determined to get Angel there before he could die. But he muttered over and again, "Mexico, Mexico." None of her arguments worked. And she finally realized that the bleeding man beside her had been taking orders since he crossed the river, probably before that, and now, wounded, hurting, he was going to give the orders. And whether from desperation or a dying wish, he wanted as quickly as possible to be home. So Jerri turned away from Santa Rosa and drove instead toward her apartment, glad in her choice not to take the poor, sick victim to the hospital. She drove for her apartment because, if she was going to drive to Mexico, she wanted to make the run in her Suburban. And she also kept hearing Fuentes's plea to return that night.

❂ Sitting in the cab of the U-Haul, Jerri looked up at the light, now on, in her living room. Then she looked at Angel. He clutched the Uzi. "Another solution. I go up. I call Immigration. They fix you up. They take you to the border. All they do is drop you off. They don't ask questions."

"You take me," said Angel.

"*La migra* would be better. I guarantee it."

She took Angel's arm and leaned over him. "*Tú, tú, tú,*" he said.

"And I say Immigration," Jerri replied, and Angel slowly shook his head. Like the wetbacks hiking through brush, cactus, and snakes, he made no sense making this journey. He refused to realize just how badly he could get hurt. But there was something noble about the ignorance and the desperation. She scooted away from him and back to the driver's seat. She yanked her purse out from behind the seat, reached into it, and pulled out her pistol. She handed Angel the pistol. "Watch where I go. Wait a few minutes, then come up to my apartment if you can. If not, I'll be back down. And for God's sake, if you're going to shoot something, use my gun. That Uzi's too damn dangerous."

Jerri walked up to her apartment and looked over her shoulder. Convinced that she didn't see Parr or whatever was left of the Toyota, she stuck her key into the lock, turned it, and opened her door. She walked into the bright light of her apartment. And she saw Fuentes sitting on the sofa with an empty bottle of bourbon in his hand. Jerri turned toward the drapes and pulled the string to open them. When they came open, she looked out into the parking lot to see if she could see Angel and to give him a chance to see her. She saw the U-Haul but couldn't see him in it. She turned back to Fuentes.

Fuentes got up and took a step toward her. "Jerri, dearest Jerri." He stopped and looked over his shoulder toward the bedroom door. Then, wavering, he held his finger to his lips and shook his fingers toward the door as though he had just dipped them in a finger bowl. He was shooing her back out the door.

"I need some explanations first," Jerri said, and stepped toward him.

Fuentes motioned again at the door. And when Jerri didn't move, he said, "Run, Jerri, run. Go." Then Jerri heard the creak of a footstep on a loose board in the bedroom and turned toward the bedroom and put her hand into her purse. She felt for her pistol, but all she felt was her brick. The little man who had followed her came out of the bedroom, holding a pistol. His *compadre* came out, holding a gun in one hand and a bloody handkerchief pressed against his nose with the other hand. "Where is Angel?" the little man with the trim mustache asked.

"I dropped him off," Jerri said, and stuck her thumb under the straps of her purse.

"See there," Fuentes said, and staggered toward the little man. "Trujillo, you have got to let her go."

The little man walked closer to Fuentes and shoved him away with the palm of one hand. "Shut up," he said to Fuentes, and Jerri thought about moving in close and taking a swipe at him with her purse.

"Where's the little Angel?" the big man said in a nasal tone, then grunted and walked to the sofa and sat. "No more fucking around," he said by forcing air through the disrupted passages of his broken nose.

"Hurt yourself?" Jerri asked him.

Fuentes let out a giggle and took two swaying steps toward the little man. "Let's all have a drink," he said, but the little man pushed him into the center of the room, and Fuentes spun around to look at Jerri. Jerri noted the way the skin on his face just seemed to hang. She heard him mutter her name as if saying he was sorry, as if saying that he loved her still. She stood still when he reached out and put his hands on either side of her face. And Jerri, out of a sense of debt, raised up on her tiptoes to kiss him. The kiss was long and passionate, with the two goons yelling for them to break it up. As she relaxed her toes and let her feet fall flat against the carpet, smiling at Fuentes, who, even with the whiskey on his breath, might have resurrected her love for him, Jerri heard a gunshot and the cracking, crashing glass of her front window.

Jerri turned toward the sound of the breaking window and saw Angel poised and aiming *her* pistol at her. "Jerri," he yelled, then gasped for breath. "Move." Then she felt Fuentes's hands on her shoulders and heard him grunt as he pushed her forward. As Jerri fell toward the carpeted floor, she heard the guns of the two goons fire and heard the dull thud as the shots hit. As she caught herself with her outstretched hands, burning her cut palms on her carpet, she heard the shot from her own gun and the thump of her bullet hitting flesh. Twisting, she looked in back of her to see Fuentes on his butt, his hand above and hesitating to touch the puffed-up, already dying flesh around a bullet hole at the juncture of his right shoulder and neck. The wound pumped up blood and soaked his shirt and her carpet. Fuentes giggled. With three bullets in his thick squat body, Angel had still gotten a bullet close to Fuentes's heart.

Jerri rose along with the two goons, who held their guns in front of them. She walked, with the Mexicans following her, toward the gaping hole that had been her front window. She stepped through the mess, over the jagged shards of glass, and moved closer to Angel. He leaned against the railing along the balcony in front of her apartment and held himself up with both hands. A red smear stained his shirt. Not yet dead, but beyond really knowing, he tried to utter some last thought. His lips separated, but instead of a word a bubble of bloodstained spittle came out of his mouth, then popped.

Angel strained to straightened himself and slowly lifted Jerri's gun. "No, no," Jerri mumbled, and closed her eyes as she heard another shot. She opened them to see Angel, now fully straight, lean backward, then flip over the railing. He did a backward gainer onto the hood of Jerri's Suburban.

Jerri turned behind her and saw the smoking gun of the man with the broken nose. Then she looked back in and saw Fuentes still trying to touch his wound. She turned away from all of them, walked down the length of her balcony to the stairs, then down the stairs. She heard the police and ambulance sirens and thought she heard the whispers of her neighbors, whose prurient curiosity mixed with fear just now let them dare to stick their heads out of their apartments. All of them drawn, like her, like bugs to light, to Angel's body lying facedown and an inch deep into the hood of her Suburban. For a moment, with no more job to do, the sting of her tissues turning to acid having its way inside her, she wished that Angel had used the Uzi. He might have gotten a few others.

CHAPTER ELEVEN

When the crippled-up, shot Mexican pointed his pistol at Jerri's picture window, Joe Parr—like Texas Ranger Captain Lee H. McNelly chasing Juan Cortina's Mexican bandits south of the Rio Grande or ol' Rip Ford chasing the Comanches north of the Red River, all guarding the sacred borders of Texas—charged with his gun drawn toward Jerri's apartment. Limping and dragging his ass, FBI agent and drinking buddy Ollie Nordmarken and San Antonio police officer Ralph Jarozombek followed Parr out of the apartment across from Jerri's, both of their guns drawn too. They didn't stop when they heard the Mexican's gun sound and break the window's glass. They didn't stop when they saw the Mexican fall back against the rail. They didn't stop when Jerri, crying, as they could see even in the dim porch lights, stepped through the shards of glass in her front window. They stopped and drew beads when the little Mexican in the too big suit and the big stupid-looking Mexican stepped out of Jerri's house.

They didn't have time and could only watch as a pistol fired and the wounded Mexican flipped backward over the rail and dented the hood of Jerri's Suburban. Then Joe pushed aside his urge to open up on the two Mexicans and yelled for them to chew some dirt. The Mexicans didn't fire, didn't drop their guns, didn't chew the dirt (or the cement of Jerri's porch). "A lot of people are going to get dead if you birds don't drop those guns," Joe said, and the big

Mexican handed his pistol to the little Mexican, and the little Mexican raised both his and his buddy's pistols up, into the beam of the dim porch light, then laid them on the cement.

People peeked out of apartment doors, sirens went off, and Joe Parr, Ollie Nordmarken, and Officer Ralph Jarozombek slowly moved toward Jerri's apartment. Officer Jarozombek took the time to check the obviously dead Mexican, and Ollie and Joe went up the steps, guns still ready, cuffed the two live Mexicans, and read them the rights of U.S. citizens. Joe smiled as he cuffed the little bastard. Inside, they found Vincent Fuentes too drunk to feel the bullet in his shoulder but staring at the hole it made in him. They left Jerri alone, let her stay outside and bend over the railing to stare at the dead Mexican on the hood of her Suburban.

Joe sat in Jerri's easy chair and kept his gun on the two Mexicans with their hands cuffed behind their backs. The little bastard never let his mouth drop out of his pissant smirk. Ollie Nordmarken stood and watched the big Mexican, who kept his head down and shoulders hunched. They let the police, who arrived in howling squad cars, open up the back end of the U-Haul rental truck to find nothing and lead the two cuffed Mexicans out of Jerri's apartment and into their squad cars. They let the paramedics doctor Fuentes's shoulder, throw a blanket over the dead Mexican on Jerri's hood, and cart the dead and the bloody off to a hospital. Joe Parr let another cop take Jerri down to the SAPD police station and let Ollie slap him on the shoulder and say, "Good job for a couple of limp-dick old farts."

Joe Parr knew Jerri, knew how she would think, knew she gave him the answer that he had wanted too quick. He could have let it all pass, could have waited at the warehouse where she told him she would be, could have gone back to Charlie Hoestadter with his tail dragging and said Vincent Fuentes had got the best of him. He could have covered for Jerri. But no matter what he did, help or ruin her, Joe Parr knew that his guts would be twisted in a knot. The Texas Ranger, the man who arrested Bud Harrelson and shot it out with Fred Carrasco, couldn't let Jerri go.

So, enough fucking around, Joe had told himself. He called Charlie Hoestadter and told him what he knew and begged for some more men. Then Joe Parr called his buddy Ollie Nordmarken and turned the case into a federal one. A couple of agents were out at the warehouse just in case Jerri had told him true. Policemen watched Palo's house and radioed in just before Palo dropped Fuentes off at Jerri's apartment. Carrillo had followed Jerri out of her apartment, and Joe Parr cussed himself and the goddamn inept SAPD when Carrillo radioed in that he had lost Jerri when she got on a bus. And Joe almost hooted when Jerri pulled into her apartment in a big rental truck, no doubt full of stolen U.S. guns. He decided to give it all just a little more time, but then he saw the wounded Mexican limp up the stairs to Jerri's apartment.

❂ Fuentes stared up at the bright circular light above him that sent an encapsulating dome of light over him. He could see nothing but the dome of light. He couldn't see through it or over it. It made no shadow, just bright endless light. It put a thin layer between him and everything outside of it. He tried to turn his head, but his head was held in place by cloth straps that kept him staring into the light. The light inside the dome began to revolve and spin. Maybe he was spinning. Maybe he was looking down into a spiral and not up into a dome. Maybe he was rapidly ascending into the light or rapidly falling into it. Then he saw the faces, which must have somehow punctured the strong light of the dome or the spiral, peer down at him or look up at him. He tried to discern whether the faces were under or above the circle of white light and its piercing brightness. At any rate, he smiled at them. Then one of them told him to count backward from one hundred.

He heard voices say that he was out, but he knew he wasn't. He felt a numb poke on his shoulder close to where the bullet had entered him and tried to lift his opposite arm to scratch or at least touch the numbness, but his left arm wouldn't move. He smiled to himself. They thought he was out. They thought he couldn't feel. To hell, he could feel the blood in his veins. The veins surged, swelling and shrinking, with gushing blood from his corrupt old family, from the old rustler, his great-great-grandfather Juan Cortina, who showed the gringos—and the Mexicans—about blood and

207

cattle and *cojones.* No, the anesthetic didn't numb him. It just helped his mind move from place to place and from time to time. Better than the powder. Better than the gin or vodka.

But the light that he was falling into or rising to shone even through his closed eyes. Open, his eyes couldn't absorb the brightness, closed, they couldn't forget it. "Turn off the light, the light, the light," he thought he screamed, but the light persisted. The light kept his mind from moving elsewhere; the light forced his mind to remember.

He remembered getting shot in Jerri's apartment. He didn't hear his laugh, but he thought he chuckled. Wounded in action, in the apprehension of an enemy of the government; he was a hero. Literary wonder, prominent speaker, and secretly a fighter for the PRI. He was a hero. He was also a villain, thief, and liar like Palo and Juan Cortina.

He remembered Jerri. She had the *cojones* Palo talked about. She had courage. And he wanted to show her courage. The thought that he had thought in her apartment came back to him and throbbed behind his skull like a boozy headache. He could show her courage and, besides, he could escape the fright that sent his mind on trips and would, he knew, send him through a series of speaking tours and stays at luxury hotels, accompanied by Trujillo and Natividad or other keepers. Or his fright and resulting pretense would be found out, and he would no longer stay in the luxury hotels. So he shoved her to the ground and took the bullet Angel then fired.

Dead, his mind would then be free from body and thought, or it would simply be numb. Maybe it would be constant sojourns and no reality. He had once been a priest and believed in stranger things.

Angel's finger slipped, he twitched, God intervened, whatever, take your pick. In the bright light, in the white light of his open eyes or in the orange light of his closed eyes, Fuentes's mind got bogged down and couldn't move, and he knew that he had missed his escape again.

He felt pain in his shoulder cutting through the anesthesia as the doctor sliced into his wound. Five years before, in his naiveté, he had abandoned Jerri Johnson. He believed that his cause was greater than this physical, strong, real woman. He should have looked at her and seen that she was worth the world. She was greater than the feeling of the blood in his veins. He cringed from the pressure that the doctor put on his shoulder and from the pressure that he put on his head. Jerri could have made him forget about himself. He would rather have obliterated himself, gone back to prison even, than to have seen Jerri hurt. Loving Jerri so completely, back when he could have, would have been greater than any of his causes, ideas, or books, greater than the truth that the telephone book whacking him in the face gave him. And he had stuck his fingers through a picket fence and felt himself superior for the strength of his celibacy. Five years before, he had missed not just his escape, but his salvation.

❷ Joe Parr had just about goddamn near had enough. When he sat across from the little Mexican in the interrogation room with Ollie Nordmarken and two other FBI agents, Officers Jarozombek and Carrillo, and the SAPD expert, the little bastard said that if just one of them would call somebody important, they'd all see just how foolish they all were. "Me and Ollie are the only stud ducks you get for now," Parr told Trujillo. But one of Ollie's fellow agents called their regional director, and he called Washington, and Washington called the CIA, and the CIA called the SAPD and told them an agent was on the way to straighten out the matter and please by-God let the special agent of the Coahuila Defense Ministry out of jail. Even a Drug Enforcement agent who had worked with Colonel Trujillo and burned some marijuana way down in the heart of Mexico called to say that Henri Trujillo was, as Trujillo himself had said, one of the good guys.

Now, near daylight, having met with the police officer in charge, having waited by the phone, then having talked to Charlie Hoestadter and a couple of FBI big shots from Washington, Parr, Ollie, and Jarozombek walked down the long hall toward the police lounge, where pissant Trujillo had an audience of San Antonio cops and was no doubt telling them about how Joe Parr fucked up the Mexican government's case, a black day for the Rangers and the man who tracked down Bud Harrelson and shot it out with Fred Carrasco.

The wall ahead of them seemed to narrow to the door of the police lounge. Joe Parr slowed his gait. Jarozombek and Ollie slowed down, too. "Goddamn Mexican heroes," Parr said. They all stopped.

"Don't do nothing stupid, Joe," Ollie said to Parr.

"Not me. I won't," Parr said, and started walking again.

As they walked down the hall, Jarozombek said, "So Jerri Johnson turns out to be a real double-dealing, quisling bitch."

Parr lowered his shoulder and shoved Jarozombek into the wall. He felt Ollie grab his shoulder, but he pulled back a fist anyway. "Hey, Joe," Ollie said. "Don't do nothing stupid, you limp-dick old fool."

"Enough about Jerri," Parr said.

"I ought to deck you, you old fart," Jarozombek said. He rubbed his shoulder and said, "What's with you and this Jerri Johnson?"

"Nothing," Parr said.

Ollie put a finger in front of his face and said, "Remember you aren't retired yet. That means you gotta eat some more shit if you're told to."

Jarozombek rubbed his shoulder. "Yeah, sure. We all got to eat some shit. Sorry I pissed you off." Jarozombek turned and walked down the hall.

Joe leaned up against the wall, and Ollie put his palm flat against the wall, next to Joe's face, and leaned into the wall. "Jesus, I'm tired," Ollie said.

"I don't like the taste of shit, Ollie," Joe said to his buddy.

"Official orders. You have to apologize on behalf of yourself, the Texas Department of Public Safety, the Texas Rangers, and on behalf of the great state of Texas itself," Ollie said, and straightened up. "Come on. Get your spoon ready."

Parr looked down the hall and saw Jarozombek, who had to do his own ass kissing, stop and wait at the lounge door for him and Ollie. "Somebody might want to prosecute Jerri," Parr said mostly to himself, but Ollie looked at him. "And we could confiscate the guns, and we could still see if we could attach Domenic to those guns."

"It's over. This case. Fuentes," Ollie said, and started walking toward the lounge door.

Parr reached toward his mouth and, with just his thumb and forefinger, pulled out the small wad of gum he had been chewing most of the night. He tilted his head down to look through his glasses at Ollie. "Not quite," he said. Ollie stopped and turned to face Joe.

Jarozombek walked up behind Ollie and stared at Joe. "Come on, let's get it over with," Ollie said. Parr threw his wad of gum toward an ashtray but only hit the wall near it.

"Those shit ass Mexican *federales* piss me off. They left us looking like shit. Can you imagine what they're gonna tell people? Fucking SAPD cops and FBI will be laughing at me. And after I let the SAPD and you two guys play a little cowboy with me. Shit, I got to live in this town."

Jarozombek said, "Fucking A," and his face lit up.

Ollie hung his head, then lifted it to look at Joe. "Okay, buddy. Maybe I'd enjoy early retirement."

Parr pushed open the heavy, hinged wooden door to the lounge, and Jarozombek and Ollie followed him in. The lounge was crowded. A group of policemen surrounded Trujillo and Natividad, who held some bloody gauze over his nose. In among them was an FBI agent whom Parr recognized from his trips to the federal building. Another group of cops surrounded Jerri and fat Sam Ford. Parr left Jarozombek and Ollie and shoved through two cops to look at Jerri. "Jerri, are you all right?" Jerri looked up and spotted him. She slowly smiled. "Don't tell anybody anything," Parr told her.

Parr heard chuckles from a few cops. Someone said, "Fucking John Wayne."

"Fucking prehistoric John Wayne," someone else said.

"He did all right," he heard Jarozombek say.

Parr reached for Jerri, who looked at his outstretched hand, then up at him, as though debating what to do about him. She smiled, shrugged, and raised one of her bandaged hands. "Picket fence cuts and carpet burns," she said. "Wounded in action."

"Parr, get out of here," a cop said.

Parr stepped closer to Jerri and asked, "Can you help tie the guns to Domenic?"

"Don't you ever stop?" Jerri said.

"Give it up, Parr," Joe heard a cop whisper, but he stayed looking at Jerri.

"I'm trying to help you now," Joe told her.

"Joe, I have to work in this town. Call me in front of a judge, and I'll tell what I know. But I lose business if I tell you without pressure," Jerri said.

Sam Ford shook some flab and said, "You, sir, are harassing my client."

Jerri turned to him and said, "Sam, you're not my lawyer." More policemen laughed. Jerri looked at Parr. "Hell, ask Fuentes. For an expense paid trip, he'll talk." Again more policemen laughed, but Parr knew, from knowing Jerri, that she wasn't meaning to be funny.

Parr then stepped out from the circle of police around Jerri and pushed closer to Natividad and Trujillo. He felt a hand on his back and turned to see Jerri behind him. He faced back toward Natividad and Trujillo. "And I'm gonna need some statements from you two birds."

Trujillo stepped out from the policemen and rocked on his heels and crossed his arms. "Your own CIA has told you what an ass you are," Trujillo said. Natividad pushed his way to Trujillo's side.

"We're taking care of it," said Ollie's fellow FBI agent with the official-looking notepad in his hand.

"Ask them why they had to kill Angel." Jerri stepped up beside Parr. "Ask them that."

Parr turned to the FBI agent and said, "You gonna ask them, or you want me to?"

"Go ahead, ask them," Parr heard Ollie say from the door, and Joe Parr smiled at Trujillo.

"Goddamn it to hell, ask the son of a bitch," Jerri said.

"Calm down," Parr heard the agent whisper to Jerri, and while her attention was taken, Parr stepped between her and the two Mexicans.

"*Pinche,* you calm down," Jerri said to the agent.

"You look like you just won a sandlot football game," Parr said to Trujillo, and took his glasses off by grabbing the temples between his thumb and forefinger. He stuck the glasses in his shirt pocket, took a step back, cocked his fist, and hit the little pissant in the neck; his aim was off. But Joe Parr's blow lifted Trujillo off his feet and sent him into the wall. Natividad dropped his gauze bandage, showing Parr the bloody, twisted mess that was his nose, and moved toward him. Parr looked at him, crouched, and said, "You want some, too? I'll twist your ugly fucking nose the other way."

"Twist his fucking nose off," Jerri screamed. "He's a goddamn murderer. I'll tell all I know about that *pinche* son of a bitch. It was murder. They set him up. They were here to kill him." He looked behind him to see her moving toward Natividad, but Parr kept himself in front of her until a policeman grabbed her. Then bodies started whirling around him, and Parr felt two cops grab each of his arms, and a third moved in between him and Natividad.

Jarozombek appeared in front of Parr's face and whispered to him, "Calm down." Then Jarozombek added, "But good shit."

Ollie's fellow FBI agent ran quickly to Trujillo and helped him up. The FBI agent looked at Parr, who said to the police holding him, "Okay, fellas."

"This is a Mexican citizen and a fellow police officer," the agent said.

"Fuck him," Parr said. The policemen tighten their grip on Parr.

"Think what this could do to international relations," the agent said.

"Fuck him," Parr said, and wished he had gotten a chance to knock Natividad down, too.

Then Joe Parr felt a hand on his shoulder. "That a way, Ranger," he heard Ollie Nordmarken say. "That little fucker insulted the United States government," Ollie said loud enough so everyone could hear him, and pointed at Trujillo.

Parr smiled and shook his arms. "It's all y'all's. I ain't apologizing."

"How does it feel to fuck yourself? You don't even get a kiss?" he heard Ollie whisper to him. Joe smiled, felt less fucked than before, and shoved between the police to walk out of the lounge. Ollie would cover his back.

As he walked back out into the hall, Parr stopped just long enough to see Jerri come out after him. He stopped. Other cops came out behind Jerri, and she walked up to him. "Take me to Palo's, huh, Ranger Parr?" Jerri said to him.

✪ As Joe Parr pulled up to the curb in front of Palo's house, put his Lincoln in park, and turned the keys, Jerri fidgeted in the seat beside him. Too tired or too logical, the sting now gone, at least for a while, she couldn't be mad at anyone anymore tonight, least of all Joe Parr. So she sat in the dark of his car, waiting for him to say something. He looked away from her, out his window, and she saw his shoulder bunch up, then shake, as though a sob that he'd kept silent for a long while finally worked its way up out of his chest. For a moment she wanted to be alone with him inside his or Palo's house. But she forced that thought out of her mind because her exhaustion or logic told her to. Parr turned toward her and, in the predawn light and in the reflected Commerce Street lights, she could see the cracks and wrinkles in his face. "I'm sorry for what I did to you," Parr finally said, choked to keep another sob away, then added, "I watched your office, but I never let anybody watch your home." He turned away from Jerri and looked at his steering wheel. "Or at least not until this night." Jerri didn't say anything. "So tell me something. Cuss me out. Tell me what a bastard I am."

"It doesn't matter now," Jerri said, pushed open the door so that the dome light shocked her eyes, and looked back in to see Joe rub at his eyes, over his half-framed glasses, with the back of his hands. Jerri didn't get out but looked at his face, which was half in shadow from the brim of his cowboy hat. He turned so that she could see him, and he looked like every tiny pocket of flab on his face sagged or stretched to make new wrinkles. His eyes seemed to float in his forming tears. And Jerri felt a knotlike sob stick in her throat. "I never quite realized what we thought of each other," Jerri said. His hand tightened, then loosened on the steering wheel. "You going to be all right, Joe?" she asked.

"Hell, my heart's tougher than an outhouse toilet seat," Joe said.

Jerri giggled and stepped out of the car and closed the door. The light in the car went off, and she turned just in time to see a front porch light pop on. To hell with exhaustion and logic—she could go back in the car and end up going to sleep with Joe Parr. Or she could again go back to Palo. She walked toward Palo's light, not really knowing that she was moving and not having yet made a decision. Halfway to the front porch, she turned around and said, "Aren't you going to walk me to the door, Ranger?"

Joe got out of his car and trotted to Jerri. Even as he took her hand and walked her to the lit-up porch, Jerri still hadn't decided whom she would choose. On the porch, he stood close to her so that she had to lay her head back on her neck and look up to see his eyes, which smiled like those of a man who finally found some pleasure after a long time without it. "Guess it turns out you were as close to a good guy as any of us," Jerri said. Then the front porch door swung open, and Palo stood in the light coming out of the house. She would go into the light from Palo's house and not the light in Joe Parr's Lincoln. It was, at least for the night, inevitable. "Good-bye, Joe Parr," Jerri said. He turned quickly away and almost trotted down the front porch. As he hit the bottom step, Jerri quickly added, "AMF," and smiled as sweetly as she could.

Joe Parr turned around, and he smiled, too. In the light coming from Palo's house, Joe tipped his hat and nodded at Jerri. Then he walked back to his Lincoln, not looking back, and drove away.

Joe Parr wasn't passion, screaming sex, or an aphrodisiac for the mind. He had betrayed her and hurt her. But Joe had retrieved some dignity from the screwups they all made. Maybe, like Palo, he had a little wisdom.

◑ Joe Parr got to his big Alamo Heights house just before dawn. After taking a shower to wash off a full day's scum, he looked in the mirror at his bloodshot eyes and knew that he had to sleep. But instead he filled himself a glass with ice and scotch and lay in his bed. Then he sat in his underwear in his study; then he went out in his backyard, sat in his lawn chair, and felt, not the Gulf breeze, but the early morning dew on his bare back and legs, and he saw the sun rising.

Nothing worked. So, for the first time in years, he went into other rooms in his house and just sat in their dust. The rooms weren't haunted; no memories over came his mind. No matter where he put himself or how he tilted his mind, he couldn't conjure up Melba. He missed her. He was afraid that he had killed her. He hoped that Jerri might start walking into his mind late at night and start talking. Then just as quickly he hoped that both women would stay away. Late night visits to his mind, from either one, could drive him crazy.

EPILOGUE

The Bexar County sheriff brought in a cake, and his secretarial staff came in after him. The blue-haired ladies who did his filing and computing, who could remember Joe Parr when he first became a Ranger, all cried. The Mexican girls who cleaned out the court-house crammed into Joe's office next to the sheriff, the tax assessor-collector, two judges, an assistant DA, and most of their staffs. A couple of the jailers walked down from the jail and brought him nasty joke presents: a wool ball warmer, a potion some Mexicans believed made your peter stiffer, a subscription to *Screw* magazine. The FBI agent who warned him to stay away from Trujillo left his glass-and-chrome office building to bring Joe Parr a plane ticket and hotel reservations for Las Vegas.

Even Captain Jack Dean and his two secretaries left their offices over on the South Side to bring Joe a plaque with an ornate pistol on it as a gift from the appreciative state of Texas. Then Charlie Hoestadter squeezed in; presented Joe with a set of woods and irons, courtesy of the SAPD, even though Joe had never played golf; and said a few words about how the police department could never replace the ally it had in Joe. Charlie sounded a whole lot like he was running for office.

As the sun made Joe's cramped office golden, they drank the champagne they shouldn't have in a county building and toasted

Joe. Captain Dean made a speech that he must have sat up most of the night memorizing, and Joe got just a bit teary eyed.

They all stayed an hour after closing time, the custodians not chasing anybody out, and lined up to shake Joe's hand as they left. Joe Parr, an honorable man, because he had slugged a Mexican government official and army officer, had been told to retire early. But he retired too because he didn't feel like being a Ranger anymore. Rangering no longer seemed as positive as it did before he met Jerri Johnson, and deep down inside him, Joe Parr just didn't think Rangering was as much fun as it had been. If Melba were still talking to him, she would have scolded him for waiting until after she died to finally make the right decision.

After his retirement party, after the people had filed out, Joe sat alone in his office. He decided to visit Ollie Nordmarken in the downtown Nix hospital. A week before Joe's retirement party, Ollie Nordmarken finally had the heart attack he'd been waiting ten years to have and was still in the hospital, with doctors testing him and already telling him what he no longer could or couldn't do. When he walked into Ollie's room, Joe smiled, nodded at Ollie, who had one tube in his nose and another in his arm, and thought that the tubes sticking into Ollie looked like they connected somewhere deep inside him. Joe yanked the cord that raised the venetian blinds covering Ollie's window, pulled the visitor's chair up beside the bed, and sat in the beams of light now coming through the window. At their last visit Ollie had told Joe that he missed the sunlight that streamed in through his glass-walled office. Only Ollie's eyes rolled toward Joe to greet him. "I'm retired," Joe said.

"Good. You did just what I thought you should." The words sort of gurgled out of Ollie's throat.

"So what am I going to do tomorrow?" Joe asked, knowing that he probably shouldn't make Ollie talk.

"Whack your meat, get drunk, what do you care?" The sounds that Ollie made seemed to wrap around the tube inside his nose and slowly follow it out of his clogged-up body.

"Just wondering what I'm going to do in order to change my life for the better," Joe said, and looked down at Ollie and felt like puking. The disinfectant hospital smell that never could cover up the stench of sickness or death had nauseated Joe since he had watched Melba die.

Ollie, stiff from doctors poking things into him to shoot dye into his veins and other such stuff, slowly rolled his head toward Joe. The tube in Ollie's nose pulled taut across his cheek and kept him from rolling his head farther. A glint from reflected sunlight caught in his eyes, so he blinked. Joe held up his hand to create a shadow across his friend's eyes so that he didn't have to rearrange his tube-filled head. "You know what I'd do if I were you?"

"I never had an idea what you would do," Joe said.

"I'd go see that private detective that you got sweet on." Ollie smiled, then coughed through his smile. He rolled his head away from Joe, and Joe lowered his hand.

"I never told you I was sweet on her."

"Jesus, you think I got bad eyes and mental deficiencies as well as a bad heart and a dick that don't work when I want it to." Ollie's lips stopped moving, but gurgling sounds still lingered above his mouth and nose.

"I've tried," Joe said.

"Like hell," Ollie said. "You got no balls. You old pussy. Your dick's gone completely limp."

"Hell, Ollie, Jerri Johnson's got a stiffer dick than you, me, or Fuentes."

"All the more reason to call her."

Joe smiled at the rest of Ollie's jokes and tried to be cheerful to him. Then, when Ollie got tired, Joe drove home, hoping that this might be the night Melba would start talking to him again and hoping too that maybe he could this night call Jerri Johnson.

❷ Jerri walked down the corridor of the airport toward gate 27. She wanted to hurry, but she could walk no faster without outpacing Palo, who limped just behind her. Angel was dead, she told herself, but J. J. had his new computer in the mail. True to Fuentes's word, the whole messy job had been profitable. She got a wire for five thousand dollars from Mexico City less than two days after

Natividad and Trujillo sent Angel's scrubbed and bagged body back to Saltillo. She insisted to Trujillo and Natividad that she take care of the body. She wanted it pulled out of the police morgue, touched up by someone good, and sent back to his relations. But the shooting was a Mexican affair, and Mexican officials wanted a Mexican autopsy and a Mexican investigation. Parr had given a performance for the police chief and another for a U.S. attorney and rescued the Texas Rangers and himself from being considered wimps or pussies. He had done his job. The SAPD had done theirs. All of them knew better than to get tangled in international paperwork. Everyone involved wanted everything cleaned up as quickly as possible, so Angel's body, like prosecutions, investigations, and reparations, was swept quickly out the door. So even though she had given up on Vincent, Jerri Johnson moved in with his father.

Palo's cane tapped behind Jerri, and she saw a white straw cowboy hat. She hurried toward the cowboy hat, ignoring Palo. The face under the hat turned toward her, then pulled off a pair of dark green aviator glasses and smiled at her. She smiled, but the man wasn't Parr. She had thought that he would show up; it would have seemed proper to have Joe Parr around now.

"Excuse me, sir," she said to the man in the cowboy hat, and walked past him. Then she spotted a black-haired man with his back to her and a large arm-length cast on his right arm. An aluminum pole, padded at one end and plaster coated on the other, supported the cast that went up above the man's shoulder. When Fuentes turned, she saw his forearm sticking out in front of him and the pole jutting out of a belt on his waist and joining his cast at the elbow. With his left hand, he tried to brush back the cowlick on the right side of his head but could just barely reach it. The movement looked strange, foreign to him. He took a tentative step toward Jerri. Trujillo and Natividad stood up. Fuentes motioned with his free left hand and, with Trujillo's approval, Natividad, his nose wrapped in bandages, sat. Then Trujillo sat.

Fuentes stepped closer to her, then smiled. Jerri went through the gap in the railing and walked up to Fuentes. "What are you going to do?" she asked.

He shrugged his one shoulder. "Whatever I have to."

"And what do you think that will be?"

"I don't know yet. I don't mind writing and staying in the nice hotels."

Jerri laughed and heard the tapping of Palo's cane behind her. Jerri looked from Fuentes to his father then back at Fuentes. His face grew serious. "There at the end, when I said so, I really did love you," he said. "And I should have loved you more five years ago. Then maybe . . ." He trailed off.

Bending at his waist, he tried to kiss her. She smelled no gin or vodka on his breath. But as his lips neared her lips, the cast almost pulled him over on top of her. Jerri had to stick out her hands to catch him. She grunted as she tried to straighten him, and Palo, suddenly behind her, pushed with one hand. Straightened, he looked at Jerri as if waiting for her to kiss him. She hesitated, then decided not to. He deserved whatever cruelty she might wish to show him.

Palo stuck out his left hand toward Vincent. Then Vincent stuck out his left hand. Jerri watched as the father, missing most of a kneecap and one testicle, shook hands with the son, grunting under the weight of his nearly neck-length cast. Now both crippled, they were physically alike. And, except for shadings in the differing depths of their wayward senses of devotion, they were spiritually alike. Jerri wanted desperately to be free of them, but here she was, living with one and telling the other good-bye. There were no charged particles in the air between them. But Jerri knew she would always be attracted to some faint glow that only she could see in him and his father. It had the same hazy shimmer, the pretty pastel glow she saw in Sam Ford, her job, the West Side, and Mexico. And she knew how, like bugs flying toward light just to shred themselves through a screen mesh, they had all courted their own deep, personal, inevitable stings inside.

As the boarding call sounded, Fuentes looked at Jerri as though giving her one last chance for a last kiss. When she didn't kiss him, he turned and joined his companions. Jerri stood with Palo and watched the three of them walk into the tunnel that led into the plane. Fuentes turned to look back. His cast seemed to be propping him up, and though his eyes and mouth tried to smile, his face showed his unbearable sadness. He was begging her to somehow stop all this.

Jerri now knew that she could appreciate art but not create, for she couldn't bear the loneliness needed to make the thing that made people feel less lonely. What Royce never told her was that over the years of their marriage, she had lost the ability to comfort him when he turned away from his painting. And she remembered that when she returned to an expanded self from the world of ideas, the exciting chill eventually wore off and she found herself back with her life. While she was hiding from Parr and trying to rescue Angel, she was researching, lost in a world of calculation and plan. At the police station she felt a bit of an excited chill, despite the tragedy of Angel, because she understood the inevitability of what had happened. Now, back in the world, she just had to endure the weight of being human. She needed comforting as well as those chills of understanding and empathy. She looked over at Palo. Then she looked at Fuentes. He smiled and waved. Jerri knew, whether she saw him again or not, he was out of her life. Priest, writer, scholar, revolutionary, traitor—he was the loneliest man she had ever known. And just loud enough, so that only she and Palo could hear but slowly mouthing the words so that Fuentes could read her lips, Jerri said, "AMF."

❂ Joe Parr saw Jerri's Suburban parked in front of Palo's house. And as he walked to the front door, a short Mexican mowing the lawn jerked his hand toward the backyard. When Parr rounded the house, he saw Palo sitting under the pecan tree, cracking pecans in his wondrous new machine and sloshing his feet in a tub of water. Jerri Johnson sat in a lawn chair beside him.

When Joe Parr appeared from around the corner of the house, neither Palo nor Jerri acted surprised to see him. It was as though all three of them expected him to appear at some time. They already had a lawn chair set up beside Jerri. Parr bowed his head as he walked toward them, the typical shy cowboy, boot-toe-in-the-dirt posture. Palo nodded. Jerri smiled.

He reached them, and he quietly nodded to them and they quietly back at him. It was evening, just before dark, just as the Gulf breeze started to blow in, before the humidity and the mosquitoes. The leaves of the pecan tree rustled above them. The breeze lifted their hair and their spirits. Joe Parr stood in front of them and struggled with his words. "You can sit down," Palo said.

So Joe sat, and they all had a sense, an apprehension of scenes that had been repeated over and over in the old San Antonio plazas. It was the same type of evening with its breeze and its promise of a little relief to the summer that the Spanish missionaries had enjoyed when they sat outside with the Coahuiltecans they were trying civilize and Christianize, that their mixed-blood descendants felt when they learned they had become Mexicans, that the German, Tejano, Scotch-Irish newcomers felt as they became Texan, American, Confederate, and then American all over again. Just a little relief from the harshness, their intertwined histories, their conflicts with each other and themselves.

Jerri spoke first. "Where you been, Joe Parr?"

"Been busy," Joe said.

"Well, is this business or pleasure?" Jerri asked.

"I see it as business."

Jerri's smile dropped. "I'm sorry I disappointed you."

"Hell, my heart's tougher than an outhouse toilet seat," Joe Parr said.

Jerri's smile completely disappeared. Palo stopped with his pecan peeling and looked at Parr. Joe Parr looked down at the short woman, nearly twenty years younger than him, light blond hair gray near the scalp, taut body with a behind that was having its own way and spreading out a little. "What's your business, Ranger Parr?" Jerri asked.

Joe didn't answer but took off his hat and sunglasses. "I retired. I'm not a Ranger no more. I'm investigating into other businesses."

Jerri cocked her head. "Well, I'm still working, Mr. Parr." Jerri's smile spread across her face, and Palo went back to cracking his pecans, a serenade, of sorts, for the other two. "But Sam Ford is going to retire soon, too. And he desperately needs someone to help me out. Do you think that you could qualify for a private investigator's license?"

"They got an age requirement?" Ol' Joe Parr squinted to look at Jerri Johnson, then gulped to talk. "Sometimes at night, I try to talk to my dead wife. She used to answer me."

Jerri shrugged, then smiled. "My son's flunking English; most of the men I meet are self-absorbed jerks; in fact, I've had too many men; the cosmetics industry doesn't make the color I like my hair to be anymore; and worst of all, my butt's getting wider and drooping."

Parr put on his hat and sunglasses. "I don't mean to have no love affair. But I'd appreciate your company."

"I love it when you talk pretty, Joe Parr," Jerri said.

A particularly loud pecan burst and sent bits of shells cascading around Palo. Both Parr and Jerri turned to look at him. "Lili makes the chicken enchiladas tonight. You stay for dinner."

So Jerri had several dinners with the two old men whom she could help and who helped her. And then Joe Parr invited her to his house over in rich Alamo Heights. So Jerri Johnson told Sam Ford to go to hell, took off work early, and bought a new sundress at the Dillard's in the downtown River Center Mall. And the light cloth of the full dress that draped nicely over a fortyish woman's body flowed behind Jerri as she flowed through Joe's house, turning on the lights in the unused rooms. After dinner they both settled into his den. Still later in the evening, after their second time at making love, they sat in Joe's backyard in their underwear and sipped beers. They let the nightly Gulf breeze bring them the cool spray from the neighbors' sprinkler and the smells of honeysuckle and chlorine. And between the hedges, they watched the shimmering lights reflected in the neighbors' pool.